MW01633259

Dishes Can Be Deadly

Carrie,
Enjoy!

Dishes Can Be Deadly

Ellen D. Torrey

Published by:
Four Season Mysteries

Printed by:
Walch Printing
Portland, Maine

Dishes Can Be Deadly

Books may be ordered
or by contacting the author

Ellen D. Torrey
31 Cloutier Rd
Lancaster, NH 03584

(603) 636-2294

ISBN: 978-0-9840224-1-0 (pbk)

Printed in the United States of America

Four Season Mystery rev. date 02/10/2012

This book is dedicated to my family. My husband for his years – decades - of watching me write in all those Mead notebooks we carried from home to home until he convinced me that the computer was easier. My son, Ben, and daughter, Samantha, for those same years of wondering why Mom was so groggy in the morning after spending most of the night writing even though she was still able to produce pancakes and eggs Benedict before they went off to school.

Acknowledgements:

Special thanks go to Susan Becker for her creative cover, Ed Solar for his computer savvy in creating the layout, Susan Solar for her encouragement, Samantha Millman for giving me the inspiration for 'Samantha' and her curiosity for me to explore 'what happened in Rockville?' as well as all those who read and reread the stories and encouraged me to take that next step – Rick, Joanie, Elaine, Betty, Jane, Jean, Karen and Ellen. Of course, last, but not least, Steve for his assessment of 'I'm not like that.'

CAST OF CHARACTERS

Samantha Warren- author
Wayne Dunham- her husband

Peter Frost- her publicist, lawyer
Lisa Frost – his daughter

Jack Parnell - police detective
Liz Parnell – his ex-wife
Gabe Johnson - policeman

Chris Nichols- District manager of Wentworths
Gisele Fournier- Assistant manager of Wentworths
Jessica Lupine- manager of Wentworths
Holly Bush- sales supervisor at Wentworths
Jeffrey Fuller Stewart- sales supervisor at Wentworths
Betty Ann Mitchell- sales associate at Wentworths
Louisa Perez- sales associate at Wentworths
Tony Yang- newly hired associate and warehouse man at Wentworths
Melanie Friis- newly hired associate
Andrew Barker – visual merchandiser at Wentworths
Hector Rodriquez – warehouse manager
Elaine Newcomb – sales associate at Wentworths
Debbie Clinton – manager from Hagerstown
Maria Starosta – visual manager

Jake English - professor at AU in mythology and the occult

Andrea Sharp- friend who lives in GA
Greg Sharp – her husband, Navy Industrial Hygienist

Prologue

Philip Watkins grinned the grin of a soon-to-be-wealthy man as he eased his Corolla onto the 270 local lanes preparatory to merging into the light, but steady traffic of the main thoroughfare. He wouldn't normally travel the usually congested highway, but the late hour of ten thirty promised smooth sailing to his apartment in Gaithersburg. There'd be traffic, just not as much as rush hour. 270 was always busy.

Okay, so five thousand dollars wasn't exactly going to make him wealthy, but the well wasn't going to dry up all that soon. Philip knew he had the thief by the proverbial balls and would do everything in his power to soak this for all it was worth. How fortunate was it that he was asked to take out the trash that night? How even more fortunate was it that he didn't hand the job off to Hector as he normally would?

He thought of Wendy and how he could afford to buy her that ring she was hinting around for – hell, he probably could wangle some nice dishes out of the deal as well. They were Wentworths after all – even a hump like him has heard of Wentworths.

The rain began once again to fall in earnest and he flipped the windshield wipers to the 'high' setting as he narrowed his eyes and moved forward to see better. He didn't have much further to go. He'd keep to the right despite the slow Caddy in front of him and he'd be fine. At least they were lucky this stuff wasn't snow.

He tapped his brakes to let the car behind him know that 'grandma' or 'grandpa' was ahead of him, then glanced in his review to see if the car took notice. It didn't seem to, so he tapped them again – okay, he hit them a bit more forcibly. The last thing he needed was another accident on his record. He certainly didn't need any cop questioning his alcohol intake for the night.

The car behind him stayed close.

No matter, he'd be exiting in a mile and the guy could deal with Caddy.

He flipped on the blinker when the half mile warning showed for the exit on Montgomery Village Road and kept an eye on the car still on his tail. He shook his head. The world was full of them, especially in this area. Maybe he'd take Wendy back to the quieter environs of Cumberland. His mom would let them stay with her until they got squared away with jobs and a place of their own. Maybe he'd even go back to school – who knew?

He guided the Corolla toward the exit and breathed a sigh of relief as he left the highway. He may even have increased his speed slightly as his anxiety level lessened. He hated the highway.

He started to hydro-plane and searched his mind for the proper way to overcome the action of the water coming between his tires and the road. He took a few quick breaths and concentrated on staying on the road.

It was then that he was hit from behind. It hadn't been a light tap either.

His last few seconds of life – for that's all he had left – were spent trying to regain control of the small vehicle as he first slammed into the jersey wall on his left and then flew across the road toward the stand of trees meant for beauty on his right. He had no time for thought – no thinking about how his imminent death would affect his mother or Wendy. No thought of what a bummer it would be to loose the five thousand dollars in cash that had been promised no less than a half hour earlier.

He saw the tree looming before him and he hit it.

End of story.

End of life.

Holly Matilda Bush slammed the door of the locker and jumped at the noise it made. She hated being this nervous, it was – well, it was nerve-wracking. She just wished she could get the hang of managing! She'd been doing it long enough after all. After a year, you'd think the procedure would just sink in to her muddled excuse for a brain.

Saturday's meeting just complicated everything. Not only did they now have to actually <u>*do*</u> *bag checks and proper company procedure, but now they had to do it with fewer personnel. There had been a mass exodus Saturday. Those spineless wonders that didn't want to own up to their incompetence.*

At least management had stayed in tact, per se. She did miss Alphonse, she had been sorry he'd left. He was nice to her. She had noted that he didn't leave until after the big Christmas employee sale. He was always ogling the ugliest stuff! Gisele was okay, but just. Holly didn't think she'd like Jessica much although Jessica <u>*had*</u> *helped her out of that jam with the money shortage. And she couldn't forget that Jessica seemed to have been her only advocate when the others were pointing fingers Holly's way. Jessica had pointed out that Holly was fond of her Corelle and had no need for the expensive Wentworths china so couldn't possibly be the thief. Holly had spent a good five minutes with eyes narrowed and brow furrowed studying Jessica Lupine and measuring an ulterior motive. She hadn't found evidence of any.*

Of course, Jessica had been right, there was absolutely nothing Holly wanted with the inventory Wentworths carried. Why did people want all this crap anyway? Why would anyone buy a twenty or even a fifty dollar plate? Wouldn't you worry whether or not it would break for God's sake!

It was going to be a long night. She had Louisa working with her. Louisa was too bubbly, way too happy to be working here, let alone working at all. Louisa had seen the inquisition as a training exercise. She had sat before Chris and the corporate lawyer and answered every question with honesty and determination. Holly was certain it was because of Louisa the Home Office had started to insist on them following procedure to the letter. As if any of the other stores bothered -

She sighed as she clipped her name tag to her suit coat and then grunted because she'd put it on upside down. It wasn't the first time, but because of the first time, she would check it each and every time since. They had made fun of her that day, Andrew and that Jane woman –

She wouldn't even venture into the world that was Andrew Barker. Suffice it to say, she hated him and it wasn't because of his sexual bent. He was mean to her, plain and simple.

Well, enough of this! She had work to do and Louisa wouldn't stand being out on the floor for too long by herself.

Maybe they could close a couple minutes earlier tonight. Who would know?

As she neared the doors that swung out onto the sales floor, an alarm sounded. She frowned as she looked toward the back door in the warehouse – it wasn't that one. Louisa was running back from her register with the same scowl Holly sported and the same question on her lips.

"What is that, Holly?"

"I'm not sure, it's not the back door," she replied as she let the warehouse door close with a swish.

"It sounds as though it's coming from the door over by the bathrooms," Louisa said as she pointed the way needlessly.

Holly nodded curtly. "You go back to your register and I'll check. You shouldn't be away from it for long."

Louisa leaned toward her rubbing her arms absently. "I should call the police."

Holly shook her head, annoyed at the suggestion. "What do you think is happening, Louisa? Do you think the thieves are crazy enough to be stealing stuff now after we were all questioned?"

"Couldn't be a better time, it's just the two of us," Louisa replied matter-of-factly. "I'm going to ring 9-1-1, you do what you want. If I were you though, I'd wait for them to respond." Louisa turned on her heels and headed for the telephone at the front register just as a customer came through the door.

She thought she should have locked the doors as she picked up the telephone receiver, but she hadn't. She spoke to the customer before dialing.

"We're experiencing some difficulties with the alarm system. I'll be with you shortly."

The customer glanced furtively toward the back seemingly trying to decide what he should do. Louisa shook her head thinking he'd be foolish to stay, the noise was deafening. He left as Louisa finished explaining to the 9 1 1 dispatcher what was happening.

Holly had waited a few ticks before she moved off toward the back door and the offensive alarm, all the while cursing Louisa for her actions. What would it cost to have the emergency services come at this hour? she thought as she approached the door with her key at the ready. This door had been triggered once before when she'd been alone on the floor. It opened onto a stairwell with another door beyond that opened to the back alley. Chris Nichols had reluctantly told her how it was silenced. It used the key same as all the other doors. Why it was such a state secret, she would never know, particularly since she was a manager. She pushed on the bar and met with resistance on the other side.

She pushed harder, the door wouldn't budge.

She tried a third time and applied all her fury and indignation along with the push and was surprised and shocked the door gave way easily, sending her hurtling forward. She stretched out her arms before her to break whatever fall she may experience as the outside door slammed shut. She hit that one full force. Next she knew, she was sprawled out on the cold cement floor.

She didn't think she had lain there long, but when Louisa showed up with two policemen in tow, she thought she might be wrong. They prevented her from sitting or standing and told her she should wait for the ambulance that had been summoned.

"I'm all right!" Holly avowed. "Just let me up!"

"You've been hurt, ma'am, you need to wait for the EMTs," one of the police officers said. He knelt beside her and gently, but firmly held her in place.

"Did you see who did this, ma'am?"

"I am not a 'Ma'am' and, no, I didn't see anyone because nothing was done. The alarm was going off and I came to silence it."

"I heard the outside door slam, Officer," Louisa said firmly. "She was struggling with the door like someone was on the other side and then she wasn't. You – or she – can't tell me that someone wasn't holding it. We had some problems with thefts recently. I, for one, am not fooling around with any possibility and that's why I called."

"For God's sake, Louisa, it's nothing," Holly grumbled. She stared significantly at the officer, but he refused to budge.

He smiled tentatively as he looked back at his partner. "Why don't you check out back, Ray?"

Ray nodded and proceeded forward while Holly scowled after him.

"Gisele is going to be furious with us," Holly said as Ray returned and shrugged.

"I'd rather have her furious over this than angry we put ourselves in danger," Louisa declared as she glanced backward and saw the two paramedics approach. "I'm going home," she announced and then looked at the officer who had risen from Holly's side. "I can, can't I?"

"Let me just get a statement from you – Louisa, is it?" he said smiling. "It won't take long. Should you call in someone to take care of the store closing?"

"I can do that," Holly said as she slapped one of the paramedics who was trying to clean her head wound she'd sustained.

Louisa shook her head and rolled her eyes. "I'll call in Andrew, he lives just across the street and he can do all the reports."

The officer smiled and nodded and walked with her to the front. "I'm Gabe Johnson, by the way, Louisa."

Louisa held out her hand. "Louisa Perez, when you question me, you can ask why the hell I think I ought to continue working here."

Gabe laughed. "I'll do that."

CHAPTER 1

I grabbed my canvas bag and purse, slipped from the seat of my green Dodge minivan, and hunched down into the collar of the too thin jacket as I hurried towards the Caribou Coffee shop. It was new - the coffee shop - built in the corner of a recently overhauled strip mall and giving a nice alternative to the Starbucks shops that seemed to be everywhere. The offerings didn't cost less, mind you, but it was a nice substitute.

I liked this one because it had a fireplace - perhaps they all did (Starbucks didn't). The February day was raw after a week of spring-like weather and the fire would feel good. I laid claim to a small table and two easy chairs before I stepped up to the counter and ordered a caramel laced drink. I don't normally drink anything in my coffee, opting for the rich black taste of it over sugary syrup and cream, but this day seemed to scream for sweetness and comfort.

The place wasn't crowded. It was between the early morning rush of those heading for work and the lunchtime few that came for coffee or rendezvous, so I didn't think I'd have to wrestle anyone for the spot before my own assignation. I was meeting a new publicist. I'm not entirely clear as to what happened to my first one.

Perhaps I should introduce myself. I'm Samantha Warren and I'm a writer. I'm married and though I'm faithful to my husband, it doesn't necessarily mean that he returns in kind. I'm of the 'don't ask, don't tell' frame of mind there. I'm about five foot five if I stand up straight, with long brown hair and green eyes. I don't think I'm bad looking. I try to keep fit and I try to hold Wayne's interest (the husband). It's not that he doesn't particularly like *me*; he just likes every other woman, too. I guess if he beat on me or was abusive in some other way, I would consider ending our nine year marriage. He's wayward – some wouldn't see the distinction between that and other forms of abuse.

We currently live in Maryland in Rockville. For those of you unfamiliar with the area, it is a large city that probably started as a bedroom community of D.C. (it's north and west of our nation's capital) and has boomed and flourished in its own right. Wayne Dunham - I didn't take his name when we married - is a defense contractor. I'm not exactly certain *what* he does, but we move around a lot just like the military. In fact, my father was a defense contractor also – so I've been moving around for as long as I can remember. I have this dream that someday I'll (*we'll* – is that Freudian or what?) settle down in one place. I envision a house with a white picket fence and gardens and the like. I envision harmony - peace, love, serenity – I guess that's why I write. It's the 'reality bites syndrome' that I try to avoid. Don't get me wrong, I'm not unhappy with my life – having much to do with the blinders I wear.

My parents are gone. I have no brothers or sisters, aunts, uncles (therefore cousins), grandparents, etc. This is depressing. Wayne has family in the west and I haven't met them all as yet. We correspond, usually at Christmas, and everyone seems content with that. We did receive a visit from his sister, her husband, and daughter when we lived in Florida one Christmastime. They had shown up unannounced on our front doorstep on Christmas Eve morning; of course we invited them in – I wouldn't have thought of doing any differently. Wayne took them to Disney World and I went to the mall to purchase gifts for them as well as to the grocery store to bulk up our stores for their stopover. They stayed with us for four days and I was declared the consummate hostess by Chloe (the sister); Wayne was pleased. She and I had gotten along well I thought, but I haven't seen or heard from her since.

I sipped at the sweet-laced, milky coffee and was rewarded with a mustache of cinnamon-coated whipped cream that I slowly brushed off with my tongue. Talk about orgasmic –

I wondered what Peter Frost looked like. Harry Beckwith, my former publicist, was a kindly old guy with white hair, faded blue eyes, a round body and a tendency towards the easy way out. He negotiated me a contract that barely provided me a profit with a publishing firm that set strict rules on what I wrote. The publisher provided the formula and I added a bit of my own personality and they made the big bucks off it. Harry signed me up for each and every seminar available and never accompanied me anywhere, so I footed the bill (thus the slim profit margin).

I would have complained if I wasn't doing what I'd always wanted to do. If I really needed to, I could pick up a job in retail. There were certainly enough businesses out there starving for my limited expertise. I may not have many skills, but I was a good worker bee. I would do anything anyone asked of me and I would do it well. Of course, I had to find a business that would be willing to work around my seminar schedule.

Wayne never held back from me. If I wanted anything from him, he would willingly give it to me. I think he thought it his obligation as my spouse - and he probably felt a little guilty as well; at least I'd like to think that.

Wayne Dunham, what can I say? My husband makes my heart skip a few beats. He's blond and blue-eyed, not overly tall, standing at just less than six feet. He has moderately broad shoulders, a washboard stomach and, unfortunately, not much of an ass. I think I'm an ass girl. He runs, bikes, and does the gym thing religiously. He likes – no, I have to qualify that and say, he *loves* - to clean. Believe me, that *is* a big plus because I don't, although he does it to the point of obsession.

We met roughly nine years ago when we were both on vacation and the attraction was – well, it was amazing.

Those three days were probably the best three of our whole relationship because there hadn't been a lot of talking done. Our connection could best be described as stormy though, if we could have managed to keep our mouths shut, you would log us in at passionate.

If we hadn't rushed into marriage, maybe we would have come to our senses and not married, but by then it was too late and we were stuck with one another.

He loves to entertain. We fit together nicely there because I love to cook. We've put on some good parties. When we did, we were well synchronized and we knew our places collaborating on the menu and going to the grocery store together. Then Wayne concentrated on the cleaning and setting up and I did the cooking. The kitchen was my domain (although I did allow him to enter when the dishes piled up too high – which was always - and he willingly took care of them).

He could even occasionally manage to pry me from the safety of my kitchen haven with a firm hand to my back so we could mingle among our guests. Of course, at first opportunity, I would be back in my kitchen. I liked my kitchen!

I was staring at the blank white screen of my laptop, glancing up when the door would open, as I waited for Peter Frost. I was trying to decide on character names for the next book that was due to the publisher by June. My original contract was for five. I wondered now whether or not I was still obligated since Harry had left the picture.

Any distraction, ranging from a buzzing bug to a nuclear disaster, would result in a glance at the *other* novel I'd been working up off and on for two years. I brought it up on the screen, studying the notes I'd made in caps. I was so immersed in the tale I was creating that I no longer paid attention to who was coming and going; I was no longer aware of anything else. At least not until I glanced over and saw the black boots attached to jean-clad legs standing just to my right. My gaze traveled up the legs to the blue and green plaid flannel shirt covered by a khaki colored suit jacket. He stood tall – maybe six foot four or more. He was a large man with arms the size of my thighs and had brown hair that was cut in a severe crew-cut; grey eyes on a smooth, tanned face. He carried a briefcase and one of my books in one large hand and a cup of coffee in the other. He was reading the computer screen.

"That's good," he said pointing to the computer. He set the coffee down on the side table and his briefcase on the floor beside the other easy chair and held out his hand. "Peter Frost; you're Samantha Warren, I presume."

"Sam," I said rising and clutching his hand firmly.

"Good handshake, I like that," he glanced at my cup. "Would you like another coffee or whatever that is?" He made a face when he stared into my cup and I shook my head. I didn't need any more coffee; I'd had my full quota of caffeine for the year at that point. I was studying him as he folded and sank into the chair. He looked like an enforcer; someone a loan shark would hire to break legs if you tried to default on a loan. A bodyguard type that would put his own life on the line for the protected. A big gruff father bear that would –

"How am I doing?" he asked showing a nice set of teeth behind his smile.

"I'm sorry, I tend to wander away, forgive me."

He waved a hand of dismissal and pointed to my laptop. "Is that your newest then?"

I trilled my lips. "This? This is just play. The next romance is -" I searched for the right word. "It's coming along," I lied.

"I like *that,*" he said again pointing to the screen.

Exactly how long had he been standing there? I wondered.

"I like that better than the romance stuff," he jabbed his finger at the book he held in his lap.

"But I'm contracted for two more."

He nodded, but said nothing as he opened my book and slipped on a pair of half glasses. Somehow for him, it didn't ruin his overall image.

"What's the story there?" he asked as he read.

I sighed. "Harry wasn't aggressive and I allowed him not to be."

He looked over his glasses with a bemused look. "I didn't mean with your contract, sweetheart, I meant with the story you're working on. But that tells me a lot."

I reddened under his gaze. Sweetheart?

"Okay, then tell me about Samantha Warren."

"There's not much to tell."

He sat back and rested his chin on his hand. "How would you characterize yourself?"

I snorted a laugh and sat back myself with a shrug. "I don't know – let's see – I'm five foot five if I don't slouch." I looked his way. "My mother always threatened to put me in a back brace if I didn't straighten up. Actually she and my grandmother vied for the top spot when it came to telling me to stand up straight." I blushed again. "I have brown hair though I can't remember exactly what my original color is. I wear it long because my husband doesn't care for it long. I'm … ah, let's say, fit," I said hesitantly and grinned. "I wish I was sultry or skinny or even well-endowed. I guess I could be in fiction if I was the heroine of the story." I groaned at the thought of that impossibility. "I have green eyes *not* hazel as my license decrees. I know they're green because my grandfather called them cat eyes." I searched the air for more. "I'm married - have been for nine, nearly ten years."

"Do you love your husband?" Peter's voice drifted into my brain.

I nodded, hesitating ever so slightly.

"You aren't certain?"

"That's an odd thing to ask."

He shrugged. "You didn't mention him until the end."

I grinned. "I love him. I just don't think he cares for me very much." I held a hand up while I searched for the right words. "I suspect that Wayne isn't monogamous."

"Suspect? You're not sure?"

"I don't think I want to know; the 'ignorance is bliss' thing." I chuckled. "I do know that I maintain a separate bank account." I did an intense study of the floor. "I don't miss him much when he goes away," I said and let my voice trail off. "Don't get the wrong picture here; he's very attentive when he's home."

I caught his gaze. There was no reading this one.

"Tell me about this novel you're working on, Sam," he said quietly.

I shrugged again. "It's a murder mystery or at least I want it to be. I don't know enough about the workings of the police world to do it justice. I always thought I should " I paused and shook my head.

"Always thought what, Sam?"

"I wrote a short story a long time ago about this writer that attaches herself to a policeman – you know – she follows him around on cases. They get caught up in this drug thing and she gets kidnapped by the bad guy and awaits rescue." I looked up at his grey eyes. "You see somewhere along the way she fell for him – anyway …" I waved a hand in the air and stopped my discourse.

Peter leaned forward, "What happens?"

I sighed again. "The story is in the first person so she doesn't know that he's been searching for her since the moment she went missing. She's been writing the story as she and the policeman go along, all the while toting around all these notebooks. Anyway, the bad guy that has her keeps giving her injections and she ends up dying before the police guy finds her." I ran my hand through my hair. "Like I said, I don't know the inner workings of a police investigation and I get bogged down in the romantic story thing. I guess that's why Harry set me up in Romance Novels."

"So you thought if you could follow around a police guy that you'd pick up story material," Peter said thoughtfully as though he was considering the prospect.

I threw a hand out in the air. "I don't think it would work well."

"Is that how the story ended?" He asked taking me back to my short story narrative.

I shook my head. "The policeman finished it, telling about how she died before it could be finished and, of course, how he'd fallen in love with her." I pointed at the book on his lap wordlessly explaining again why I write romance novels.

He nodded – was silent for some time and then seemed to shake himself and pointed to my laptop. “I want to read that,” he said finishing off his now cold coffee. “Can you print it for me?”

I regarded him and nodded. “My house isn’t far; we can go there.”

He nodded and unfolded himself from the chair. “Let’s do that then. You lead the way.”

Actually, I drove.

As I drove, I assessed my opinion of my new manager. I knew I liked him. I rely a lot on first impressions and he’d impressed me even before he’d shaken my hand and I think he liked me, too, which was a good start. I liked him even more after he told me what he’d done already.

“I’ve started renegotiations with your publishing company. You may still have to give them the last two contracted novels – as yet, I don’t know. I will meet with them again early next week. I wanted to hear from you what you wanted to do; whether or not you wanted to stay with them or have me look for someone else. One thing’s for certain, you need a better contract. Harry Beckwith was lousy!"

"How do you know Harry?" I asked as I turned left onto Drake Drive and wound my way up the hill before turning right on to Castaway Drive. Harry Beckwith lived in Tennessee, I thought.

"It's not important," Peter said as he looked at the neighboring homes. "Nice neighborhood. Have you lived here long?"

"Almost a year now; we don't stay in one place very long. Wayne's a government contractor."

"What exactly is that?" Peter asked as he slid open the door.

"Beats me. We move and he travels a lot." I picked up our morning newspaper from the driveway. "I personally think he's a government spy," I said off-handedly.

Peter was scouting out the landscaping most of which I'd done since we moved in. A large wisteria bush I'd grown from seed shivered in the February breezes; its fragrant blossoms in hiding until the warmth of March and April would bring them bursting forth. A split rail fence adorned the curve of the corner lot where Shippers Lane and Castaway met. At the base of the fence, running adjacent to it, I had planted daffodils, tulips, daisies, irises, and peonies. A larger oval garden was centered on the slope of the hill where the ranch style house sat built up with a high, stone retaining wall. This was home to more perennials of chrysanthemums, iris, rhododendron, peonies, daisies, and assorted others I'd thrown in forgetting their names long ago. Black-eyed Susans lined the two driveways and there were groupings of blueberry bushes, peonies, rhododendrons, and hydrangeas about the lawn with two dogwood trees along the neighbor's fence line.

"I love my flowers, but it's a bitch to mow the lawn," I said as we took the walkway to the front porch.

"I like how the house sits above the others," Peter said as he turned at the top step.

I laughed. "Wayne likes to sit out here and spy on the neighbors." I opened the door. "When he's home."

Peter Frost held the door and waited for me to precede him inside. I was glad for the fact that Wayne had been home the past week; the house would be clean and uncluttered. Left to my own devices, I tend to let stuff like that go ... forever. That's not exactly true – at times I can go on cleaning binges - just not lately. Let's say, the past five years.

We stepped into a short hall that opened into the living room. The dining area sat a step up and to the left. Wayne and I had ripped up the carpeting here and down the hall and sanded and stained the floors ourselves before our furniture had arrived. I was very proud of those floors.

There was a large bay window straight ahead that looked down onto our back patio and the neighbor's yard beyond the fence. To the left was the L-shaped kitchen which we had modernized before we moved in with oak cabinets and all new appliances. We had made the wall between the kitchen and living room a half wall for the express purpose of opening up the chopped up rooms to create the illusion of space. To the right was a corridor that led to three rooms and a bath (originally, I'm sure, they were meant to all be bedrooms). The stairwell that led to the finished basement sported a half wall against which the couch sat. The master suite was in the back corner to the left, my office was straight ahead and Wayne's to the right. The rooms weren't overly large. In fact, we were considering taking out the wall between the bedroom and my office to expand the master suite.

"Did you want to see the downstairs? I'll start printing off the story. There's not much – mostly notes so it shouldn't take long." I pointed below as I continued on to my office. Peter moved down the stairs and I mentally moved with him. At the bottom of the stairs, he would step onto new beige Berber carpeting and face the hunter green sectional couch which dominated the elongated room and faced the sixty inch big screen television. The TV was Wayne's personal wet dream - HDTV, Tivo, surround sound with Bose speakers suspended from the four corners of the ceiling, Blu-ray DVD player, VHS player, and on and on and on …

Beyond the far end was the laundry room which in turn opened up onto Wayne's play room that sported a wet bar and a humongous pool table in dark pine sitting under a rectangular Tiffany lamp suspended just over the table.

The Berber was in there as well, and beyond that, tucked in the corner, was a spare bedroom and half bath; rarely used.

"The place is a lot bigger than I'd thought," Peter said from the doorway of my office and I jumped. I hadn't quite kept up with his circuit of the lower level, I guess.

"It helps having the basement finished."

He was looking into our bedroom (the bed was unmade) and stepped back to glance in Wayne's office all neat and tidy and then back to my office which was a disaster. I reddened under his grin. "Wayne was home for a week before he headed for San Diego so don't get used to the look of neatness."

Peter laughed rather heartily. "Does that mean you'll keep me then?"

I looked over to him – perhaps a bit flustered – and watched him grin again.

He nodded. "Yes, Sammy, you do have that choice. You're not just a bit of chattel." He leaned against the doorjamb and stuffed his hands in his pockets. "You have talent and it's my job to make certain that people read your stuff and you make money. That was Harry's job, too; he's just not as good at it as I am. I'm also a lawyer, by the way, and hope you'll entrust me with your legal needs."

I laughed. "I trust you to do anything and everything for me, Mr. Frost. I guess you could say I'm naïve that way. First impressions do that to me."

"Call me Peter," he pushed off the door and accepted the packet of papers I handed him. "I'll start on this. Can you get me more by the end of the week?"

"You haven't read it yet."

Peter smiled again. "Can you?" he asked again.

I nodded.

He sketched a salute. "I'll be in touch," he said and headed down the hallway.

"Maybe we can have dinner, Wayne will be home Friday."

"Sounds good, I'll set it up," he tossed back over his shoulder and was gone.

Okay then.

It wasn't until I was a half-hour into my writing that I realized that *I* had driven us from the coffee shop. Great! Good first impression. I considered trolling the streets for him, but figured by then he had made it back to his car with disdain for me on his mind.

CHAPTER 2

Peter called at ten, two mornings later. I should explain that at times when I get to writing, I often don't stop for anything - including sleep. So when Peter's call came through, I was deep in slumber. Very deep. The kind where you're burrowed into the pillows and quilts and, in order to even find the telephone, you have to literally climb and claw your way from the depths of the bedding. The kind where you wake up sleeping in a puddle of your own drool - Get the picture?

"Hello?"

"Sammy? Did I wake you?" Peter asked with a hint of amusement.

"Of course not," I replied with a yawn, scratching at my head absently.

He laughed.

Jerk.

"I'm sorry about you having to walk the other day, I was writing."

"No need to be sorry. I didn't think of it myself until I saw I didn't have a car; the walk was good for me. Do you have plans for Saturday night?"

I sat up and tried harder to infuse some life back into my brain. "I don't think so."

"I've made us reservations at the North Woods Lodge in Gaithersburg. I have someone I want you to meet and you're to bring your husband along."

I nodded, trying to think if Wayne had told me we were committed to anything. If I could pull myself from the confines of the bed, I could check Wayne's calendar. "Sounds good, we'll be there."

"Seven o'clock, see you then."

Again I nodded as if he'd see me do it. He'd already hung up and I still held the receiver as I stared zombie-like at the green quilt that covered our bed. It was the one thing that Wayne had allowed from my household when we meshed the two together. I should have had some clue then that he was particular. I replaced the receiver and scrunched my eyes closed debating on whether to get up or burrow back in when the telephone rang again.

"Hello?" I admonished myself for not checking caller ID first, but knew I'd never *not* answer a ringing telephone, I'm too damned nosy.

"Hi, sweetheart," Wayne's voice sounded as sleepy as mine.

I leaned back against the pillows. "How's the trip?"

"Same old, same old, the weather's nice though," he answered while I tried my damnedest to remember where he was this week. I couldn't exactly, but my foggy brain tentatively came up with California.

"It's not here. It's cold again."

Wayne laughed. "I suppose you're keeping the heat down. I picture you all bundled up wearing those abominable sweats and your hair all askew. Have you used the gas fireplace?" We'd also just had one of those installed as a fireplace insert. And no, I hadn't used it yet.

"I haven't been downstairs much, just writing."

Wayne's ensuing silence spoke volumes. He thought the writing was a waste of my time. I had been educated to the fullest extent of my being and he thought, though I certainly didn't, I should be able to pick up any professional job I wanted. Problem was – writing is what I wanted.

"I have a new publicist. I think he may have won me in a poker game with Harry," I replied pleasantly – or as pleasantly as I could muster. I'd even plastered a smile on my face.

"Great! Another hump that can bleed you dry."

I couldn't picture Peter as a hump or even bleeding me dry. "You can discuss it with him. We're having dinner with him Saturday night."

More silence followed. My mind wandered back to his comment about picturing me bundled and I smiled. Wayne was thinking of me.

"We didn't have anything planned, did we?" I asked biting my lower lip as I waited for his answer.

"Nothing that can't be rescheduled, I guess." He sighed heavily.

"What was it?"

"I was thinking on the lines of you and me alone and naked, sweetheart," Wayne replied quietly.

I blushed. "We can do that all day Sunday."

He sighed again and I knew what was coming. He was going to tell me he had to go somewhere else. "I'm off to Georgia Sunday. Maybe you can go with me?"

"Can't. I leave Monday morning for a seminar that Harry arranged. Perhaps I can cancel though, I'm not sure how much of Harry's plans I have to keep up with."

"Don't sweetheart, we'll try another time. I should get ready. I had to hear your voice. I will see you Saturday morning." He broke the connection and I recradled the receiver. Slick the way he did that - telling me he wouldn't be here until Saturday instead of the Friday I had planned on. I may not remember where he went, but I always registered when he'd be back home. There was also the fact that he knew my schedule better than I did. *He* knew I would be going to Chicago.

Maybe.

I scrolled through the caller ID and found Peter's number and hit the dial button. Peter's deep voice answered. "Hi, Sammy."

I chuckled; Peter had checked his caller ID. "Peter," I shifted in the bed. "I was wondering if I'm supposed to keep my appointments that Harry set up for me. Like the seminar in Chicago this coming week?"

I could hear the shuffling of papers and Peter's even breathing. "The Romance Writer's Guild thing?"

"That's the one."

He sighed. "Why?"

"Wayne asked if I can go with him to Georgia. I've a couple friends down there I'd like to see, if it's okay, that is."

"I'm not your den mother, Sammy. Of course you can go to Georgia. Give me the info on the Chicago trip and I'll cancel your reservations for you."

"I can do that."

"I want to make certain they don't charge you," he said.

I frowned at the phone and then shrugged. *Made no difference to me who actually did the calling*. "I'll get the numbers - hold on."

"You are in bed, aren't you?" he said bemused.

"It's your fault, you said you wanted more. I've been writing," I said and could feel the scowl on my face. I walked to my office shuffling through the papers on my desk, searching for the information Peter had requested. I had no idea where it was.

He seemed to sense that.

"What hotel is it in?"

I shrugged. "I don't remember." I scanned all the surfaces in the room and then the floor, "The Marriot, maybe."

"There's probably a dozen or so Marriots in Chicago, Sammy." He laughed again. "Don't worry, I'll find it. See you on Saturday."

Good one, Sammy. Now not only does he think you're a slug, but he thinks you're absent-minded and disorganized.

Okay, so I was that anyway. He would have discovered that sooner or later; better that it was sooner. I wondered if I had to buy something to wear for Saturday and talked myself out of that while I made a pot of coffee. It still looked frigid outside - a good day to write.

Chapter 3

Hector Rodriquez was deep in thought as he wheeled the loaded cart out the large warehouse door. He negotiated around the small patches of snow that remained from the last storm and carefully lowered the rickety handcart to street level and pushed his load of boxes and trash toward the two dumpsters situated between Wentworths and Barnes and Noble. The night air was chilly, but welcome. He'd spent the morning breaking out stock at the bookstore and the afternoon and the better part of the evening checking in a truck for Wentworths. He didn't mind the two jobs in the least. For one, the stores were right next to each other. The other? They were only four blocks from his small apartment.

Also, neither business minded his need for supplemental income; they trusted that he would do an equally superior job at both places. Hector owed that trust to the fact that he was an honest, hard-working man. He'd never given any place he worked cause to doubt his integrity. As Mr. Nichols told him, he was an asset and a good example of what the American dream exemplified. Hector smiled; it had certainly not been his dream – American or otherwise – to have to work two jobs in order to subsist.

No matter. He loved Washington DC and took every opportunity he had to avail himself of the deep history it afforded. He couldn't fathom how most of the people he encountered had not seen the Museum of Natural History or the war memorials which were literally right under their noses. Besides the fact that all these monuments and museums were free for any who wanted to see them.

He shook his head sadly as he tossed the mound of cardboard into the large green container after previously disposing of the day's trash in the smaller compactor. His fellow Americans, at least in this little corner of the world, were fat, lazy, uneducated and content to remain that way.

He would also have loved to live in downtown DC, but instead settled for the suburb community of Rockville.

Of course, the only factor that allowed him to live in Rockville was that his landlady charged him low rent for a one room bed-sit in return for his handyman services. Rockville was becoming almost as expensive as the District to live in.

He wheeled the empty cart back toward the door and decided he could probably make a sizeable dent in at least the first couple pallets of the ten that had been delivered before he would call it a night and go home to sleep. Obviously, he had no family to get home to - a depressing, but true fact. He couldn't seem to get a girlfriend either. Then again, he had no time for one.

He pulled down the heavy metal door and slid the padlock into place then hung the key on the nail to the left of one of the four light switch boxes. Ms. Fournier had been adamant that he shouldn't need the full complement of lighting when he worked at night and he would do nothing to incur her wrath. He could see what he needed to see with just the center lights on.

At times like these, he wished he'd had help, but Ms. Fournier had not deemed it necessary. Perhaps he'd approach the new manager or even Mr. Nichols. Not now though; now was definitely not a good time. The store was dealing with a major crisis that he, Hector Rodriguez, had brought to the attention of Nichols.

As he sliced through the plastic that held the boxes of merchandise in place on three of the pallets, he pondered his recent conversation with Mr. Nichols. Hector had noticed large discrepancies in the inventory as well as an inordinate number of empty boxes on the upper shelves. He wanted the management to know of the discrepancies as soon as possible and, equally, didn't want to be blamed for the losses. Nichols had listened to him attentively and, Hector felt, had heeded his words. Mr. Nichols said he would pass on the information to the new manager, Ms. Lupine. Hector hoped Nichols would keep it from Ms. Fournier; he didn't care for her at all.

The inventory they'd conducted the first of the month confirmed Hector's suspicions and accusatory meetings had ensued. A lot of people had quit, but the thief had yet to be found.

He imagined he heard the scrape of a shoe and straightened up to listen. The huge warehouse was silent, but Hector sensed someone there with him. He decided he would silently slip from his position behind two of the pallets and surprise whoever lurked. He grinned; perhaps there would be a large reward for uncovering a thus far sneaky thief.

He was negotiating his way around the second pallet when he heard a grunt of exertion. He looked up just in time to see boxes hailing down from above. He raised his arms to protect himself; a futile and useless gesture as the corner of one of the heavy boxes struck his temple. At least he was unconscious before the other boxes followed and crushed the life out of him.

CHAPTER 4

Wayne chose his 'baby' to drive us to the restaurant; a silver Audi TT convertible with a black roof. We had three vehicles; the TT, a tan Pontiac Aztec and my green Dodge Caravan. I had been successful in warding off Wayne's efforts to buy me a new car for a couple years now. In fact, every time he obsessed about it he bought himself a new one. Perhaps that was his aim all along. In deference to my hair and the fact that it was cold, he kept the top up and the heat on, and, as was his wont, when he wasn't shifting, he held my hand. It was kind of cute.

"So what's this Frost guy like?" he asked as he negotiated the turn off Gude Drive.

"I like him," I replied.

Wayne snorted a laugh. "That doesn't exactly answer my question, sweetheart." He raised my hand to his lips and kissed my fingertips.

I don't know why, but I was irritated with his comment. Perhaps it was because I didn't have a great 'first impressions' track record even though my everyday life depended heavily on them. I tended to take people at face value and that was probably the reason I'd ended up with Harry Beckwith - and Wayne Dunham, for that matter. Something Wayne wasn't going to let me forget anytime soon I was certain – well, the Harry part anyway.

When irritated, strike back at the object of your irritation.

"Why were you delayed? You were originally scheduled to arrive home yesterday morning." I thought I felt him tense. Unfortunately, my lack of detective skills were right up there with being able to sense those who might or might not be out to rook me (or better still, how to keep my husband from wandering).

Wayne smiled easily. "It figures you would remember that, sweetheart. I should have explained when we talked. I had a quick trip to Port Hueneme via Camp Pendleton. The extra day saved me from a trip next month. I didn't think you'd mind." He squeezed my hand. "Next time, I'll keep you apprised."

I regarded him as he turned into the parking garage and retrieved the ticket. I did love the man, only God knew why, but I found myself wondering how I could check up on his story. *Oh hell*. I fought with myself to return to the 'don't ask, don't tell' mode as we walked hand in hand towards the North Woods Lodge.

The North Woods Lodge was the newest of a spawn of restaurant chains that had the good fortune to occupy the meager space around a manmade lake (pond anywhere else in the country) on fast developing prime real estate in Gaithersburg. The restaurants would never lack for clientele. In the surrounding two square mile radius were several high-rise apartment buildings and as many communities of townhouses with cute historical names heralding their proximity to the nation's seat of government. The residents alone could support several dozen such restaurants without fear of closure. The fact that they were surrounded by shopping, a ten screen theater complex and ample parking only added to the restaurants' safety nets. Target, Kohl's, Barnes and Noble, and Galyan's anchored specialty shops that changed hands as often as the Peach Orchard did in a one day battle at Gettysburg. All were well within walking distance. Though, judging from the full to over-flowing parking lots and garages, most patrons chose not to walk. The D.C area population did value their cars highly.

The Lodge sat on a hill whose slope was frequented by water fowl ranging from wood duck to Canada geese. The grass was definitely not a place where humans would sit or stand to wait for tables to be ready, for fear of stepping in a pile of goose poop.

The Lodge was constructed with huge over-lapping logs reminiscent of the Lincoln Logs that were thrust upon me as a child, fronted by a set of wide rough hewn wood steps, rails, and porch. The porch, heated with free-standing heaters this time of year, was where patrons waited clutching an electronic square pager that would vibrate, light up, and be generally annoying when tables became available. You waited everywhere to eat in Rockville and those pesky pagers were the norm.

I scanned the hordes on the porch and didn't see Peter so we pressed on through and stepped inside to an equally congested foyer. The post and beam ceiling rose up to heights I hadn't thought possible from the outside. The faint scent of pine emanating from the new logs made me wonder if they used some artificial scent to enhance the effect.

"Rustic," Wayne commented dryly.

"It had good reviews," I managed as someone pressed an elbow into my back.

"You're a better cook," Wayne added. My husband had said several times in our marriage that he would rather I cook than go out to eat. He scowled at the guy that was standing too close and he backed off a bit – evidently, Wayne was an imposing presence. Wait until he met Peter.

A standing-room-only bar was directly in front of us and the hostess desk blocked any unescorted entry into the dining area. I managed to forge my way forward to the desk. It wasn't easy to be heard as the din made normal conversation impossible. I had to really lean into the face of the black and red plaid flannel shirt clad hostess.

"The Frost party? I'm not sure he's arrived."

She nodded and smiled and indicated we should follow without her actually speaking. I have to say this, the difference in volume between the waiting area and the dining room was phenomenal. I have no idea how it was achieved, but it was like night and day. It was as though there was a glass wall separating the throngs waiting and the diners dining. The tables were spaced widely apart with booths lining the perimeter. Squares of ceiling were suspended above each table and even though the entire dining room was open, each table seemed intimate. It was a nice effect.

The hostess (her name tag read Belle) wore a long khaki colored canvas skirt and black boots. She turned to me as soon as we'd cleared the noise and held out her hand for me to grasp. "I hope I'm not making a fool of myself, but I'd kick myself if I didn't ask. You're Samantha Warren, aren't you?"

I took her hand firmly and smiled.

"I thought so, I love your books."

"Thank you, Belle."

She blushed and waved a hand. "I'm not really Belle, my name is Christy. We use different names." She didn't explain why and I didn't ask. As we approached the table, Peter stood, bent to buss my cheek, then held his hand out to Wayne as I introduced them. Belle faded away and I noticed Peter's friend.

"You've got to have a bit of pull to manage this table," Wayne was saying to Peter as he held a chair for me. *Wayne was impressed.*

Peter merely shrugged. "Sammy, I want you to meet a friend of mine. Jack Parnell, this is Samantha Warren." I shook the man's hand while taking mental notes of him. He was at least in his early forties if not more, sporting a thick gold band on his left hand. Reddish brown hair dusted his forehead and he peered at me through dark green eyes. He laced his fingers together and studied me as I sat.

"Pete's told me a lot about you, Mrs. Warren."

"It's not actually Mrs., please call me Sam. This is my husband, Wayne Dunham."

He nodded at Wayne and they shook hands.

The waiter, Bart, appeared almost immediately to provide Wayne and me with drinks and menus and replenish Peter and Jack's.

"How long have you been here?" I asked scanning the multi-page menu after ordering coffee.

Peter waved a hand. "Not long."

I'll bet. "Have you eaten here before?" I asked.

"Couple times, they're known for their steaks."

I watched Peter studying Wayne and didn't think Wayne was measuring up very well. I'm not at all sure whether or not that was wishful thinking on my part. Probably so.

I liked the waiter; he hovered without giving the appearance of doing so. I was fairly certain that Bart wasn't his given name any more than 'Belle' was Christy's. I liked the fact he dressed in black (Black Bart?). Anyway, he kept our drinks flowing and when we were ready to order, he was spot on to take them. He didn't write anything down, a sign that *I* thought meant he was a good waiter. For my husband, it meant that Wayne was going to do his level best to make his order as difficult as possible to test Bart's limits and abilities. He had done it numerous times before and I always slipped the waitperson an extra twenty or so for having to put up with Wayne's crap. I caught Peter's eye and he winked at me knowingly.

Did I say how much I liked Peter Frost?

The guys ordered steaks, baked potatoes with all the fixings, and salads. I ordered corn chowder that was billed as the Lodge special and a salad with homemade blue cheese dressing. Wayne offered to buy a bottle of wine wanting desperately to display his newly acquired knowledge of vintages and bouquets, but the offer was countered by Jack Parnell's order of a loaded nachos appetizer. They all decided beer would serve them better with that. I knew then I was the designated driver, at least for our vehicle. I could feel the testosterone emanating from their every pore. I found myself smiling and shaking my head.

Peter leaned back against the soft cushioned seats, cocked his head and smiled. "You look like you're storing away notes," he said as he raised his glass in salute.

Wayne snorted. "She used to bring along a notebook until I put a stop to that."

Peter ignored Wayne's comment and continued. "Do you remember what you told me you'd always wanted to do, Sammy?"

I frowned in his direction and waited for him to continue.

He jabbed a finger towards Jack. "Jack is a detective with the Montgomery County Police Department's homicide division. He's agreed to let you follow him around and pick his brain."

"I haven't agreed to it yet, Pete," Jack said, eying Peter.

"You will Jack," Peter answered him without looking his way. Peter had my attention *and* interest.

"Jack's an old partner of mine," he explained further.

"You're a cop, too?"

"Was – until I went to law school."

Jack laughed. "Until it was in his best interest to attend law school, he should say. He wasn't the most disciplined of cops."

"Like you are," Peter replied sarcastically in Jack's direction.

I had to smile at their banter. I could see the two of them playing the 'good cop, bad cop' roles and was easily formulating a story line that would reflect that when Wayne slid his arm around my shoulders and spoke.

"You want my wife to follow this guy around? Won't that be dangerous? Are you sure you're working in *her* best interests?"

The look Peter leveled at him was rather venomous - and delicious – and entirely in my imagination.

"I wouldn't do anything to put Sammy in danger," Peter answered him evenly.

"Couldn't tell that by me, buddy. I don't think I agree with your plan here."

I looked at Wayne and tried, unsuccessfully, to control my anger. "I don't think you have any say in this, Wayne."

"Of course I do, sweetheart, you're my wife. What this hump is proposing is dangerous."

"It was *my* idea, Wayne, and *I* want to do it."

"Sorry, babe, I'm going to have to disagree," Wayne replied.

My nostrils flared and even Peter Frost reared back in surprise. "Did you just call me 'babe'?" I hissed in Wayne's direction as quietly as I could which wasn't very.

He smiled indulgently towards me, but said nothing. I hated when he did that, didn't rise to the bait of an argument. Of course, this wasn't the time or place and certainly not in front of Peter and Jack and the other diners, but that was beside the point.

"I need to go to the rest room," I said through clenched teeth. Wayne slid from the seat and let me up. I knew he wanted to say that was a good idea – that it would give me time to cool down.

He didn't though. Damn him!

What I wanted to do was leave, but I returned to the table and sat in silence. The three of them managed some small talk quite nicely. At least I think so – I didn't listen. I was attentive to Bart when he approached, but that was it. *Screw them.* And they didn't seem to mind. They all probably thought I was quite the bitch. I wished I had brought a notebook.

The chowder was delicious, a nice blend of corn, multi-colored peppers, and rosemary in a creamy base seasoned with cracked red pepper; no potatoes to provide bulk that it didn't need.

I was aware of someone's eyes boring into me and I looked up at Peter.

"You all right, Sam?" Both Wayne and Jack were absent from the table

I nodded.

"Your husband is …" he searched for the proper word.

Possessive? Over-bearing? "A jerk?" I provided.

Peter laughed. "I was going to say skeptical."

I looked around the restaurant. "Did Jack take him off to shoot him?"

"No, Wayne's in the men's room and Jack got a call," he tipped his head. "You really zoned out there. Get some good ideas?"

I reddened under his gaze. "Sorry."

"Don't be, I'm learning a lot about my new client."

"Well, I'm sorry anyway. I try not to let him bait me and I fail a lot."

Peter nodded his head and finished off his beer. "You're out of that seminar by the way."

"I may not go to Georgia. Wayne hasn't broached the subject of me going with him again."

"You should go and see your friends anyway. I can make the arrangements if you want."

I shrugged. "How many clients do you have?" I asked as he looked past me. I felt Wayne slide in beside me placing his hand on my thigh. Peter slid from the booth and smiled. "Just one, Sam. Order me some coffee and a piece of apple pie a la mode, I'll be right back."

I grinned and signaled for Bart.

"One what, sweetheart?" Wayne asked.

I didn't answer.

"I don't think you should do it, Sam," Wayne renewed his protest on our drive home. Too bad, I was considering going with him to Georgia again.

"Why not? I could use the technical advice." I sailed down the hill over the stretch of Norbeck Road that spanned Rock Creek Park and nearly sideswiped a deer.

"Isn't your new boy an ex-cop?" Wayne said with a sneer (not really, I was still a little mad at him).

"Wayne, you could at least treat my writing as a viable profession – and stop being such a jerk. The way you treated the waiter was unforgivable. Just once I'd like us to go out to eat without you having to try to trick someone into messing up. The kid was really good tonight."

Wayne snorted. "Is that why you left the guy a hefty tip?" He sighed as we waited for the road to clear on our turn onto Bauer Drive. I stopped just short of laying on the horn to move an obstructing car from my path. "You've always wanted to write professionally and I'm trying to be encouraging."

I may have grunted.

"What's wrong with the fluff novels?" he tried capturing my hand. I brushed him away.

"Nothing is wrong with then, but you think that's all I can do, isn't it?"

Wayne hesitated a hair too long before he answered. "No."

Too late.

I made the turn onto Russet Road – perhaps a bit too fast. Wayne yelped and grabbed the door handle and the action and his reaction made me feel better. We were silent until I pulled the car into the garage bay and turned the key. Okay, Wayne was actually holding his breath. He expelled air as I pushed open the door and slid out of the seat when he found his voice. "Don't slam the door," he said.

Yeah right.

Needless to say, we didn't do the nasty that night.

Chapter 5

I slept in my study, first curling up in the chair and then stretching out on the hard floor. It was cold, but I was damned if I was going to open the door in search of a blanket and pillow and something soft. I woke up cranky and it was probably best Wayne had already packed and departed. I found his itinerary on my desk. He had slipped in and left it along with a note that said he *thought* he'd be back Friday. He also thought we should plan on being alone and he wouldn't say anything if I didn't. Like I said, we were always best when we didn't talk.

He didn't write he was sorry. Wayne never apologized because he never thought he did anything wrong. Perhaps it *was* me. I scanned his schedule and booted up the computer to bring up a map of Georgia just as the telephone rang. I hadn't had my morning coffee yet and debated ignoring it. The machine would take a message until the caffeine ritual was taken care of.

Who was I trying to kid?

"Hello?"

"Hi, Sam," Peter said.

"Hey."

"Everything all right?"

Well, it had been right up until that point. I leaned my head on my hand and fought to control my emotions – unsuccessfully. Peter waited on the other end of the line. I would come to love that about him; his patience and silent understanding of me even when *I* didn't understand me.

"I'm sorry," I finally said, swiping at my eyes.

"Why should you feel sorry?"

I shrugged pointlessly.

"Had coffee yet?"

"Not yet, I just woke up."

"I have some for you. Take a shower and dress and we'll go to breakfast. Jack says he'll have some time this morning. We're to meet him at the Pancake House."

"When?" I loved the Pancake House; they had pecan waffles to die for.

"Twenty minutes. I'll drive."

"When will you be here?"

"I already am," he replied. I padded to my window and moved back the curtain waving to him and getting a hand in return.

"Come on in, I'll be ready in ten or so."

Rather than answering, he broke the connection and pushed open the door of his dark red Ford Explorer. I smiled. I would have expected him to have nothing less than a Hummer, Peter was definitely a Hummer person.

I grabbed some clothes and waited at the bedroom door for him to come inside and hand me the coffee. He said he'd wait in my office and I let him. I had no qualms about leaving him to his own devices while I showered. I trusted him. And he didn't show a reaction one way or the other when he saw the state I was in. As I said, I really liked the guy.

I did my best with my hair and the hair dryer. My lack of good sleep hadn't done much for my complexion, so I didn't figure any effort would have been worthwhile. It was better Peter and Jack realized my shortcomings early on. I tossed on some jeans and a sweater and hoped it wasn't the same set I'd had on when we'd first met. I don't do a lot of shopping and – well, it doesn't really matter I guess – it goes along with all those other shortcomings. I did have on clean underwear (a pair of Wayne's silk boxers - I loved his boxer shorts).

When I emerged from the bedroom, Peter was reading the computer screen, twirling a pen end over end in his hand as he did so. I don't think he realized I was there.

"What do you think so far?" I asked and noted that he didn't startle easily.

"I like it. Want me to turn it off?"

I nodded and shuffled through the pile on the floor extracting a black and white notebook and a pen. "Ready?"

I was down the front steps when he asked. "You don't lock your doors?"

I turned. "Not usually - much to Wayne's chagrin." I sighed and came back to do so after checking that I had my keys in my purse. I smiled thinly his way and he laughed.

Men were all alike.

I figured our trip to the Pancake House would be a good opportunity for me to learn a little more about him and wasted no time in pursuing that.

"Are you married?" I asked, directing him to turn onto Dowlais Drive and then left onto Flint Rock Road.

"Divorced, I have a daughter though – Lisa. She's nine," he said and grinned.

"You see her often?"

"Not often enough, but the divorce was amicable and Tracy lets me have Lisa whenever I want – and can. You have no children?"

I shook my head. "Wayne didn't want the complication," I answered and left it at that.

"I take it he got off early this morning," Peter observed.

"He could have left last night for all I know," I said in a way that hopefully would curtail any further discussion. Peter looked at me sideways and shook his head.

"I take it then that you definitely aren't going to Georgia with him."

We crossed over the Metro tracks and slowed for the line of traffic turning onto Chapman Street. I didn't want to talk about me or Wayne. "So does Lisa live around here?" I asked.

Peter chuckled. "She lives in Arlington." He waited at the light at Bou Avenue and I frowned, the Pancake House was to the right across the Pike. I opened my mouth to say so when he interrupted. "We're picking Jack up. He's right over here," Peter pointed to a store on the corner.

"His new case," he explained as he turned the corner and stopped before Wentworths. It was a fairly new store, by virtue of being at this location for six years or so. It sold dinnerware and crystal and sat on a corner of an upscale strip mall. I'd heard of Wentworths (it was part of a chain) and seen the advertisements, but had yet to go inside. The store name was in lights above the two double door front entrances and proclaimed '*Wentworths – Synonymous with fine dining since 1898*'.

"Is Wayne staying with your friends you mentioned?" Peter asked.

"No, they don't like him."

Peter laughed. "I think you should go see them then, take a couple days."

I shrugged.

We could see Jack talking with a chunky, well-dressed blonde before one of the entrances. She eventually opened the door for him and let him out. Evidently, Wentworths wasn't yet open for business as I watched her twist the lock closed behind him. He opened the car door and nodded to us as he slid into the seat with a sigh.

"What happened?" Peter asked as he inched the Ford forward waiting for foot traffic to clear.

"Their warehouse manager was found crushed beneath a pile of boxes. It happened last night after they closed. We're ruling out suspicious death," Jack said without further comment.

I was going to learn he played everything close to the vest – or at least he would try.

I cocked my head. "How could someone die underneath a pile of boxes?"

Jack Parnell's head snapped in my direction. "They sell dinnerware, most of the sets average fifty pounds. It's a big warehouse and they have tall stacks," he answered curtly and probably hoped he was dismissive.

I reared back in mock surprise. "OSHA inspectors must have a field day in there," I remarked. No retorts from either one though, when I looked Peter's way, I thought he was smiling. I wondered if I was going to get any information from Jack Parnell. Then I decided I just had to ask the right questions. Of course, this was all contingent on whether or not he agreed to help me. He hadn't done that as far I as was aware.

The Pancake House was crowded; then again, it was always crowded. It was open from seven to two every day and sold breakfast foods ranging from a simple piece of toast to fried dough covered with a multitude of gooey, sugary fruit toppings. It had been in this location for sixty years and would probably be around – and busy – for a hundred more.

Peter asked for a table (I lie, not *a* table, *the* table). It was in the back corner and, when we were shown to it fifteen minutes later, I could see why. It was the only one that wasn't butt to cheek with all the others. If there was any privacy in the small restaurant, then this was it. It was a small rectangular table with a padded bench that arced around three sides with the capability of having two more chairs brought in. I slid in the middle and was flanked by the two men. The hostess who had led us here had been followed by a tall, wiry man decked out in a three-piece grey suit with a maroon shirt and maroon and navy tie. Definitely a Mafia type (hey, cut it out; I deal in fantasy).

He had neatly coiffed brown hair and sharp brown eyes and he was angry, extremely angry.

As the hostess handed us our menus, he tapped her on the shoulder; it didn't appear that he was being gentle about it.

"Excuse me, Miss, but I was here before they were. I demand this table."

The hostess was of indeterminate age, short, thin, dark hair curled around a tired face with hollow blue eyes and pale cheeks. She didn't wear a name tag and she no longer wore the tired smile she'd pasted on when she greeted Peter. She looked as though she could handle herself in a confrontation. I envied her.

"There'll be another table for one available shortly, sir; you'll be first in line for that."

"I don't want the next table, I want this one."

"I'm sorry, sir, but I'm not going to ask them to leave. Come back with me and I'll seat you as soon as possible." She certainly wasn't going to tell him Peter requested this table.

The man grabbed her arm and spun her around. "You don't understand, sugar, I want this table!" He measured his words carefully - or should have.

The woman looked down at Jack and then back at the man. Her knee came up hard in his nuts. Frankly, I was impressed that she could reach that high. She pressed his head on the table as he bent low and leaned in so he could hear and understand her.

"These fine people have this table. If you wish me to seat you at another, we will go do that right now, sir. By the way, if you ever call me or any other woman 'sugar' within my earshot, I'll do worse than this. Got it?"

"I'll sue your ass off, *sugar*," the man said back, albeit in a slightly higher voice.

The woman laughed. "You go right ahead and do that, *darling*, but I can guarantee you that no one here will bear witness for you. You've been such a pain in the ass this morning that every person here will back me up." She straightened and let him do the same. "Now, do you want that table?" She smiled sweetly and then watched as the man stormed from the restaurant ranting the whole way out.

Jack Parnell shook his head. "You know someday someone's going to call your bluff, Liz."

Liz shrugged.

"And both Pete and I are officers of the court; we're duty bound to bear witness."

Liz patted Jack's cheek and turned. "You have a pleasant breakfast now, you hear?"

Peter chuckled as our waitress timidly approached with a pot of coffee and filled our mugs with more of that heavenly elixir.

"*That* was amazing!" I said after we'd given our orders. "In fact, I think I'll write it down." I looked sidelong at Jack. "You know her?"

"Know her?" Peter laughed again. "He was married to her for three years. It was the best three years of his life." Jack didn't look as though he was enjoying Peter's joke very much. I jotted down a few notes and then for good measure noted down some questions that I wanted to ask Jack later when he was more amenable, or not. I'd ask them anyway.

Jack brooded to my left and Peter watched me as he sipped his coffee. "This is what she does all the time. She's either writing them down or taking mental notes, Jack. She'd make a good cop I think."

I stuck my tongue out at him sideways and had finished my notetaking by the time the waitress approached with our breakfasts.

Jack dove into his eggs. "So what is it you want to know, Sam?" he looked up at me. "It's okay I call you Sam, isn't it? I mean your husband will think that's all right?"

I leveled my best PMS stare his way as I munched on a piece of my pecan waffle. I shrugged. "I need to know police procedure; maybe follow you around on a case." I stabbed my fork in his direction. "Like this warehouse guy -"

"Hector Rodriquez," Jack supplied the man's name.

I reddened, embarrassed at being so cavalier with the man's life. "Sorry. Do you really think that he was crushed accidentally or do you suspect that it was foul play?"

Peter smiled, but said nothing as Jack held my gaze.

"I don't *think* anything until I get forensic results." He pointed his finger my way. "That's one thing you could clarify when you write this stuff. Make it plain that cases aren't solved within an hour's time frame. Evidence takes time to process and results are days and weeks in getting back to us. I really hate these shows that make it seem like the detectives have second sight. We don't. We're plodders and most of the time, we stumble onto clues." He took a sip of his freshly topped mug. "Another thing, crime scenes aren't pristine. People mess stuff up all the time trying to revive the victim or just simply trying to confuse us. I hate …"

Peter chuckled. "I think this means that he'll take you on, Sammy."

I nodded, but didn't take my eyes off Jack. "But – do *you* think it was more than accidental?" I asked again.

Jack looked annoyed and then he slowly nodded his head. He waggled his finger at me. "This doesn't mean you go blab this to anyone, do you understand?"

I sat back. I hadn't realized that I'd been on the edge of my seat (literally and figuratively) throughout his little speech. "Of course I wouldn't, who would I blab it to?"

"Your husband, for one," Jack answered without hesitation.

"No fear there, Jack; its okay to call you Jack, isn't it?" I asked as I cut off another piece of the now cold waffle. Peter sniggered to my right.

"This is a match made in fucking heaven," Peter commented as he signaled the waitress for more coffee.

Jack's cell phone rang and he pulled it out of his breast pocket, put it to his ear, listened, and then folded it back up. "I have a thing," he said. "How do you want to work this, Sam?"

I shrugged and looked to Peter. "I may be out of town for a couple days. Peter will let you know when I get back and we can get together again."

Jack nodded and went for his wallet.

Peter held up a restraining hand. "We'll get it, Jack, I'll be in touch." Jack wove his way through the narrow restaurant and disappeared out the door.

"Where do your friends live?" Peter asked, pulling out a leather-bound notebook and a pen from his pocket.

"Kings Bay; Greg is attached to a submarine there," I finished off the coffee.

"So you'd fly into Jacksonville then?"

I nodded. "And I'll need a rental car," I sighed "You sure I should take time then? Shouldn't I be slaving away at the computer?"

Peter smiled. "I think you need diversion."

"I was just going by what my publish –"

"We're changing your publisher just as soon as you've met your obligation with him," he said curtly.

Can we do that? I thought.

A ghost of a smile appeared on his face. "Yes, we can do that, Sam. I believe you've been misrepresented and I'm going to change that." *Great this guy reads minds!*

"But I still have the last two books."

He waved a hand of dismissal. "You'll get them done, I have no fear."

I grinned and stared at the table. "Actually I had an idea for one last night. Can I run it by you?"

"I should hope so." Peter rested his elbows on the table.

"I want to explore mythology. I don't think that justice has been done to the romantic angle of mythology."

Peter waited for more and then spoke up when nothing more was forthcoming. "But you don't know enough about mythology," he stated with a grin.

"Exactly." Have I mentioned how much I like this guy?

He stood and tossed a few bills on the table. “I know a guy; I’ll set up a meeting.”

I smiled and slid from the booth. “That’s what I thought you’d say.”

CHAPTER 6

I took the coastal route (Route 1A north and then over to Route 95) from Jacksonville to Kings Bay. The sunshine was brilliant and warm and a welcome change from the chill that still gripped the D.C area that morning when I'd left. I needed to see the ocean again. It was both exhilarating and calming to see the sun glinting off the gentle waves. I opened my windows so that the fishy brine could fill my nostrils and purge my winter mindset.

Armed with a Mapquest map of the area and my friends' address - they actually lived in the town of Kingsland, I wove my way through their development to Laurel Landing Boulevard. They lived on a golf course, their house one of the few that didn't back up to one of the holes. I saw that as an advantage as there would be less chance of a stray golf ball striking their windows. I had met Andrea and Greg Sharp when we all lived in Florida. Greg had been stationed at the Naval Systems Center in Panama City Beach and Wayne had been based there for a year. Andrea (and Greg) and I had hit it off immediately. Both of them had tolerated Wayne. It probably had something to do with the fact that Wayne had tried to proposition Andrea, but I could be wrong. She was the only friend (that I'm aware of) that Wayne had approached. Because of this transgression, he had lost out on strong friendship with the Sharps.

The community was less than three years old, built up around the newly established submarine base. Similar communities had grown and prospered with epic proportions in other areas around the country. Before the base, there had been the town of St. Mary's and little else save for the occasional shack or two all the way to the interstate.

I slowed so I could read the house numbers and then spotted Andrea kneeling in a small garden to the side of her new home. It was stucco – as were all of them in the area – a one story home with two story height. Neighbors were close, but not too much so and a large white fence separated them from construction of another phase of the development going on behind them. I pulled up to the curb, turned off the car, exited, and waited for her to notice me.

Andrea was a beautiful woman with fine chiseled features and a healthy tanned complexion. Her black hair was cropped short and framed her head; I've never seen her with a hair out of place. She had deep violet colored eyes and thin lips, a slim body, and a perfect shape. Greg was her antithesis – stocky, fair haired with pale blue eyes; their only similarity was that they were both the same height – both slightly taller than me.

Andrea was working on pulling up a particularly stubborn weed when she glanced up and saw my rental car. She frowned and rose to wipe her brow on her pink cotton shirt sleeve. Recognition dawned and she approached me with arms outstretched and a wide grin on her face.

"As I live and breathe, Samantha, is that you?"

We hugged, and then she bent over searching inside the car for signs of Wayne. "Please tell me you've come to your senses and left him."

I laughed. "I haven't come to my senses, but I have come to visit." I spread my arms out. "It's good to be in warm weather again," I declared. "Can I see the house?"

"Of course, how long are you here?"

"A couple days, I have a place in town," I lied.

"Bullshit, but nice try. You know you're welcome to stay here any time for as long as you want, especially if you left Wayne behind."

It had been Andrea that had persuaded me to set up a separate bank account when the meager royalties from my writing had started coming in. She said I should trust

Wayne about as far as I could throw him. I think I honestly thought she was wrong about him, but I followed her advice anyway.

I laughed to myself. There wasn't anyone I knew that thought I should stay with Wayne. I knew why. Frankly, being alone scares me, even though I was alone in fact most of the time. It's the security issue I guess. "Actually, he's around here somewhere on business."

"I shall call Greg and tell him to request a couple days off then, so we can show you around and so he won't run into Wayne." She pushed open the door and let me precede her.

It was warm in Georgia, but not so warm that the air conditioner was a necessity. Andrea had windows open and a gentle warm breeze flowed through the house. The front door opened into the living room/dining room with vaulted ceilings dominated by two large, dark stained fans that circulated the fresh air. There was a half wall section separating the dining room table that faced the front and the living room grouping that faced Greg's entertainment system. That was the only thing that Greg and Wayne had bonded over, entertainment systems and the best brands of speakers etc. etc. etc. Any other unrelated topic had been off limits.

To the left was the kitchen with a dining nook that faced the small back yard and a white fence. There was another door that led to the garage through a utility/laundry room. Beyond the kitchen was a corridor that led to a full bath shared by the bedrooms on either side of it. One bedroom served as a guest room with pale blue and green decor; the other was full of exercise equipment and a small television for diversion when the treadmill was in use. From the breakfast nook, we walked onto a screened-in lanai full of huge potted plants. Interspersed among the Dieffenbachia, schefflera, jade and a banana tree was white wicker furniture with plush dark green cushions. We continued on through and entered the master bedroom suite. Andrea had decorated the room with pale salmon and sea foam green. Behind the white headboard of the bed, she had painted a large palm tree with a setting tropical sun as a backdrop. The effect was breathtaking.

"I love this, Andy," I said as I turned toward the back wall. Between the two windows was a mirror that reflected their bed and background – an even nicer effect. I stood there speechless.

"I love it, Greg's not too happy with the mirror when we have sex, but he makes allowances and I make him forget it's there."

We passed back through to the living room and completed the tour in Andrea's office which faced the road at the front and the garden she'd been working in on the side.

"It's beautiful," I said, trying not to get too mired in self pity. We'd both spent our married lives moving from place to place, each time setting up household in what we could only imagine as a permanent place yet knowing full well it wasn't. We had lamented countless times with one another about our nomadic lives and our wish for permanence. Andrea would never tell her husband about those discussions; I wasn't so sure I hadn't mentioned it to Wayne (a few dozen times).

"Let me call Greg and you bring in your things. I've been remiss in not offering you a bathroom. He'll be so happy you came, Samantha." She hugged me and I went to avail myself of the facilities and retrieve my suitcase.

We ate chicken cordon bleu, fresh asparagus, and roasted potatoes then retired to the lanai for coffee and dessert. I skipped the dessert of cookies and ice cream and settled back in the wicker rocker closing my eyes and listening to the sounds of the southern night.

"I have been given a couple days off," Greg declared off in the distance. "I thought we'd take you to the Okefenokee Swamp tomorrow if you're up to it."

"Sounds heavenly," I commented.

"I have some literature on it if you're interested. I know how you like to bone up."

I nodded. I think.

"So what have you been up to, Sam?" Greg pressed. He wasn't about to let me drift off to sleep – not yet.

I repositioned myself bringing a leg up underneath my butt and sitting sideways to face the two of them on the wicker settee. "I have a new publicist, a real nice guy. He thinks I can write mysteries and has set me up with a police detective friend of his who's agreed to let me shadow him for a while."

I told them about Peter and Jack Parnell and Wayne's objections of my association with them. Then I slipped easily with no compunction into the case in which Jack was involved. He certainly didn't mean that I couldn't tell *them*. What harm could it do? They were at least five hundred miles away. "Jack doesn't think it was an accident."

"It seems as though you have a plan in mind, Sammy," Greg said as he poured me more coffee and gathered up dishes preparatory to taking them to the kitchen.

I did an intense study of the white fence and then my eyes met his. "I was thinking on my way down here that I might apply for a job at the store; preliminary stages of thought, mind you. What do you think?"

"I think you should stay on the fringes, Samantha," Andrea answered with her usual air of common sense.

Greg and I, however, were made from the same adventurous cloth and he shook his head vigorously. "That's what I thought. You could be on the inside and give your detective friend some insight to the personalities."

Andrea rose and shook her head, taking the dirty dishes from Greg's hands as she crossed the threshold into the kitchen. "I swear you two are related; you both have hair-brained schemes and absolutely no sense."

Behind her back, Greg and I did a high five and hunkered down to formulate a plan of attack on my return to Rockville. We conspired until 2 a.m. and then surrendered to bed. I thought for certain I was too juiced to sleep, but next I knew Andrea was gently shaking me awake at seven.

"It's too early," I grumbled, burrowing deeper into the bed.

"You can sleep in the car, we're going for breakfast." She swatted at my butt. "Come on, Samantha, get ready."

She left the room and I squeezed my eyes tight, but it was too late. I was awake and there was nothing I could do to change that. I slid from the bed and padded to the bathroom to shower. I could hear Andrea in the distance urging Greg awake as well.

We breakfasted at The Waffle House and were soon heading west along State Route 40 towards the town of Folkston. On the way over, I read the brochures and printouts that Greg had obtained from the internet before their last trip there, glancing up every so often to catch a glimpse of the passing countryside. It was evident that this part of Georgia was not prospering. Modest homes, trailers, and shacks stood side by side with dirt and gravel lawns and drives. One modern convenience prevailed though – practically every one of the residences had a cable line or a satellite dish.

We traveled up the long drive of the entrance to the National Wildlife Refuge where stately southern pines stood sentinel over palmetto bushes.

“Keep an eye out for wildlife in there,” Greg whispered.

I guess he didn’t want to scare any away. It worked. We saw numerous fox, deer, an odd looking squirrel, turtles alongside the road, and I’m pretty sure we spotted an eagle.

I dredged up my reading in my mind. The swamp covers somewhere in the vicinity of 440,000 acres – it would be a hard place to miss when traveling east-west in southern Georgia. It was a natural peat bog formerly part of the ocean floor; the peat having formed from layers of decaying plants in the water. Because of the unstable peat, the land moves. In fact, the name Okefenokee is derived from the Choctaw for 'quivering earth'. Hey, my mind is filled with a gazillion useless facts.

"We'll go buy tickets for the boat ride first and then do the loop road. There's a boardwalk we can do as well, depending on the time the boat leaves," Greg said as he pulled into the parking lot of the Visitor's Center. There were several raccoons hurrying along by the picnic tables before us. Two buildings were visible; one the museum and the other the inevitable gift shop where we would purchase the boat tickets. A canal ran alongside the museum and out past the gift shop where the boats sat. In the water were several logs; on closer inspection, these logs took the shape of lazily drifting alligators. Some faced the concrete ramp that led up to the deck outside the museum and others faced the docks where the boats were moored. I think they were licking their chops just waiting for someone to slip in the water.

Several school buses were parked behind us and we could hear the screeches of kids when they realized what the lumps in the water actually were. It took all of the chaperones to keep the kids from skipping out onto the none-too-sturdy looking docks for a closer look. I was getting a whole new appreciation for teachers and the parents that volunteered for that shit.

It was a pleasant day as we drove the loop road trying to spot more alligators in the channels of water alongside the road. All the ones I spotted turned out to be logs caught up in the current. Andrea spied a snake crawling up the side of a tree – eww.

We parked the car and took the boardwalk into the observation tower positioned about a mile in. I didn't think much of its close proximity to the water until we climbed the tower and saw at least a half dozen very *large* looking (even from that height) alligators below us in the marsh grasses. On the return trip, you can be assured that I walked in the dead center of the five foot wide walkway. I'd also read in the brochure that alligators could rear up quite high out of a floating position in the water. I wasn't about to walk the edge, let alone bend over it to be up close and personal to something that could snap my head off without a second thought.

We actually witnessed an alligator-rearing-up incident as we neared the end of the boardwalk and were about five hundred feet from the car. There was a group of school kids standing on an observation deck overlooking a rather large pool. An alligator watched with detached interest just hoping for one of the tender morsels to make a mistake. One of the kids hung out over the railing, clicking his fingers and making kissy noises. The alligator swung up around sideways coming within inches of the outstretched hand; or would have if the hand, body, and child hadn't been snatched backwards by a chaperone. I heard, as we ran hell-bent for the car, that particular student wouldn't be going to the observation tower.

Our boat ride tickets were for two o'clock, so when we returned to the Visitor's Center we had a couple hours to kill. We used the facilities (keeping a vigil out for bathroom snakes), toured the museum, watched the floating alligators through the glass of the back deck, and had lunch before we headed over for the boat.

Each boat held fourteen people. I diligently checked the height from water to the boat's edge and thought perhaps it was high enough to be out of danger before I settled back in my seat. The water was brown and murky and I could just envision a hundred or so reptilian eyes staring up at us from just beyond our range of vision. The water was brown because of the high concentration of tannic acid – dissolution of the peat and other vegetative materials. It smelled … well, swampy. We glided along the Suwannee Canal (you remember the Stephen Foster hit?) deep into the swamp as our guide recited a perhaps canned, but very entertaining speech in his thick-as-molasses southern drawl. He explained about the water color and mentioned several times how important it was for us to keep our hands and arms inside the boat. He told us how the canal was dug back in the early 1890's in an attempt to drain it for logging purposes and how, fortunately, the project was abandoned. I'd like to think that the native habitat had some say in that and shuddered at the thought of how many workers' lives were lost while the bigwigs debated.

He pointed out plant life (golden trumpet, hooded, parrot and trumpet pitcher plants, sundews, bladderwort and butterwort) as we glided along searching for alligator and wild boars. He spun tales of growing up in the swamp and mentioned he was sixth generation swamp rat on his mother's side and seventh on his father's. Then our guide pulled up in an open stretch of water and cut the engine. He fell silent and so did everyone else as we drifted there listening to the sounds of frogs and birds – and probably alligators. It was mystical. This quiet, unspoiled wilderness just miles from modern civilization still existed despite man, just as it had for seven thousand years.

I was humbled.

The guide broke the spell, restarted the engine and we headed back in silence. We didn't actually see any alligators or wild boars, but I don't believe anyone there minded one bit.

CHAPTER 7

Elaine Newcomb carefully smoothed out the newsprint as she strained to listen to the hushed conversation between Gisele and Andrew. She was never any good at being subtle, so she tried not to spend too much time at the same thing. She moved from the register area and started to straighten some fixtures that Andrew had just finished merchandising.

"I think that looks fine, Elaine," Andrew said softly, making her jump. She hadn't realized that he'd moved her way. "I'll tell you later what she said," he added with a wink of his eye and then proceeded to clean up his mess.

Elaine smiled sheepishly as she turned to greet the two elderly ladies who had just entered the store. She did like Andrew even though she knew he didn't like her – well, sexually that is – he seemed to like her as a person. Most of their colleagues didn't like him and she didn't think it was because of his sexual persuasion. He didn't suffer fools well. The fact others didn't like him bothered her. Hell, all she wanted to do was look anyway – he was certainly enjoyable to look at. Elaine wasn't the most beautiful of women, but Andrew always managed to make her feel special. She had been instrumental in introducing him to Fletcher.

"Can I help you, ladies?" she asked pleasantly. They looked as though they may have been sisters. They stood about the same height and definitely had the same eye color of blue and, of course, the same hair color of silver grey.

The one – Elaine would learn she was the spokeswoman of the two – nodded and smiled. "We're looking to purchase something from a bridal registry for our grand-niece. We believe that she is registered here."

"I can certainly check that for you. What is the bride's name?"

"Chelsea Lawson."

Elaine smiled. "Yes, I know she has a registry, we've been getting requests all week. The wedding is next weekend, I believe," she said as she guided them to the customer service desk where Gisele Fournier was finishing up with a telephone order.

Elaine seated them at the registry desk, introduced herself, then excused herself to ask Gisele if she would cover the front desk so Elaine could take care of the women.

Sales at Wentworths were not based on commission, but there was an unspoken and unbroken rule that whoever greeted the guests would serve them.

Gisele nodded curtly and rounded the customer service desk to go up front with a, "let me know of you need any help, Elaine."

Elaine returned to her customers with a smile and brought up Chelsea Lawson's registry on the computer.

"You say Chelsea is your grand-niece, Mrs. Potter?"

"She's our brother's granddaughter, yes."

"Let's see now, what price range were you thinking?" she asked as she printed the registry.

"Somewhere in the vicinity of seventy-five dollars each though we're willing to pay more if we have to," Mrs. Potter spoke. As she said it, she glanced at her sister who nodded her confirmation.

Elaine scanned the list for items that had not yet been purchased. "We have a vegetable bowl in your grandniece's pattern for eighty-four dollars. She needs two more place settings of her cutlery – those are fifty dollars each. There are some pieces of stemware still available and a vase she particularly cherished for one hundred and seventy-five."

Elaine looked toward them expectantly.

"Lordy, I just don't know what we should do; you said she has all her place settings of china? That's what we really wanted to buy."

"Yes, ma'am," Elaine replied and rose. "Let me gather some of these items so you can see something tangible. Perhaps that will help you decide. I'll be right back." She rose and left them seated in the comfortable chairs and entered the warehouse.

Chris Nichols and the new manager, Jessica, were busy processing a truck. Jeff was rifling through some dinnerware sets searching for a pattern a customer requested. Holly Bush was readying to come on duty, fiddling with her name tag in obvious consternation. Holly's beady little eyes flitted to Elaine as she ran a finger along the place settings of flatware looking for the Malvern pattern. Elaine slid two off the shelf and then crossed the warehouse to the location of the stemware, quickly removing four boxes.

Elaine turned toward Holly as the sales supervisor approached. She hesitated slightly and then pressed forward.

"Holly, could you take these out to the registry area while I look for a vegetable bowl, please?"

Holly scowled.

Jessica approached and smiled. "Holly would be happy to help you out, Elaine. Wouldn't you, Holly?"

"If Hols doesn't want to help, Jess, I will," Andrew said as he pushed through the double doors with a load of broken down boxes and two bags of trash.

Holly grabbed the items from Elaine and nearly mowed Andrew down as she headed for the door.

Andrew turned on his heels to follow Holly. "Don't worry, Elaine, I'll make sure she doesn't smash them against the customer's head for you."

Elaine proceeded down the warehouse toward the back door hoping she wouldn't have to climb to the top of the shelving to retrieve the bowl. She hated heights.

The lighting in the back corner was dim at best, but she felt she would be able to find what she needed without extra light. She searched the lower levels of shelving and knew after a few moments that she'd have to climb the ladder. Most of the accessories were on the top. The platform ladder she preferred was on the other side of the warehouse and, therefore, not available for her use with the truck pallets were in the way. One of the taller step ladders was, thankfully, nearby and she maneuvered it into position below the spot she felt the pattern would be located. Rather than opening it to the scissor position, however, she leaned it against the top edge of one shelf and wedged it against the lower shelf opposite. Elaine took a deep breath and held tight to the railings as she ascended the steps. She was able to lean over far enough to check the few boxes in the immediate vicinity without having to climb on top. The box she needed was not there.

She shuffled a few more around and met with more failure as she repeated the mantra that she was all right and she'd soon be down on firm ground once again. It took her a few more moments - and several repetitions of her mantra - before she found the inner strength to crawl onto the shelving. It took her a few more moments of deep breathing before she dared to stand to resume her search of the boxes. She tread carefully, picking up and squinting at the numbers that would tell her which pattern she was holding all the while wishing she had flipped on more lights.

A box, unusually light, threw her off balance. She grabbed for the top of the ladder to steady herself and let her heart return to its normal rhythm – or at least as near to normal as it would get until she returned to the floor. The box should have had merchandise in it, but it was empty. She frowned.

She had countless times complained that no one seemed to clean up after themselves. Here was a perfect example. How much effort could it have taken to toss the empty box to the floor? She did so with an angry shake of her head. She liked working here, but wondered if it was worth it. Would the work ethic be different anywhere else? Probably not.

Two things happened in quick succession. Elaine once again hefted a box with the notion that it would be heavy and the ladder scraped along the cement floor. She toppled sideways when the weight difference threw her off balance and continued to the cement floor below when the ladder she reached for was not where it had been. Whether or not she saw the figure that had moved the ladder ever so slightly out of her reach may never be known.

She struck the unforgiving cement floor with her shoulder followed closely by her skull.

CHAPTER 8

I traveled that canal over and over in my dreams after a dinner out of pasta and wine. At times I was there searching for Wayne, other times just searching for peace. Our guide on the trip had mentioned that he hired out to feed wayward husbands to the alligators. That offer seemed to be on my mind when I was searching for Wayne. I guess that would be considered Freudian, too. I woke confused and lay there for some time trying to sort out what I would do next. I had mentioned at dinner trying to locate Wayne and the suggestion was immediately shot down by both Greg and Andrea. I wasn't so sure that I agreed.

A soft tap sounded on my door and I glanced at the digital readout of the clock and saw it was nearing ten.

"Samantha? Are you awake? You have a telephone call."

I tossed off the covers, pulled on the short robe I'd packed wrapping the tie around me, reached for the door and then the receiver Andrea held out for me. I know I thought it was Wayne.

It was Peter.

"Hi, Sam, I've been chatting with your friend, she seems very nice."

I sat back heavily on the bed. "Peter," I said trying to mask the sound of disappointment in my voice. I've never been able to do that from the first unwanted Christmas or birthday gift to this day.

"You're not happy to hear from me," he said with his hint of amusement.

"I thought you might be Wayne," I confessed.

"Sorry, but that's why I'm calling. He contacted me wondering where you were. I wasn't certain whether or not you wanted him to know your location. He was quite perturbed when I wouldn't divulge your whereabouts."

I closed my eyes tight. How did Wayne have Peter's number? Did I? "Did he leave a number?"

"Yes, have a pen?"

I padded out to the kitchen and spied pen and paper by the phone stand. Greg and Andrea were drinking coffee on the lanai. As I jotted down the number, I frowned. "How did you get this number?" I know I hadn't told him their names – at least I didn't think I had.

"It took a little doing," Peter said. "I had to break into your house and find your address book."

"You broke into my house?"

"Not really difficult, sweetheart, you left the door unlocked."

Sigh.

"Are you going to call him?" he asked next.

I had the feeling there was an underlying current of concern on his part. I shrugged. "I don't know," I answered truthfully.

"I don't think you should, evidently Andrea agrees with me." Peter paused. "But you're a grown woman, aren't you."

It wouldn't seem so.

Andrea had appeared at the doorway and stared. I stuck out my tongue at her. "How's Jack doing?" I asked.

"He was asking after you. There's been another accident at that store – nonfatal this time, although the girl is in a coma. A dangerous place. When do you think you'll be back?"

"A day or so."

Peter had made my airplane reservations open-ended. I chewed the inside of my mouth wondering if I should tell him about my idea to apply for a job at Wentworths. Not yet, I decided. "I'll give you a call."

"You do that, Sammy. I'll see you then."

"Could you lock up for me, Peter?" I added as I checked the caller ID and smiled when I saw he was calling from my house.

"Will do. Bye."

Andrea handed me a cup of coffee and leaned against the counter while I mused. "Well, are you going to?" she asked.

I raised my eyebrows.

"Are you going to call Wayne?" she posed.

I considered the option and then finally shook my head. "I don't think so. I'll call when I get back. He thinks I'm in Chicago and I'll leave it at that." I slurped at the coffee and then slapped the counter. "What's on the agenda for today?"

As it turned out, there hadn't been much on the agenda as they hadn't been certain how long I would decide to stay. We improvised. We visited a nursery and I helped Andrea pick out both annuals and perennials for a new garden as well as to plump up the one she'd been working on when I'd arrived. It was nice working in the dirt, getting grungy nails and a smudged face.

Greg had opted for a game of golf. When he returned and we'd cleaned up, he took us into St. Mary's to a tea room that had just opened called the Mad Hatter. They served a multitude of flavors of tea (and coffee – but I stuck with the tea to be sporting) plus platefuls of tiny sandwiches and desserts. We gorged ourselves on cucumber, ham, crab, and watercress sandwiches, fruit tarts, scones with jam and clotted cream, and tiny cream puffs.

Then we walked to the waterfront and caught a ferry to the Cumberland Island National Seashore where we visited the Plum Orchard Mansion and the First African Baptist Church where John-John Kennedy had married. It was another beautiful, warm, sunny day.

I was glad that Peter had persuaded me to come down and probably, deep down, was happy that I had not called Wayne. I was thinking along the lines of 'absence makes the heart grow fonder' – who knows whether I meant for me or him.

CHAPTER 9

I rose early the following day, promising Andrea I'd come back and making them promise they'd come visit me and then headed for the Jacksonville airport. It would be five o'clock that evening before I slid the key in my door exhausted, happy and hustling for the ringing telephone.

"Sam? Where the hell have you been? And please tell me why your hump wouldn't tell me where you were and why you didn't have your cell phone with you."

"I was in Chicago, remember?" I said trying to catch my breath, temper my anger, and keep myself from telling him the truth. Peter is not a hump, Wayne.

There was silence on the line – for the longest time – so long I thought perhaps he'd hung up. "Wayne?"

"I'm here, I forgot about Chicago."

I doubted he'd forgotten, but thanked God he hadn't tried to find me there. "Apology accepted. I told Peter I wasn't to be disturbed. I have to crank out another book and it's due soon." Very soon. Like by the end of the month. "How's your trip?"

"All right." *Noncommittal.*

"Did you call Greg and Andrea?" I asked with tongue in cheek once again thankful that the video phone idea had never gotten off the ground.

"No, I ended up in Jacksonville and now I'm headed south for Miami. I didn't think they'd want to hear from me anyway."

I couldn't think of a military base in Miami, but I didn't question. Evidently Wayne was into mind reading.

"I'm spending tonight there and then continuing on to Key West, I fly out home from there," he explained.

Oh.

"Everything okay, Sam?"

Peachy. "I'm tired, you have a safe trip and I'll see you Friday."

"Saturday – afternoon," he answered and then hung up before I could protest. I'm paranoid enough that I believe he knew exactly where I'd been – and would anyway when he returned home because I'd tell him.

I stood in the doorway of my study for a good half hour staring at the blank screen of my computer finally deciding that it would be in my best interest to relax a little and have a good, long, soaking bath. Maybe a margarita, too. I've never had a margarita, but I'd always thought they looked good when Wayne made them. I knew we had the ingredients for them because we'd had a Mexican themed party about a month ago.

As I was thumbing through the cocktail recipe book, I landed on the page that had a picture of a strawberry daiquiri and thought that looked even better. I searched the liquor cabinet for rum and the freezer for strawberries and scored a can of frozen strawberry daiquiri mix as an added bonus. Bless my alcohol drinking husband!

I read the directions carefully – well, sort of carefully – and ended up tossing said ingredients in the industrial sized blender that Wayne had bought. Perhaps I splashed in a little too much rum. It's really hard to say. I reached for a glass – a martini, I think - and thought the big tall tumbler looked like it would hold more and poured the slushy into it.

That was my real downfall as I carried glass and blender beaker towards the bathroom. I thought of it as a slushy. Big mistake for a person who rarely drinks. Never think of an alcoholic drink as something fruity and harmless. I spun the hot water knob to full force and gave the cold water knob a quarter turn and took a sip of the drink.

Yum.

Then I spread towels on the floor, added a generous dose of bubble bath, and turned on the stereo in the living room. I grabbed my robe from the closet, went into the bathroom, stripped down, and lowered myself into the almost boiling water carefully setting the glass on the edge of the tub after taking another sip. This was heavenly. I laid my head back and closed my eyes thinking how good it was to be queen.

When I woke up, the telephone was ringing in the distance and I swore. Worse than that, the water had turned frigid and I resembled a goose bumpy prune. Let the machine get it I thought, as I pulled the plug on the tub and turned on the shower to warm myself up. Unfortunately, I wasn't having great success in standing. I frowned towards the blender beaker and the glass and wondered for a brief moment who exactly had drunk all the strawberry stuff.

I pondered the two empty glass objects as the warm water pelted me from above. Pelted me, the floor, all my towels I had lying on said floor, and my nice cushy warm robe (it was a pretty turquoise color that Wayne had bought me for Christmas last year); all because I hadn't put the shower curtain liner inside the tub. A few interesting moments followed as I struggled with getting the liner on the right side. It wasn't happening.

I sat sprawled on the tub floor in a drunken stupor. As you may have guessed, I'm not much of a drinker and I'd decided I was going to have to spend the night in here.

At least I was warm again – for the time being.

The telephone rang again insistently, cutting off just before the machine picked it up and starting right up again. Someone wanted to get a hold of me. I crawled from the tub because standing wasn't an option. I clumsily wrapped myself in one of the still damp towels (sort of) and inched to the phone in my office. I answered it somewhere around the thirtieth ring.

"Hello?" I hope I sounded annoyed. I tried not to notice that the room was spinning and whirling about furiously.

"Sammy? Are you all right?"

Yes Peter, stop yelling. My mouth was full of cotton balls and I swiped at my tongue with my hand.

"Sammy?" he said a bit louder.

"What!" I said and wished I hadn't spoken, certainly not in such a loud voice.

There was a moment of silence. "Are you drunk?" he asked.

"No."

"Liar. I'm coming over." I think he hung up. I didn't.

I was still there kneeling on the floor leaning on my chair and trying my damnedest not to move anything when Peter strode into my office. The towel may have slipped, but I wasn't about to move to rewrap it.

His hands touched my arm and he sucked in his breath. "Jesus, you're cold, Sammy!" he said – it could have been quietly, but it sounded thunderous. "How much did you have?"

I held up my thumb and forefinger a fraction of an inch apart.

He was trying not to smile. "You left the water running, did you know that?"

I could have shaken my head if I wanted to, I just didn't want to.

"I'm going to have Moira get the shower ready and then I'm going to carry you in. Is that okay?"

"Moira?" I said mortified. "Someone's here with you?" I shouldn't have tried such a long speech along with so much sudden movement. I hurled – big time – and it was red.

Gross.

I think I missed him. I certainly didn't miss the rug.

Peter scooped me up and carried me to the bathroom. There was a tall woman there, blonde with perfectly chiseled features and a twinkle in her amber eyes. She was laughing at me, well, smiling, and maybe it was at Peter. I wasn't certain I liked her and wondered if she liked kids. Peter had a daughter you know.

"This is Moira, Sam, Moira Finley," he stood me in the shower and slipped off the towel holding me up while he stood behind the curtain. Just what I needed was more prune skin. I heard him ask Moira to make coffee and look for something for me to eat. Eventually, he turned off the water and threw the curtain aside wrapping me in Wayne's robe and winding a towel around my head. It seemed as though he'd done this kind of thing before.

The bathroom had been cleaned of wet and soggy towels and robe.

"You need to vomit again?"

I shrugged. Not at that particular moment – no.

"You had anything to eat?"

I shook my head and then held it in both hands as Peter steadied me. "Does she like kids?" I asked.

"What?"

"Does …" what was her name? Moira. "Does Moira like kids?"

He smiled and helped me toward the kitchen seating me at the table. Moira slid a plate in front of me with unbuttered toast as Peter poured three cups of coffee. He lifted the rum bottle and noted the level.

"How much of this did you have, Sammy?"

I didn't answer him. He could see as well as I that it had been a new bottle, the seal was sitting right next to it.

I nibbled at the toast and when my stomach didn't protest, I bit off a little more. I wasn't sure the last time I'd eaten. I think it was in Georgia that morning before I left, maybe at the airport. I glanced back – moving very slowly – at the clock on the stove and saw that it was eleven ten. Wow.

Then I felt guilty. "I'll be all right, you can go home," I said.

Peter was leaning against the bench watching Moira at the stove. Whatever she was cooking smelled good. It was she that spoke.

"We'll just see you to bed, Sam, after you've eaten," she slid a plate of eggs in front of me and went to find a fork. I could have eaten them without one.

"I don't normally do this," I said, forking up some egg onto the toast that I had left "The drinking thing, I don't handle liquor very well."

"No kidding," Peter commented as he took his cup to the sink and rinsed it out. "You had me worried. I knew you were home, but I couldn't get a hold of you. Moira thought it was a good idea that we come over."

"How did you know I was home?"

"I called Andrea and then the airline. You should have called me to come pick you up."

I raised my shoulders.

"You talked with Wayne," he said.

I didn't answer. I was beginning to feel human again – as long as I didn't have to move much. Should I tell Peter of my plan to work at Wentworths?

Naw.

I finished my plate stopping just short of licking it and dutifully went to bed. Actually, Peter put me to bed.

CHAPTER 10

Next I knew it was daylight. I stared at the digital clock and frowned at the time – *2:23* – I looked out the window at the grey day. It was two twenty three in the afternoon. I hadn't slept *that* late in a very long time. First order of business was to call Peter and apologize and then Andrea to tell her I was home safe as well as what a big dolt I was. I vowed I would sit through the chastisement silently and did. I was a little surprised that it had lasted so long, however – from Andrea, not Peter. My transgression hadn't seemed to faze Peter at all.

Having accomplished those tasks and taking my second dose of aspirin for a headache that hovered about the fringes of my brain, I set out to seek part time employment at Wentworths. I toyed with the idea of mentioning that I was researching for a book just in case someone recognized me. I'd learned, much to my surprise, people actually do look at the pictures on the back of books. I can't say I'd know Tom Clancy if I fell over him, but I would know Martha Grimes or Janet Evanovich.

It was raining steadily now; a cold rain whose dampness seemed to seep into the bones. I'd had the car heater blasting which only made me colder when I hopped from the car. I probably should think about a heavier coat.

As I'd mentioned before, Wentworths occupied the first floor corner of one wing of an elongated strip mall that had grown building by building until it occupied some prime real estate in four different sections.

Wentworths sported windows on two sides – one facing the entrance of the parking garage and the other facing the new Italian restaurant across the parking lot. Above it on the second floor was a sporting goods and camping supply store, next door was a Barnes and Noble, and attached to that was a Starbucks. There were two banks that fronted the Pike (that's what the natives called Rockville Pike, the main drag in Rockville – Route 355. 355 was continuous, but the street name changed depending on the town you were in. On one end of Rockville, it turned into Hungerford Drive and the other, just beyond the National Naval Medical Center, it became Wisconsin Avenue). The closest wing consisted of the parking garage, a discount store, a Sports Authority, and a Giant Food Store. Construction on the two other wings was progressing along with another entrance/exit onto Randolph Road.

Signs in the front window, on each door, and on the front register proclaimed that Wentworths (*Synonymous with fine dining since 1898*) was looking for eager employees. No shit, I bet they're looking for a warehouse man and – did Peter say what the recent accident victim had done?

I decided to look around before I approached the employee I saw as I walked in. There were two double door entrances with an elaborate display in the window between them. The display heralded what had to be a new pattern of square dishes in rust, purple, black, white, and navy blue accompanied by square sided stemware and tumblers with coordinating placemats and napkins. Whoever was doing the merchandising was excellent at their craft. It made *me* want to buy them. I wasn't much for changing dishes; I still used the same ones Wayne and I had purchased when we were married. Who knew, perhaps I'd see something I liked. I walked toward the left and peeked into the center section that was set off by four curved walls and housed dinnerware exclusively in whites. There were at least seventy patterns represented on the walls and floor displays.

I continued on toward the far wall (by the second set of doors and another pair of registers) and found myself looking at geometric patterns in pastels, bold colors, and black and white. There were a couple of patterns I liked, but for the most part didn't care for the modernness of them. The back corner was clearance items as neatly and tastefully displayed as the rest of the store. A corridor beyond the clearance section had an emergency exit, bathrooms, and another door that I would learn went into the warehouse.

I turned right (the white dinnerware was now to my right) and passed a display of wooden trays, boards, salad bowls, and napkin holders interspersed among large generic white and green platters and serving bowls. I assumed they were generic as they were not labeled with names as the rest of the patterns had been.

I faced another desk and register and noted it was the Customer Service counter. Behind that was a curved section displaying bone china with platinum and gold edges. This section was centered by a bridal registry table with a computer and four upholstered chairs which were surrounded by displays of lead crystal vases and candlesticks. Beyond Customer Service and facing the side road where I'd entered the mall, was stoneware in dark browns, blues, and ecru.

The floor displays in front of the customer service desk held glass platters, vases, candy dishes, and candleholders of varying degrees in price. Completing the circuit of the store, I came back to the front where the crystal stemware was displayed. I browsed through the area picking out a couple styles that I liked while I waited for the cashier to finish with the customer she was ringing up.

The cashier was short – maybe five feet – with dark hair and a deep voice; I judged her to be somewhere in her sixties. She chatted amiably with the customer who was talking on a cell phone throughout the transaction. I thought that was rude of the customer. The cashier wore khaki slacks and a black polo shirt with the name *Wentworths* emblazoned on the left and her name tag – Betty Ann – over that. She wrapped the customer's purchases and boxed them before sending the woman out the door with a thank you. She turned toward me and had just about rearranged her face from the grimace she'd given the departing woman's back to the smile she pasted on for me.

"Can I help you?" she asked pleasantly.

"I'm checking into the employment you have advertised," I said while I studied her further. She had blue eyes and, on closer inspection, I was pretty sure the black hair was a wig.

She nodded and reached in the file box between the two registers for an application. "We certainly do have openings," she said with a heavy sigh. "Fill this out and I'll page the assistant manager; perhaps she can talk to you now."

Without further thought, I accepted the paper and pen and leaned on the counter to fill in the blanks. I was faced with a dilemma when I read 'current occupation'. *Don't get your shorts in a twist, Sammy; you're self-employed,* I said to myself as I wrote it down on the application.

"Do you enjoy working here?" I asked her after she hung up the receiver. I assumed she used that to page the assistant manager since the telephone hadn't rung.

She didn't answer me, so I looked up. Her face was a study; a cross between fear and resignation. She slowly nodded.

"I work just nine to two Monday through Fridays. It gives me mad money and a chance to get out of my house." Slowly the fear faded. She glanced towards the back. "It's just that we've been having some troubles of late," she said quietly.

"What sort of troubles?" I asked.

She was busily smoothing out the newsprint she used to wrap the stemware and worried the corner of one piece with her fingers taking pains not to look at me. "There's been a couple accidents, the police have been here and everything," she responded.

"Really? What happened?" I inquired, trying to be encouraging. We both heard the swish of a door in the back and she made herself look busier as she turned my way.

"Please don't tell her I said anything," she whispered.

It wasn't long before a woman stood beside me holding out her hand.

"I'm Gisele Fournier, the manager here at Wentworths. You are?" She was an inch or two taller than me and probably twenty pounds heavier with a cap of blonde hair and hazel eyes and modestly applied makeup. She looked the part of the consummate professional with a tailored black suit and a pale green silk blouse and low heels. She was the woman that had let Jack out the door the day we picked him up.

"Samantha Warren," I said.

While she shook my hand, she regarded me. She had that look; she knew me from somewhere - she just couldn't place where. I may have to use the research angle.

"I'm interested in a part time job and your door said you have openings."

"Of course, if you'll just come back with me to my office," she held her hand out for me to precede her. I saw her glance suspiciously towards Betty Ann probably trying to discern what Betty Ann may have told me.

We passed through the double doors near the customer service desk and into a warehouse of gargantuan proportions. It stretched side to side the length of the store and was at least twenty feet wide from the showroom door to the cargo door in front of us. Heavy duty shelves made from rough hewn thick wood covered the bulk of the floor space and boxes were stacked on them at three levels. The first level was floor to about chest high, the second level to about five feet above that, and the top level reaching upward toward the ceiling which was probably twenty feet above. It wasn't a finished ceiling, just steel jousts with large metal lights hanging down. We passed by a few stacks of boxes and I moved one to gauge its size and weight, deciding I wouldn't want any one to fall on me let alone a stack of them.

We entered the kitchenette next with refrigerator, sink, microwave, and table where I assumed employees took their breaks. One wall was covered with a cork board that held the requisite OSHA and minimum wage posters plus pertinent notices for employees that included a schedule. The opposite wall was devoted to the employee pictures. I took note that Gisele Fournier was not the manager, she was an assistant as Betty Ann had said. I also noted there were several holes in the grouping. I glanced back at the schedule and noticed numerous black lines through names. Had there been a mass exodus of employees? Did it make me rethink my plan? Of course not.

"Please have a seat, Mrs. Warren," Gisele said as she took the chair at the desk.

"It's not Mrs. – either Ms. or Sam," I said.

"It says you're married."

"I didn't take my husband's name."

I looked about the small office. It was ten by ten with shelves lining one wall above two computers, a printer, and a fax machine. A tall file cabinet was tucked into the end on the right. Gisele's desk sat by the door and the chair I took was in the back corner next to two small two-drawer file cabinets. Under the bench was a cut out scrap of rug. I gazed at that for some time and wondered its purpose finally deciding that it probably concealed a safe.

"Why not?" she asked.

I regarded her thoughtfully trying to remember to what she was referring. *Oh yes, my name.* "Is my employment contingent on that answer, Mrs. Fournier?" I suppose I should have been charitable and not assume she was married. What the hell. I didn't like her much.

We had a little stare-off for a few seconds which was broken by the entrance of a man. He stood maybe five eight, five nine with sandy blonde hair and rather intense blue eyes. He was slim (not skinny), well dressed in a three piece grey pinstripe suit covering a white shirt. (I think I started drooling). He flashed me a dazzling smile and came toward me with hand outstretched.

"Chris Nichols, I'm the district manager; my office is across the warehouse," he grasped my hand firmly as he pointed out which direction his office sat.

"Sam Warren," I think I may have stammered a bit.

"You're applying for a job?" he asked.

Why else would I be here? I nodded. "Something part time," I managed.

He nodded back. "Good, make sure Gisele treats you right." He glanced back at Gisele and then nodded towards me before he headed for the door.

"Will Jessica be in today?" he asked Gisele, turning.

"She didn't say," Gisele replied. I think she was trying to keep the iciness from her voice. If so, she wasn't succeeding.

"Have her come see me if she does," he threw a wave my way and left. Steam was coming from Gisele's ears as she watched him stride across the warehouse floor. My mind returned to the wall of pictures and I mentally picked out Jessica at the top. Jessica was the manager, Gisele was not happy with that fact.

"Ms. Warren then, what brings you to Wentworths? Why is it you want to work here?"

Could I tell her it was because I liked melodrama? Danger? Perhaps I could get a romance novel out of this if nothing else. I certainly wouldn't mind being caught in the dark with Chris Nichols. It seemed to me that Gisele wouldn't be averse to that either. I shook my head to clear it of these thoughts, folded my hands in my lap, and tried to remember all those things I'd been taught in high school and college about giving a good interview.

I think I passed with flying colors!

The only thing required of me was take a pee test which I knew I'd pass as long as they weren't hoping for teetotalers. Could they detect how much liquor a person consumed the night before?

Gisele Fournier called me two days later (Saturday) and told me I had the job if I wanted it. No surprise there, they probably would have hired any baboon off the street. I was to start the following Monday.

In the intervening time, I had been in relative seclusion rattling off chapter after chapter. Peter Frost was my only contact with outside civilization; contact limited to the telephone and very minor conversations.

Oh, I forgot. I received a call from Wayne in Key West saying he was traveling west again and wouldn't be back in Rockville until the following Friday. So much for combining trips when he was out in California. I failed to mention my new job to him. I failed to mention quite a number of things to him for that matter. Good thing I was busy writing or I would have finished off the rest of the liquor. When I wasn't writing, I thought it best not to even go near the cabinet.

CHAPTER 11

Wentworths requires its *sales associates* to wear a uniform - that's what I was by the way, we aren't mere cashiers – Sales Associates. The uniform consisted of khaki slacks or skirt with a choice of a black, navy blue, or white polo shirt with the company name on the left side. It was up to us to buy said shirts after they issued the first one and we had to keep them clean, so I ordered two more each of the black and navy blue. I didn't wash clothes all that often and figured four would be a reasonable amount. I also didn't know how long I'd actually work there and thought I'd be able to pass them on to someone else after my employment was terminated.

Name tags were also required. I hated name tags. If someone wanted to know my name, I'd happily tell them on request. However, in the interest of being a model employee, I tacked the damned thing above the embroidered Wentworths' name.

The first couple hours of my first day were spent filling out paperwork and boning up (no pun intended) on the intricacies of china (bone and otherwise), flatware (it was never referred to as silverware), and crystal stemware. The company had a nifty manual that detailed the differences between fine china, bone china, stoneware, and the like as well as the varying degrees of crystal from just a notch above glass to full lead crystal. The manual made it easy so I wouldn't have to try to bullshit my way through a sale. I could just consult that handy dandy manual and make my life simple.

Gisele had hired two others who started the same day. It was nice to know I wasn't a rookie all by myself. Tony Yang was Vietnamese, third generation in the United States. He was about twenty two and short (well my height) with dark hair and brown eyes. Melanie Friis was Danish-American, around the same age as Tony. She had pouffy, perfect brown hair, brown (the color of milk chocolate) eyes, big chest, and little waist. Sigh. If I didn't immediately take to her in a positive way, I would have hated her. In fact, I thought the three of us would get along famously.

We had an extensive lesson on safety in the workplace covering not only the normal regulations, but delving into how high boxes should be stacked and safe handling of them as well as being cautious on the shelving. Hmmm, I wonder why.

After the paperwork and lectures, we were given a tour that started with the assignment of a locker and padlock. We were encouraged to keep our valuables secured inside whenever we were in residence and were told the locks would be checked periodically to make certain we were in compliance. It seemed a bit excessive to me, but what did I know.

As I mentioned, the warehouse was as wide as the store itself. Looking from the store entry towards the freight door, the kitchen and Gisele's office were to the left. All stock on that side was dinnerware and accessories. Each pattern had an alpha-numeric designation and the stock was stored alphabetically. Made sense.

Being one of the larger stores, we carried more accessories than others because we had the space. Along the wall that formed the kitchen and office were the lockers and three plastic shelves that held the silverware – sorry, flatware. Beyond that was the 'damaged goods' station where we would bring anything damaged when unpacked or anything was broken either by us or a customer. We were told during our tour that no one was charged for breakage. Managers had to handle the reporting of the damages. I looked at the piles of boxes and bins of broken glass and thought perhaps none of them had bothered for a while.

The side door opened into the corridor I'd seen on my first go-round where the bathrooms and an emergency exit were. Going back to the center of the warehouse and to the right were the shelves that housed the crystal; crystal vases and platters were to the left and stemware to the right. These were also alpha-numeric.

On the far end there were two offices. One was Chris Nichols', the other was used for storage of glass shelves and floor fixtures. Over these rooms was space for overflow of stemware and vases.

It was very organized (I learned later this was due largely to Hector Rodriquez). Back by the front door was the shipping station where periodically one of the staff was detailed to ship out orders. From the looks of it, shipping hadn't been done in a while either. Perhaps Hector had been the one to do it.

Melanie and I were directed to the sales floor and Tony had been recruited to help Chris with the shipment that had arrived while we filled out paperwork. I would have liked to do that. The deliveries were shrink-wrapped onto pallets, lowered to ground level from the truck by an automatic scissor lifter and then wheeled inside the warehouse. It looked like fun.

I was paired with Betty Ann (full name Betty Ann Mitchell) and Melanie was stuck with Gisele. I suppose I should be fair, I really didn't know her that well, but thus far, Gisele hadn't impressed me much. We were to learn the finer points of working the registers and generally helping customers. It was odd, the one overlying theme of my training was the 'meet and greet' – where each and every customer was greeted the moment they walked through the door. It hadn't happened when I'd come through the doors. Maybe Betty Ann had been too distraught because of the accidents. I strove to ask her about them sometime in the course of my training.

The store opened promptly at ten (eleven on Sundays). Other employees started to filter in around nine-thirty. Holly Bush, who I was told was a sales supervisor, bustled in just before Andrew Barker. Betty Ann explained the hierarchy to me as we prepared the register area. Jessica Lupine was the manager, Gisele the assistant, Holly and Jeff Stewart were sales supervisors. Those four were the management staff that had the keys. Chris Nichols was the district manager and reigned over a dozen stores in the DC, Virginia, and Maryland area. These were the people I answered to –

Holly was tall and skinny and extremely nervous. She looked to me as though she was on drugs, but of course couldn't have been because of the screening. She had to be six four, all skin and bones under a drab brown suit that hung terribly off her shoulders. She had a limp handshake and a nervousness that I wanted so badly to attribute to the drug thing aforementioned. Her dark eyes darted left and right as Betty Ann introduced us. The eyes finally settling on Gisele Fournier at the customer service desk. She seemed fearful of Gisele.

Andrew Barker stood at the desk and chuckled. No, I lie; he laughed at Holly and she in turn gave him a withering look of disdain before she hurried on to the warehouse.

"I'm Andrew," he said taking my hand. He didn't shake it, just gave it a squeeze.

So you are I thought appraisingly.

He was handsome, as tall as Chris, but definitely more muscular. He had light brown hair with blonde highlights and deep blue eyes that were almost violet (I was pretty certain they were contacts, but I could be wrong). He had a washboard stomach and a very nice ass. Working here was certainly going to be easy on the eyes. I guess if I were made of the same cloth as Wayne, I'd look on this as good grazing. *If* I was so inclined – I wasn't. *What was it that Wayne always said to me?* It doesn't hurt to look.

Andrew grinned. "Thank you, darling, but I'm gay, as flaming as the day is long." He chucked me on the chin. "But it certainly is nice to be appreciated." He waved a dismissive hand towards Holly. "Don't be put off by Hols, she's just nervous," he cocked his head sideways. "You have heard about the unfortunate chain of events at our humble establishment, haven't you?"

I attempted my most innocent look and shook my head.

He flashed a wrist in my direction. "Then I insist we do lunch today and I shall fill you in. Nice to have you here, Samantha Warren."

He walked towards the back casting a dismissive wave at Gisele as he passed. I liked him. I turned towards Betty Ann – I don't think she did.

"So what does Andrew do here?"

"He's the visual merchandiser, he does all the displays."

I nodded my approval. "He does good work," I commented.

Betty Ann just shook her head. Evidently she didn't like Andrew's work either.

Fortunately, running a cash register isn't all that difficult. It tells you everything you need to know as long as you hit the right buttons. In between customers (who were few and far between – it being Monday, I'm sure), Betty Ann and I toured the store more thoroughly than I had my first visit. There were five registers, one and two were at the front door, three was at the customer service desk, and four and five were by the other set of doors. The latter were put into service at holiday time and when there were big sales so the main ones two were not tied up. From what I could see that morning, Andrew used the further ones as a base of operations when he was merchandising.

The different 'shops' actually had labels, i.e., the White Shop, Country, New Age, Stoneware, and precious metals (the gold and platinum edged stuff). There was the clearance area and, off the stoneware section in the right front corner was a small round room devoted to odds and ends pieces from sets that had been broken down either due to damage, replacement, or return. I learned that there were customers who visited here weekly to snatch up all the new patterns they could at a discounted rate. Mismatched pieces were collected, certainly a good source for anyone collecting cups and saucers and the like.

By lunch time, boxes from the shipment started to trickle out for us to unbox and price – and ogle. Wentworths sold quality product. Betty Ann showed me how to check to make certain the bar code scanned. If it did, we just ticketed them; if it didn't, we had to make bar codes and price labels at the customer service desk. A place setting of any new patterns had to be given to Andrew so he could set them up in the appropriate shop.

Andrew hummed his way through two displays while we worked then came to me at eleven. "Tell me when the Nazi lets you off for lunch and I'll go with you."

I nodded and suppressed a smile. And here I thought Betty Ann would be my source of hot gossip. Little did I know.

CHAPTER 12

"I take it no one has recognized you," Andrew opened when we sat down in a booth at CiCi's both with trays loaded with salad and pizzas.

I debated giving him the look of confusion, but didn't want to waste it. "How come you didn't say anything?"

He shrugged. "So what are you writing then? A romance about dishes?" he leaned forward, his eyes sparkling. "Would you put in a couple homos for me? Romance novels just don't give us any due."

I chuckled, but didn't answer as I sampled a ham and pineapple pizza.

Andrew started laughing, a deep laugh that emanated from his gut as he pointed a finger at me meaningfully. "You're doing the accidents aren't you?

You're writing a story about our," he sketched quotes in the air, "our 'accidents'."

"So you don't believe they were accidents?" I ventured.

"No, darling, I don't. Hector Rodriquez worked here for six years and he was at the Seneca store before that. He was the personification of careful. He certainly wouldn't stand under a stack of dinnerware sets and wait to be crushed."

"Did you tell the police that?"

"I thought about it, but I like my job. I'm not sure enough about it to say anything."

"How about the other accident?" I queried as I stabbed a piece of lettuce.

He regarded me for a while and then grinned. "I did say *accidents,* didn't I?"

I didn't enlighten him that I knew about them already. "So?"

"The latest was a girl who'd worked part time for us since Thanksgiving. She goes to Montgomery College and came here nights and weekends mostly. Her name was – God, is – Elaine Newcomb. She supposedly fell off the top of a shelf in the warehouse trying to get back onto the ladder. She's in the hospital with a broken back and a coma, poor thing."

"You're sure she didn't fall?" I couldn't look up at him for fear I'd be told to mind my own business.

"Oh, she fell and it was awful – the scream, that is – the ladder was leaning against the shelf when they found her. It was the standard twenty foot tall model. Elaine normally used the mobile one with the platform, have you seen that one? She felt a little more sure-footed on it and she could stay on the platform and reach for anything she wanted from the top rather than getting off onto the shelving. Also, *if* she did get up the twenty-footer, she wouldn't step out onto the shelf. I've seen her two steps up on a ladder and she'd go white as a sheet."

"What if that was the only one available?" I asked as I forked up some salad and held it to my lips.

He dropped his voice. "She didn't get off it willingly," he held my gaze.

I don't know what he was waiting for from me, but he sat with lips pursed.

Me? I couldn't wait to report to Jack. *Wait a minute? He said 'the latest'* – I opened my mouth to ask the next question.

"You aren't keeping Samantha out too long are you, Andrew?" Gisele's voice said to my right.

I jumped, Andrew didn't. Perhaps that's why he'd gone to silent mode. We looked towards her and found she wasn't alone. Chris Nichols stood next to another woman he introduced as Jessica Lupine. *Ah, the Manager*.

Jessica was short, not as short as Betty Ann, but close; spunky seemed to fit the bill for description. She had short blonde hair with dark roots, a small waist, and a pixie-ish face with blue eyes framed by eye shadow and mascara.

I had worked with a girl from South Jersey once who looked just like her except Flo's hair was fluffed high. It gave her at least five more inches in height. Jessica wore a tight black skirt and a multi-colored, even tighter sweater and three inch black heels. From the way Chris looked at her, he must have thought she presented a nice package.

"So pleased to meet you, Sam, Gisele has given you a rave review," she pumped my hand and looked back at Chris Nichols with the grin still plastered on her face. "And Mr. Nichols as well."

"The seal of approval then," I said trying to pull my hand from hers.

"Well, it's surprising with all that's been going on," she said. I watched Chris' hand touch her back and she bit back words. Jessica didn't seem to be afraid to talk about the accidents.

I saw her silence as my cue to get up. "I have to get back, wouldn't want to be late, especially on my first day."

Andrew slid from his seat and followed me out keeping his mouth pursed shut until we reached Bou Avenue where we stopped to wait for traffic so we could cross.

"I hope we weren't overheard," he said looking away from me.

Yeah, I just bet.

"Have there been other accidents, Andrew?" I asked as we approached the front door.

"I'll fill you in later," he replied opening the door for me and letting me precede him through the door.

CHAPTER 13

Betty Ann left at two, and Melanie and I were pretty much left to our own devices which was a scary thought. Luckily, we didn't have many customers. I suppose we could have pried Holly from her siege on the customer service desk if we'd had to. She was doing her level best to stay away from us.

Melanie cut open a box of vases and spoke in a stage whisper. "How'd you like to go through life with the name Holly Bush?" she asked bemused.

I laughed. "She seems a bit up tight, perhaps that's why."

She reared back in surprise, "You mean you don't know?"

"Know what?"

"Well, for one thing, how we were so easily hired."

"You mean it wasn't because we're so good or the accidents?" I'm sure they had been written up in the papers.

"Not just those – the thefts. A friend of mine worked here, her name was Jane Willis. She and I submitted our applications in at the same time. Anyway, there was a big to-do after inventory, everyone had to come in early one Saturday morning before the store opened and go through questioning, an initial internal investigation. I'm not certain whether management would have called in the police, but they hinted it may happen. Jane said that close to fifty thousand dollars worth of merchandise disappeared."

"Overnight?"

She shrugged.

"All I know is that Jane was so incensed, she quit along with four others that day. *But* only after they were cleared of suspicion."

"How long ago?"

"Just after Christmas and their inventory – so around the first of January."

"So why is Holly so tense?"

Melanie leaned toward me conspiratorially. "Holly is top of the list of suspects, I heard."

A customer came in the store and Melanie moved away to begin her sales pitch. Not only was she pretty, but she was a natural born retail person.

Andrew was working in the back corner by the stoneware, Holly was brooding at the customer service desk, and I still had an hour to work. I sighed and slit open another box. I guess I couldn't expect to learn everything in one day. I took out a sheet of paper from the fax machine and jotted down a few notes keeping an eye on the door, Holly, and the time. I wrote down the names of those I'd met thus far and their positions, then I made a column of 'victims' and their 'accidents' smiling as I put that word in quotes and thinking back to Andrew's elaborate air sketching. I noted the heist - I love that word as useless as it is - and vowed to do a little internet research when I got home that night.

Then I jotted down a few questions for Andrew the next time we were off by ourselves. Top of the list was how stock is accounted for from its departure from the main warehouse to its departure from each store. There had to be some sort of checks and balances applied, some way for the company to know where their product was and how it left any given store. I gave myself a head slap; *of course there was you idiot, that's how the thefts had been discovered.* Well, I'd still ask. Fifty thousand dollars worth of merchandise couldn't be too easy to conceal in your purse. I had a brief moment of pause wondering why I thought the thefts important.

They had to be -

I caught movement from the customer service desk and stowed my notes in my pocket. Next I knew, Holly stood before me with her hands on her hips.

"It's five o'clock," she said impatiently. She was definitely not a people person, maybe she was more outgoing to customers.

I smiled at her and waited for her to continue.

"I have to count out your drawer before you go home," she said next then snapped out a key from her pocket. "You have to watch me count it in the office."

I nodded. "They covered that in the training this morning."

She took a large bag and inserted the drawer inside and then grabbed the paperwork envelope from the plastic file box next to the fax machine.

"Can I carry something for you?" I asked.

She merely spun on her heels and exited the register area. I followed her to the office.

On our way, I met another sales associate, Louisa Perez. She was short, stocky, jet black hair, and brown eyes – not as pretty as Melanie's. I also met the other sales supervisor, Jeffrey Fuller Stewart (I swear to you that was how he introduced himself). He was a bit taller than me, thin and pale. It looked as though he never saw the sun, let alone stood out in it long enough to get color. Then again, it could be just the time of year. His brown hair was styled neatly, his hazel eyes danced as he shook my hand.

"Nice to meet you, Sam, I was talking with Andrew," he said winking, letting me know he knew me and my secret was safe with him.

Holly had continued on to the warehouse and now stood tapping her toe at the door waiting for me to catch up.

"I'd better go, nice meeting you, Jeffrey."

He shook my hand again. "Good luck."

I stood at attention at Holly's side while she counted through the drawer twice. Evidently everything was in order and we both signed off on the register tape she'd created.

It was then I'd realized that I hadn't seen hide or hair of Gisele, Jessica, or Chris since Andrew and I had returned from lunch. I regarded Holly and figured she wouldn't kill me if I asked.

"When do you get off?"

"Six," she answered snappishly.

"Whatever happened to the big three?" I asked.

Her head whipped around toward me so forcefully I thought she'd give herself whiplash. "What do you mean?"

I waved my hand in the air. "The big three, Chris, Jessica, and Gisele; I haven't seen them since lunch."

"They have – things to discuss," she answered, trying to be dismissive and not quite accomplishing the endeavor.

"Oh, it must be the thefts – or the accidents maybe," I said as dismissively, letting her know I knew and she could certainly confide in me if she wanted.

She frowned at me, but didn't answer.

"That's why we have to do this, isn't it?" I waved my hand over the cash drawer.

Holly rolled her eyes. "This is company procedure," she said evenly as she pushed back the chair.

She waited for me to leave closing and locking the door behind her. I watched her go out toward the sales floor. All this may have been procedure, but I didn't think the store had been following it previous to the thefts, at least not down to the letter. I couldn't remember whether or not this had been done with Betty Ann. How could I ask Holly without raising her ire?

The back doorbell rang as I pulled my coat from the locker. I was closer, so I went toward it with the intention of opening it.

Holly called out a warning, "I have to do that, Samantha; the alarm will sound."

She surrendered the bagged drawer to me, peeked through the peephole before she slid the key in the lock, and pushed open the door for Chris Nichols. He noted that I held the drawer and glanced toward Holly without saying a word. She relocked the door and grabbed the drawer from me before she scurried off towards the sales floor. Chris cast me a curt nod and headed for his own office.

I played and replayed that little scenario a couple times and missed the significance. Perhaps I wasn't deemed worthy enough to hold a register drawer. I shrugged and retrieved my pocketbook.

Before I was released, Holly did a cursory search of my purse. Given her red face as she did so, I didn't think that particular procedure had been followed previously either.

Chapter 14

I went home, wishing Wayne was there for several reasons – and the major one was not because I knew how messy the place was. I don't like it when we fight and I truly hate it when he goes off and we have unsettled issues (which lately was always). Damn it, I missed him.

I changed from my Wentworths' uniform and pulled on some old sweats of Wayne's ignoring the clutter on the way to my study. I was thinking that after I did some research, I could probably throw a load into the washing machine, maybe run the dishwasher, and maybe even pick up some and make the bed.

When I was in the safe haven of my study where the clutter was commonplace and expected, I figured I'd just hold off and wait out this sudden urge to clean. I did take note of the fact that the rug in the study didn't have that red hue any longer and smiled to myself. Peter must have taken care of the cleaning of it. I'd have to remember to thank him.

I spent the next hour or so accessing newspapers trying to get an account of the Wentworths' thefts. There wasn't much from any of the rags. There was a blurb about Hector Rodriquez's accidental death and a small write-up about Elaine Newcomb and that the police had been called in and an investigation was being conducted. There was also, curiously, mention in the police log that a cruiser and ambulance had been dispatched to the store long before Elaine's accident. Very curious. That was it and it wasn't much. OSHA should be deep into its own investigation at the very least, but no mention was made of it. I suppose a business such as Wentworths would do all they could to keep that hushed.

My stomach growled and I glanced at my watch and was surprised to see that it was nearing eight. I'd make myself a sandwich and give Jack a call.

I opened the refrigerator with caution knowing Wayne hadn't been here long enough between trips to do any grocery shopping; a bit afraid to see what I'd find. I should explain that I don't do a lot of foraging for food when Wayne isn't around. Take out is the norm. I've had some very promising potential science projects growing in my Glad and Zip-loc plastic storage containers in the past when he's been away too long.

I opened the meat drawer and took out a package of deli ham. I didn't have to smell it to know it was bad, I could feel the slime through the bag. I retrieved the garbage can from under the sink and tossed it. I peered into another container and cautiously opened the cover, whatever it contained was fuzzy and I didn't think saving the container was worth the trouble so I tossed everything. Another container revealed an evil smelling glob of brown something; that followed the fuzzy thing. When the milk cap popped off and emitted a gaggy sour smell, I resigned myself to the fact that nothing in there was edible save for the eggs and maybe the jar of pickles. I didn't even let myself think about Moira searching for something to cook for me.

So I cleaned it out – everything – except the eggs (and they should probably have gone, too, but I needed something to eat). I filled two garbage bags and carried them down the hill to the buckets by the garage door plopping them in with a sigh. I was cleaning. I wanted to be eating.

As I walked back up the hill I decided that eggs were not what I wanted for supper. It was nine o'clock now; I should go to the grocery store. A scary venture. It was never a good idea for me to grocery shop when I was hungry. I tended to buy things like Twizzlers and Pepperidge Farm frozen cakes rather than things good and nutritious. *Okay – so tell yourself you're going to eat right. Buy a frozen dinner or something.* Yeah right, like fried chicken with the mashed potatoes and heavily buttered corn and the brownie. Yum. Healthy Choice just didn't sound like it would fill me up.

Dilemma. My stomach rumbled again to remind me I still hadn't fed it. *Oh hell.* I trooped into the house and grabbed my keys and purse.

I was actually proud of myself. I managed to steer clear of the candy aisle and the frozen food section bringing home sandwich meat, cheese, bread, and skim milk. Of course I'd gotten some strange looks and mothers with small children - *what exactly were they doing out so late* - steered clear as I repeated the mantra of 'no candy, no cakes, and no fried chicken.' I had a revelation on my way to the store that I might be able to obtain more information if I ate in the employee's lounge – or at best overhear something from the office next door, thus the sandwich meat purchase served a dual purpose. I made myself a sandwich, cursing myself for forgetting mayonnaise, and carried that and a glass of skim milk back to the study to call Jack Parnell. I gave no thought to what time it was. I doubt it would have stopped me from calling anyway.

How would I broach the subject without actually telling him I was working at Wentworths?

"Jack, this is Sam Warren, how are things?" Good start.

He didn't answer. He also didn't hang up. Okay.

"Peter called me in Georgia, he said that someone else got hurt at that store."

"Yeah."

Oh, you're a font of information. "Are they all right?"

"She's in a coma, broken back," he replied noncommittally.

Hey, guess what I did? I got a job at Wentworths! "I did some research on my own to be helpful. Did you know Wentworths had a big heist?" I felt like an idiot calling the thievery a heist.

Jack chuckled - evidently he thought I was an idiot, too. "I had heard that," he answered.

Oh.

"Anything else I could look up for you?" I ventured. "You know – background stuff."

Hey Sam you know what would be great? You could get a part time job there and be my inside source. What do you think?

"Nothing else, but I'll let you know."

"Good. Maybe we could go out to dinner again sometime?" I said and I think he grunted before he hung up. "You could bring your ex-wife," I said to the dead air space between our telephone lines. "She could kick my ass for you."

Okay, that went well.

I stared at the telephone – should I call Peter? Ask his advice; chance that he was with Moira again and that I'd be disturbing another evening?

I guess not.

I pouted and then sighed. It was late, I should go to bed. I had another busy day tomorrow. I had a job. I had responsibilities.

I typed well into the night.

CHAPTER 15

Betty Ann was dusting the front display table when I parked my van out front, opting for the open air parking rather than the garage. She waved and smiled and unlocked the door as I approached.

"Good morning, Samantha.

"Yeah," I answered irritably. "Do you want some coffee?" I hadn't bought coffee at the Safeway and I was fresh out. It's not good when I don't have coffee first thing – especially after staying up most of the night.

"No thank you," she said cheerily.

Yech. I hate early morning cheerfulness.

"I'll just go get some and be right back," I didn't wait to see if it was all right.

She nodded – I think – and probably cheerily, too.

I turned back about four steps into my journey. "Who else is here? I'll get them something."

"Gisele and Andrew," she answered. "And Holly is due in."

"Any idea what they like?"

She shrugged.

I'd improvise. I slogged the rest of the way to the Starbucks and pushed open the door to stand in line. Tony was three people ahead of me, he waved, and gave up his place in line to come back. Another cheery morning person. I was surrounded. I found myself wondering if Peter was one, too.

"Hi Sam."

"Tony," I'm not much of a conversationalist in the morning either.

"You ready for another day?" He rubbed his hands together enthusiastically.

I nodded.

"I'm doing shipment again," he offered as we crept forward.

"Do you like that?"

He shrugged. "It's all right. It will be better when I've learned where everything goes."

Light bulb! I smiled at him as we stepped closer. "How is the shipment processed?" I asked.

"It's different than what I'm used to," he started as it came our turn and he ordered a latte with a triple shot.

I kept him from paying. "I'll get this," I said and ordered myself a black coffee and then tacked on four cappuccinos before I paid. Someone would drink them.

"Thanks," Tony said as we waited.

"You've done warehouse work before then?" I asked, trying to get him back on track.

He nodded. "At Barnes and Noble, I do their shipments." He grabbed his latte and the tray they'd placed the four drinks in while I grabbed my coffee and took a sip. Heavenly.

"You said receiving stock was different at Wentworths?" I pressed.

He held the door open with his butt. "Most places have a scanner and they record the receiving electronically. At Wentworths it's all done manually. Each pallet has a printout sheet attached with the numbers and we check them off one by one. I would say that's why it takes so long and they are so backed up."

Minus the fact they keep losing employees, of course. We were approaching the front door and I wasn't quite ready to go inside. Fortunately, Betty Ann wasn't right there. "So if something is missing then you'd know right off."

He nodded as he peered inside. "And if there's something extra – like from another store – each store has its own number and it's printed on the shipping label.

When everything is done, the manager makes the proper adjustments so the inventory is corrected." Tony answered as he waved to someone inside. Chris Nichols opened the door for us and accepted one of the coffees I offered him with a thank you.

I mulled over the information Tony had imparted as I stuffed my purse in my locker and closed the door. I remembered only then the fleeting thought I had I would leave my purse home rather than subject it to the search at the end of the day. Then I remembered I'd left the nice lunch I'd made on the bench in my kitchen. Oh well.

How would someone go about stealing stock? I mused. Was it so obvious that it was someone that was new to the game that wouldn't be privy to the procedure? A new employee that would look upon the merchandise with delight without thinking of the consequences? I shook my head. It had to be someone with a key. Every door and register was locked to the general employees. Even the back door needed a key before it could be pushed open or the alarm would go off.

I mused right into Chris Nichols as he stood at the end of the lockers.

He grinned and leaned against the wall of lockers. "Daydreaming, Ms. Warren?"

"Just going over the manual, Mr. Nichols – in my head."

He laughed. "I'll just bet. Call me Chris, please." He looked behind him then back at me, leaning toward me. "I was wondering if you wanted to go out for a drink sometime."

I looked at him sidelong and frowned. "Are you asking me on a date?"

He laughed again. "No, of course not, just a friendly drink between colleagues." He was too quick - and too red-faced - for it to be just that.

Like that would ever happen! I'm married, buster! Besides he wouldn't be interested in me that way.

"Sure, that sounds like fun," I said as I pinned on my name tag and fell just short of sniffing under my arms wondering if I'd put on deodorant that morning. I would have to do a wash tonight though. My other shirts were promised by the end of the week. I knew this one wouldn't last until then.

"Good then – tonight?" he posed.

I have to do laundry. "Sure, when?"

"Nine-thirty? I'll meet you at Friday's," he said and I found myself nodding. Great. I was just like Wayne. Again I admonished myself. It was just as Chris Nichols had said, a friendly drink between colleagues, nothing more.

The second day was spent pretty much as the first with Betty Ann and me unboxing stock and putting it away.

Gisele gave me a turn at the customer service desk going through the procedure for returns and exchanges. I wasn't certain why, I couldn't do them anyway because I didn't have a key. I guess I could start the process while I sought out a key holder.

She also showed me how to look up stock at the warehouse and other stores. There was a mutual understanding among all the stores that if a customer needed something from any one - or all of them - then it could be obtained. The customer always comes first. She also taught me how to operate the bar code label maker. That was kind of cool.

"How are you finding things, Sam?" she asked when she finally took a breath and, therefore, allowed me to as well.

I nodded. "I like it," I replied honestly.

She smiled. "You get a twenty-five percent discount and two or three times a year we have special higher discounts."

The telephone rang and I picked it up giving my name after saying 'Wentworths.' The caller wanted to speak to Chris. I put him on hold and Gisele told me how to page Chris.

"Chris says he asked you along tonight," she said, when the call was answered.

I tried to mask my surprise as I nodded.

She seemed to read right through me.

"We like to do this once in a while to promote harmony among employees and such. Sometimes, we go out to dinner, but most often it's just drinks. Remind me to invite Tony and Melanie, when she comes in later."

You really didn't think that he'd invite you all by yourself did you? Again, I nodded. "What is it you want me to do this afternoon?"

"I have paperwork to catch up on. I'm going to have you hang around here until Holly comes in and then I'll give you over to Andrew. He needs assistance in setting up a new display in the bridal registry. We're having a bridal show the middle of March and the newspaper is sending someone to take some pictures for our advertisement." She struck a thoughtful pose. "As a matter of fact, I believe there's some new crystal vases that came in we're to use in that display. I'll find Andrew and see that he gets them to you to price."

Okay then I thought as she walked away. I was bummed. Chris had actually *meant* that it was just among colleagues even though it hadn't seemed to me that was what he meant. I guess there would be no grilling of him over drinks. I burbled my lips and sought out some boxes from Tony. I couldn't just stand around and do nothing and could easily get two or three done before I was given Andrew's tasks.

So I spent the afternoon learning the finer points of merchandising from the master. I reiterate that Andrew was very good at what he did. There's considerable difference between placing something on a shelf and artfully displaying it, between crowding a display with stock, and making it pleasing to the eye so it would be snatched up by the drooling and unsuspecting consumer. That was, after all, why we had such a huge warehouse.

"What we try to do is have at least one of everything new prominently displayed up front here," he pointed to the rounded glass shelves that comprise the back of the customer service desk. "When registry couples come in, they see it and their eyes light up. Make certain that the price tags are discreetly hidden and that no finger prints are visible on the merchandise we display in this area, but especially on the glass shelving. That sounds impossible as far as the vases are concerned (he pronounced the word 'vaazes'), but utilize paper towel when placing them and it can be accomplished." He had been talking non-stop for a couple hours and it seemed like he was finally winding down. I had a lot of information. I just wasn't so sure it had sunk in.

"So, I hear that you're joining us tonight," Andrew said as he shifted a bone china plate and slipped a sliver charger beneath it.

"Yeah, Chris asked me this morning."

"Chris did?" Andrew asked with eyebrow raised. "Don't you rate?"

Okay – I was hungry and irritable. "Cut it out, Andrew," I retorted.

"Sorry," he replied and turned his face away from me. I think he was grinning, perhaps his feelings were hurt. I'm not sure whether or not I cared either way.

"Can I ask you a question, Andrew?"

"Sure."

"Did they find out who stole the stuff?"

He held my gaze and then finally answered. "No, they didn't."

"Okay then, how can someone go about stealing that much merchandise without it being missed?"

"Actually, it's pretty easy. We only do inventory once a year. You've seen our stock room, a box here and a box there would be easy."

"But what about the bag checks?"

"They weren't enforced much before the thefts were discovered. There was speculation that cartons were taken off the truck before they even came into the store. My theory is that there was more than one in on it. Chris felt similarly thinking it was an employee in cahoots with customers. The customers would come in and the goods would be passed on without paying for them."

"So it wasn't done overnight then."

He shook his head and looked over towards the customer service desk at Holly. She was making a good show of *not* listening to us. He bent his head closer to my ear.

"Holly was, and probably still is, high on Chris' suspect list because she was here alone the night before inventory. Her biggest defense was that all the merchandise *couldn't* have disappeared overnight." He crossed his arms over his chest. "I have to agree with her there given some of the items that went missing."

I tried my damnedest not to look in her direction. How pleasant it must be to work in a place that people suspected you of pilfering. No wonder she was so cross.

Andrew pulled me away from the gift registry. "Holly had her own accident, you know."

"How so?" I asked stealing a look her way. How much more obvious could we be?

"The alarm went off on the back door over by the bathrooms. When she went to investigate, she was injured."

"My God, how?"

"Long story short, someone was holding the other side of the door and then suddenly they weren't. When she pushed on it for the third time more forcibly than before, they let go and she went through and banged her head. I think it was fortunate that Louisa had already called the police when the alarm sounded."

Holly trotted towards the back room with her head bent.

"She's been a one woman crusade trying to find out who did steal the stuff. She's been going around accusing everyone and being real sneaky about it. I caught her once hiding among the dinnerware listening. Scared the bejeezus out of me when I bent over to retrieve a box of dinnerware and she's tucked in the back. It wasn't a pretty sight let me tell you."

"Given her accident, I would think she'd leave well enough alone."

"But she's a person scorned; someone accused her of the nasty deed," Andrew stressed.

"So they think she staged her own accident then?"

Andrew shrugged holding his hands out in supplication.

"Who accused her?"

"Well, it was Jessica that voiced it and questioned her, but I think Chris was pulling the strings."

"Who was here when the warehouse man," *What was his name?* "when Hector was crushed?"

Andrew grimaced. "None of us, he was doing the truck after hours. We were all here when Elaine made like a bird," he paused. "At least all of us that are left." He grew pensive.

I cocked my head. "You've thought of something."

He smiled and shook his head. "It's nothing – really." He surveyed our work. "I declare this complete, you are done for the day," he held his hand out as though he was the fairy godmother touching her wand to a dog to turn him into a horse.

I shook my head while I retrieved my purse from my locker. No one was here with Hector, but his killer.

CHAPTER 16

I wasn't sure why I'd agreed to go to Fridays. I was tired from the week, tired from work, from lack of sleep. I guess I thought I could get some more insight into my co-workers' characters. I smiled as I drove wearily home – it was a good thing it wasn't a far drive or I would have gone to sleep at the wheel.

I hadn't learned anything, save for the fact I didn't know what I was doing and probably shouldn't go into work tomorrow.

I parked the van in the upper driveway and slid from the seat. The house's sensor lights came on and lit my way to the front door and I absently inserted the key in the lock. Clear your mind of everything I told myself. Stop trying to make something from nothing and, for God's sake, stop trying to make a mental character list of those you're working with.

I stopped dead in the hallway in the process of hanging up my coat in the closet. (I must be tired, I was actually hanging up my coat). Something was not right. I turned and squinted into the kitchen, the light from the porch filtered in; the bench was clean. There was nothing on it, no bowl from my breakfast of cereal and no carefully prepared lunch. And I *know* I had left it there –

I stepped toward the hallway cautiously and tiptoed to my bathroom. Nothing on the floor - I'd left dirty towels and clothes. This could only mean one thing. No, not a prowler, Wayne was home. He'd cleaned and - I glanced in the closet where the hamper was kept – he had done laundry. Damn! I really needed a clean shirt tomorrow (so much for the thought of not going into work).

I tossed my bag into my study which was thankfully messy and retraced my steps down the hall toward the stairs where I saw ambient light from the laundry room. I trotted down the staircase just as I heard the dial to the washer being spun for another load. I crossed the living room and stood in the doorway ready to declare I had more laundry.

Wayne jumped a mile.

"Jesus, you scared me!" he said, holding his heart and leaning against the washer.

"Sorry, I had more to add. I need this shirt tomorrow," I pulled it off and handed it to him. He studied the logo while I slipped off my pants and then added my underwear.

"Wentworths," he mused and then looked my way and smiled crookedly. His blue eyes narrowed, he dropped the shirt on the floor, and stepped toward me. He reached out, snagged my arm crushing me to his chest, and kissed me.

Hmmm. I think he may have missed me.

"I need a shower bad," I said as he ran a finger down my shoulder.

"You go up. I'll put these in and join you shortly," he said huskily.

I was reluctant to leave his embrace – it had been too long. "Sammy?" his hot breath brushed my ear.

"Hmmm?"

"I'll be up in a minute, I promise," he whispered.

I backed away and smiled. "Okay."

It seemed like a long wait, but it was really only a few minutes before he was there. I guess he had needed to clean his clothes, too.

It was another one of those times in our relationship that I would remember vividly. When we just concentrated on the business of loving each other and didn't do any talking. It was good.

Light filtered in through the window and I turned to look at the clock. It was nearing seven. Wayne stirred beside me and wrapped his arms around me a bit tighter as he kissed my shoulder.

"Good morning," he said.

"Good morning. You got home early."

"I missed you. When I got here, I thought you were away," he moved back so he could see my face. "Where were you?"

I didn't bristle at his question, after all, I constantly asked him where he was and when he'd be home even though I didn't need to.

"Working," I answered.

He raised an eyebrow and leaned up on one elbow still holding me possessively with his other hand. He regarded me for some time and then smiled knowingly. "Wentworths," he commented and I nodded.

I made to move. "Which reminds me, I have to go put my shirt in the dryer?"

He wasn't quite ready to let me go.

"When did you start there?" he asked.

"Monday. I'm a sales associate," I said proudly. "I make eight bucks an hour."

His expression was clear. He so wanted to ask what had happened to my other 'profession' – I *knew*. I waited for it to come.

It didn't. That surprised me more than you can imagine.

"When do you have to be there?"

"Ten," my eyes traveled to the clock again. "Plenty of time," I said and he smiled waving his hand for me to go do the dryer thing and hurry back.

This was good, too.

I didn't need the belt of caffeine that morning so stood at the door waiting for someone to show their face in the other side. While I waited, I mulled over the little get-together we'd had at Fridays' the night before. Chris and Jessica had come together, I think they'd been out to dinner before their arrival, but I can't say for certain. Gisele came dressed down, obviously coming to the restaurant from home. Andrew showed up with his boyfriend, a youngish looking man about a foot taller than Andrew, husky build, bald head and pale brown eyes. Andrew introduced him as Fletcher and I had the feeling Fletcher was a bit uncomfortable, but maybe it was me thinking that for him.

Rather than going home, Melanie and I had wandered about the four or five strip malls within spitting (and walking) distance of Fridays picking up a loaded burrito at Chipotles before heading over.

Chris had commandeered a table for us and even went so far as to order a selection of appetizers to go with our collection of drinks. I ordered a badly needed cup of comfort coffee while the others spewed forth a variety of alcoholic beverages when the waiter approached. My evening with the blender full of strawberry daiquiri was still fresh in my mind.

"Where are Jeff and Holly?" Chris asked. I guess he was the spokesperson and general leader of the gathering. After all, he did invite us all – I thought with some level of vehemence.

"Jeff had reading to do for his class. I guess Holly is coming over after closing," Andrew answered. "I didn't get the impression that she would show up though." He turned towards his date. "Did you, Fletcher?"

Fletcher reddened and shrugged. A man of few words evidently.

I remembered I was just itchy to get out and go home to bed.

"Sam? Are you coming inside?" Betty Ann asked as she stood with the door open before me.

I shook my head to clear it and stepped inside while she closed and locked up behind me. She pursed her lips.

"I had to call in Gisele, she's madder than a hornet."

"Why's that?"

"Holly was supposed to open this morning and she never showed. I waited until nine fifteen and finally gave up and called Gisele."

I remembered Gisele saying something last night about her taking a shopping trip today - it was a day off. I wondered why Betty Ann would call her rather than Jessica. Then I asked Betty Ann *why* she called Gisele.

Betty Ann rolled her eyes and busied herself at her register.

I stared at her curiously and chuckled. "You know you just can't do that, Betty Ann."

"Do what?"

I leaned toward her. "You can't drop a broad hint of juicy gossip and not give me something. Is Holly usually late?"

She laughed then. It was a deep laugh and she made it sound as though she was relieved.

"You crack me up, Sam," she said and then hurriedly started straightening the newsprint she'd brought from the back. It must be her favorite diversion. I figured Gisele must be approaching.

My suspicion was confirmed when a hand touched my back. Even with the forewarning, I jumped.

"Holly has done this once too often," Gisele said, trying on a smile without succeeding. "I'm afraid she's going to find that this is strike three."

Gisele was out of 'uniform' in a pair of jeans, a blue tattered Ragg sweater, and black clogs. These were her clothes from last night. Her hair was mussed and her eyes bleary.

"You missed the best part of the evening by leaving early, Samantha," she smiled thinly. "But you do look the better for it. Jessica should be in shortly," she threw this out to the two of us, and then leaned on the counter with a clipboard. "I've outlined what you can do this morning. Andrew is due in at noon." She rubbed her face wearily. "There are a few boxes left to price. I've put them on the carts. When Andrew comes in, he can show you, Samantha, where to put the overstock. I'd like him to finish up the bridal registry area. I want him to tweak it a bit and make sure you dust and polish. The photographer will be in early afternoon."

She had every minute detail she was voicing already down on paper. I wanted to tell her I thought I could read just fine, but I didn't. I guess this was what she needed to do.

"Betty Ann, if you would, I'd like you the clean the stemware area and make certain everything is fronted, maybe show Sam." She looked towards me. "You haven't closed yet and this is one of the nightly procedures while the manager is counting out drawers."

I looked around the stemware and noted that particular procedure hadn't been followed the night before. I think Gisele noticed, too. All the more evidence against Holly.

Jessica Lupine inserted her key in the door and slipped through with Chris Nichols on her heels. I thought he had on the same suit as the day before, but I wouldn't swear to it. Gisele never missed a beat as she continued on down her list while the two of them walked to the back with only a nod in our direction. Not even Jessica displayed her bubbliness this morning.

Curious, I thought.

Gisele straightened and placed her hands on her hips. "I'm out of here then, have a good day," she threw back at us before she left without a backward glance.

Betty Ann and I stared in her wake for the longest time until Betty Ann finally became aware of a woman with a baby carriage who was staring back at us and nudged me. I went to open the doors. The day at Wentworths had almost succeeded in starting without us. It would prove to be an interesting day.

CHAPTER 17

We didn't see Jessica at all. I guess it was fortunate for her we didn't have any transactions that required her key and, fortunate for us – or me - we didn't have many customers. Although I did manage to impart my limited expertise and sell twelve place settings and a serving set of '*Monique*' to one lady. I was quite proud. My real contribution was helping her decide between the '*Monique*' and '*Rosemary*' patterns. I knew someone named Rosemary and didn't care for her; the entire basis for my opinion.

Chris emerged from the back around ten thirty and informed Betty Ann that he would be traveling to the Winchester store and probably wouldn't be back at Rockville until the following week should anyone want him.

Somewhere in the course of the morning, my husband showed. I introduced him to Betty Ann and Andrew when he came at eleven thirty on Wayne's heels. There was an odd moment there between the two men before Wayne held me possessively and asked if I could join him for coffee. I glanced at Andrew who winked at me. I assumed that was an okay and we went next door to Starbucks.

"Interesting guy, Andrew," Wayne said as he placed the two drinks on the table and sat down taking up my hand in his.

"I think he thought you so as well," I replied, sipping my drink.

Wayne held my hand up and kissed my fingertips sending a chill down my spine. "I brought a lunch for you," he said smiling and holding up an insulated lunch bag.

"You did? Thank you." Where the hell had he gotten an insulated bag?

"I figured you wouldn't have time enough for us to have one together."

"I only get a half hour. What's on your agenda today?"

"I have to go into the office for a bit, get my tickets for Alaska."

I tried not to pout. "You're leaving?" Again?

"Not until Saturday, weather permitting. It's supposed to snow, if you can believe it."

"I hope it does then - buckets."

His hand was on my thigh and I reddened. "That's cute, you haven't done that in a long time." He leaned over and kissed me and sent another wave of electricity through my body. Screw Wentworths, I was going home with my husband.

"I should get back," I said standing and kissing his lips. "I'll see you tonight."

"I'll make it worth your while."

I walked back to Wentworths – no, I floated. I hadn't felt this way about Wayne for a long time. I glanced back before I entered the store and wished I hadn't. Wayne was holding the door for a tall blonde and giving her the once and twice over and maybe thrice. He hesitated briefly at the door and then followed her back inside.

Shit.

I knew I shouldn't, but I did. I trotted back towards Starbucks and pushed open the door just in time to see Wayne and the blonde leave out the back. I walked back to Wentworths with my head low.

Andrew was rubbing his hands and smiling. "He was delicious, darling, but no ass."

I blew out my cheeks fighting to control my tears. "You can have him if you want, just let me know." I headed for the bathroom hoping I wouldn't run into anyone on the way and cursing myself for looking back and catching Wayne. I tried to justify his actions. If he's told me once, he's told me a thousand times that it doesn't do any harm to look. If I could only believe that's all he did.

I did my best with cold water and the paper towel in the bathroom debating on whether or not I should have confronted him. I laughed at my reflection knowing I wouldn't have done it.

"You all right, Samantha?" Jessica asked when I wrenched open my locker. I hadn't seen or heard her coming and, once again, I was startled. I had to get a better grip on myself.

"I'm fine."

"Well, if you need a few minutes, feel free to sit for a while," she said patting my shoulder as she headed for the bathroom. I guess she'd been waiting for me to vacate it and had probably heard me crying. I would have thanked her, but she disappeared through the door before I had a chance.

I sucked in a deep sigh and contemplated putting a dent in the locker vowing to myself that Wayne could wait until hell froze over for me to come home tonight.

Turns out I wouldn't have a choice.

I busied myself with the tasks that Gisele had lined up for us, trying not to break anything in the process. Breaking things would have been therapeutic. Andrew seemed to sense my bad mood and kept quiet only interrupting my thoughts to give me pointers on something visual. The photographer came and went. Andrew had fussed and flitted while he took his pictures. I watched the process as I carefully dusted and cleaned the glass shelves and vases that backed the customer service desk. It was a full time job just keeping them free of fingerprints.

Andrew now stood back gazing at the display we'd barely rearranged before the photographer had shown. "I don't like it," he said with his finger next to his lip.

"It looks fine, Andrew." I cautiously hoisted an etched vase to the high shelf with paper towel.

He looked at me doubtfully. "It needs something," he said absently. He searched the curved wall choosing three dinnerware patterns and bringing them to the table. He then confiscated the very vase I'd just positioned.

"Do you know where the storage room is, Sam?"

"Yes."

"I need a dozen or so of the wooden plate racks and as many of the plastic single plate stands."

I nodded. I didn't take affront that he was asking me to be the gopher; it was part of my job description after all. I took a final swipe with the dust rag and stepped off the two step ladder to stand back and admire my efforts before I went to do his bidding. It looked damned good. Glass shelves and crystal vases sparkled in the bright lights, not a fingerprint to be seen.

I grabbed a load of broken-down boxes to take back for the trash pile and then headed for the storage room. I ached. I don't think I've worked this hard at anything for a long time. I pushed open the door, snapped my head to the right and left, and stopped dead in my tracks. I opened my mouth to scream and heard only a squeak. I couldn't seem to let go of the door – my hand seemed molded to it.

I had to call the police - Jack Parnell. I backed from the room and let the door close. I tried Chris' door first and found it locked. I knew there was a telephone there. I then somehow managed to walk wobbly-legged to the telephone by the sales floor door.

I dialed 9-1-1 and waited for the dispatch operator to come on the line. "I'd like to report a body," I said.

"Where, ma'am?"

"Wentworths," I answered. She must have had a digital readout of the location because she said she'd send over an ambulance and the police.

"You might want to contact Detective Jack Parnell," I said next. "He's working on a case here, this may be related."

"I can do that. What's your name, dear?"

"Samantha Warren," I answered. "I don't think you'll need an ambulance, she looks pretty dead." *But what did I know*? I hung up the receiver and stared at the concrete wall.

Well, now I knew why Holly Bush was a no-show at Fridays last night. From the looks of her, she was probably a never-left.

CHAPTER 18

There was a lot of confusion when the police arrived and burst through the doors. Neither Melanie, nor Andrew, nor Jessica knew why they were there because I hadn't moved. I snapped out of my funk and pushed through the doors, beckoning them to the back. Jessica followed close on their heels. She made it as far as the door when one of the uniforms stopped her and told her she could go no further. The policeman accompanying him took my arm and propelled me back into the warehouse.

"Show me the body, ma'am," he said matter-of-factly.

"It's back there." I pointed to the right and held my ground.

He stood squarely before me with his hands on my shoulders. He was in his forties I guessed, pudgy around the middle and graying around the temples. I thought he had very kind eyes – they were hazel – as he bent his head.

"What's your name?" he asked solicitously.

"Samantha Warren."

"You made the call?"

I nodded.

"Will you show me where it is? You don't have to look again."

My eyes met his and I thought I could do that, so I moved towards the storage room, came within a couple feet of it, and then stopped and pointed. He brushed past me and opened the door.

"She's dead all right," he stated and looked back at me. "Did you touch anything other than the door?"

I shook my head.

"Good girl, what's her name?"

"Holly Bush," I said as he let the door close.

I thought I heard him comment, "that's what I thought."

"Who's the lady that's clamoring to come back here?" he asked.

"The manager, Jessica Lupine," I answered as my arms hugged my body.

"What did Holly Bush do?"

Other than die, you mean? "She's a sales supervisor," I responded. My mind's eye saw her again and details formed; the odd angle which her neck had been bent, the purplish tint to her face, the tongue protruding from her mouth. I covered my mouth with my hand and felt his hands forcing me to sit on a crate. He lowered my head between my legs and told me to breathe.

I don't know how long he held me there, but I was glad for his presence. The nausea passed and I told him I thought I was all right now.

"I want you to stay here until the detectives talk with you. I'm going to tell Miss Loopy she has to close the store."

"Lupine, Jessica Lupine," I corrected.

"You'll be all right here?"

I glanced at the closed door. "I'd rather wait over there in the breakroom if that's okay."

He smiled. "Sure it is." He helped me up and I was surprised that I needed the support. It's just that I kept seeing that purple face and swollen tongue. "Whoa, hold on; let me get you something to sit on," he said distantly.

"What's your name?" I asked as I settled onto another crate by the telephone I'd used.

"I'm Gabe Johnson, ma'am," he held the door open while he talked with Jessica. She started to protest his request to close the store immediately and Gabe raised his hand to stem the protest. Jessica fell silent.

"There's been a mishap, ma'am, and we'll need to protect the integrity of the crime scene. You need to close the store until we're done. We'll probably be done tonight."

"Mishap? What sort of mishap?" Jessica demanded.

"Close the store, ma'am," he insisted. "Then I have to ask that everyone here gather up front, but no talking to one another. Officer Dempsey will keep a watchful eye until we've spoken with you all. Understand?"

Jessica must have nodded then because the door closed and Gabe Johnson knelt before me. "Can you tell me what happened, Miss Warren?"

"It's Sam."

"Okay, Sam," he smiled and waited.

I shivered.

"Is there coffee? I noticed a kitchen back there."

I shook my head. "There's tea and cocoa I think – no coffee." I shuddered again and he helped me up, holding me by the arm while we walked to the breakroom. He sat me in one of the metal chairs and pulled a mug off the shelf, filled it with water, and placed it in the microwave. "Cocoa or tea?" he asked.

"Cocoa."

"Can I use one of these cups for myself?"

"Sure." I didn't know, but why not.

He busied himself with the preparation of our drinks and then sat down opposite me when he was done. I held the mug in my hands in an attempt to warm them.

"So, tell me how you happened onto the body."

"Andrew needed plate racks, he sent me for them," I answered as he pulled out his worn notebook.

"And Andrew is?"

"Andrew Barker, he's the visual merchandiser."

"He couldn't get his own plate racks?"

I smiled. "I was assisting him. I'm the lackey, he's the expert."

"So he sent you."

I regarded Gabe Johnson. "Like, did he send me so I'd discover the body?"

Gabe shrugged. "What do you think?"

"I don't know, I've only worked here three days." I blew out my cheeks. "I don't think that Andrew killed her."

"When's the last you saw Holly Bush?" he shook his head and grinned. "What a name," he said under his breath.

"Yesterday at five, Melanie and I – that's Melanie Friis, she was hired the same day as I was. She and I left and went shopping until we were to meet at Fridays at nine-thirty."

"Meet who?"

"All of us, the staff here. We were meeting for drinks." Not just Chris Nichols and I, but everyone.

"Why so late?"

"The store closes at nine, it probably takes a half hour or so to do everything."

"Like what?"

"Closing, you mean?"

He nodded

"I haven't done that yet. The tough stuff is done by the managers, such as counting the money - and I'm sure they have to file a report with the mother ship."

He grinned. "Who was there at Fridays?"

I told him and he asked who arrived when and with whom, carefully writing the names down as I recited them, noting each person's position in the pecking order of Wentworths' Rockville store.

"And this Andrew saw Holly last?" Gabe asked.

"He and his friend, Fletcher, went over to Fridays from here. When they left, Andrew said that Holly was counting out the drawers." I shifted in my chair. "He said he didn't think that she would show."

"Is it common for a manager to be here alone?"

I shrugged. "I don't know really. I think they were frowning upon it because of the thefts. You'll have to ask Jessica that. You're aware of the thefts?"

He nodded and studied me. A smile formed on his lips. "You seem to have a theory."

I laughed. "It seems that the safety precautions -" I held up a finger for each point I made "- the vigilant counting of the drawers, the bag checks that are written company policy have been only recently adhered to. Holly particularly wasn't comfortable checking my bag the first two nights. I asked her if this was something new and she snapped back that it was company policy." I held my hand out with palms up.

Gabe nodded. "Did anyone leave Fridays while you were there?"

I shook my head. "Not for long, at least while *I* was there. Bathroom breaks I would guess, certainly no longer than that." I took a sip of the cocoa and it was cooling. I placed it back on the table.

"When did you leave?"

"Around ten, maybe ten fifteen, I didn't want to be there as it was."

"And everyone else stayed?"

I nodded.

"And Holly Bush didn't show?"

"Holly Bush didn't show before I left." I looked toward the room she now occupied and shivered.

He jotted down more notes and looked as though he was formulating another question when Officer Dempsey appeared in the doorway.

"Johnson? Detective Parnell is here and wants to see the body."

Gabe nodded and tucked his notebook back in his pocket. "I'm done with you, Sam. I'm pretty sure that Detective Parnell will want to talk with you."

I nodded and pushed back my chair. "I'll wash up the mugs."

He didn't comment as he followed Dempsey through the warehouse. I washed out the mugs and left them to dry in the dish drainer all the while remembering how Holly looked. A tear escaped down my cheek.

I heard voices in the warehouse and knew that Gabe was showing Jack and the coroner the body. I wiped up the table and went to my locker to retrieve my coat. I was still freezing. The cocoa just hadn't been satisfying enough and I wanted to avoid going home to Wayne. Starbucks seemed like as good a place to go as any.

I shrugged on my coat and pulled my purse from the locker looking up to see Jack Parnell staring tight-lipped at me from the center of the warehouse. He didn't look happy.

"I'm going over to Starbucks for coffee," I said as I passed by him and three others, Gabe among them, and pushed open the door to the sales floor. None of them stopped me. Jessica, Andrew, and Melanie waited at different spots at the front as I walked resolutely towards the door. Officer Dempsey spun the lock and held it open for me as he stopped two woman from coming inside. I knew Jack was following me, I didn't stop to wait. I really needed a cup of coffee – and maybe one of those sticky bars they sold there – or maybe a scone. I swiped at my cheeks and shoved my hands in my pockets.

CHAPTER 19

Jack Parnell pushed past the throngs of coffee seekers and sat in the chair opposite me with a sneer.

"Just what the hell do you think you're doing, Sam?"

I sipped at the large Caramel Macchiato I'd ordered and savored the triple shot I'd opted for. Caffeine is good, more caffeine is better. I offered to buy Jack one, too, but he had mumbled something about foreign coffee. Actually, he'd said 'God-damned foreign coffee.' To my knowledge, no state grew coffee so it would all be foreign, wouldn't it? Maybe Hawaii grows it, I'd have to check. He really should have something though, he did look as though he could use it.

"What do you mean?" I asked.

"Why did I just go into Wentworths and find you working there?" he sat back and regarded me.

"Because I am?" I said raising my eyebrows. "I thought it would give us an inside track." I was going to add 'remember'? But he actually hadn't asked me to get a job there.

"It seems as though I'm conducting a murder investigation there now, Sammy, there is no 'us', you're not involved. Get out." He now leaned forward with one elbow resting on the small table. I think he was trying to be intimidating.

"I can't quit now."

"Of course you can."

"No, I can't," I answered levelly. "I'm already on the schedule and they need the help. They've had three people hurt - *it sounded better than dead* - and five or six quit because of the thefts. Besides, I think I'm involved by virtue of discovering the body."

His balled fist rested on the table and I felt mine going into the same mode matching his stubbornness with my own. I should have warned him that I would win. I, in turn, leaned toward him coming within inches of his nose.

"I can help you here, Jack, let me. You need to know how these people think and work – and possibly murder. You have to admit that this puts a different slant on the other two 'accidents'," I sketched quote marks in the air. "You and I both know it has to be an inside job."

"What if the murderer realizes that and chooses you to be next? What if the murderer thinks that's exactly why you came to work here?" Jack countered.

I suppose it made sense.

"He won't – or she." I had my suspicions about Gisele Fournier. As well as Jessica Lupine - no one is that cute and bubbly.

Jack Parnell snorted. "Don't bet the farm on that, darling." He shook his head. "I'll talk to you later after I'm through there," he jabbed his thumb towards the store then pushed off his chair. I watched as he walked towards Wentworths talking on his cell phone.

I frowned. "What's that supposed to mean?" I called after him only serving to alarm those around me.

I debated returning to the store. He had said he'd talk with me later. Did that mean I could go home? I slumped back in the chair holding my head in my hands trying not to cry. What in hell had I gotten myself into?

I don't know how long I sat there. I know my drink got cold and, when tested, it tasted as good cold as it had hot. I felt the presence of someone standing to my left and thought it was probably Jack. I eventually looked up. It was Wayne.

He didn't speak. He curled his hand gently around my arm and helped me up. He held my coat for me and then steered me toward the door with his hand at the small of my back.

It wasn't until I was buckled in his car and he was backing out of the parking space that I spoke.

"Why did you come?" I asked, too exhausted to say anything further. I had renewed anger over his following the blonde that morning.

"Your boy Frost called me; said that I'd probably want to go to Wentworths and pick you up. What happened, Sam?"

"One of the managers was murdered," I answered leaning my head against the cold glass of the Aztec's window. "I found her."

His hand reached for mine. "You okay?"

I nodded, fighting off the urge to jerk my arm away.

Wayne was quiet a mile or so. "Sam, are you angry with me?"

Gee, what gave you that idea? "No."

"Yes, you are," he stated as he negotiated the turn onto Veirs Mill Road.

Okay, so I am.

"What did I do?" he asked.

Maybe it was the day that I had. "It might have something to do with the blonde at Starbucks," I spat out while I bit back the tears.

"Blonde?" Wayne slowed to make the left into Aspen Hill.

"The blonde, after we had coffee and promising conversation, I looked back and you were eating up the blonde in the doorway. Remember?"

He laughed. I wrenched my hand away from his and would have opened the door and flung myself out if I wasn't assured that it would result in personal injury. He continued to laugh.

"You followed her. I went back; I saw the two of you leave out the back door, Wayne," I explained vehemently.

He sobered some and looked my way, reaching over to recapture my hand. I pulled it away and shrank against the door.

"Sammy, I was giving her directions," he said quietly.

"Yeah right," I hadn't meant to say it aloud, but I did.

"Really. She asked me where Congressional Plaza was and it was just easier to show her. She was parked out back. All I did was point the way," he sighed as though I was a spoiled child he needed to indulge.

Shit. There's nothing like wasting a perfectly good bout of righteous indignation on a false observation. Well, not totally false, he had ogled her *and* followed her.

"Then why had she come through the front door?" I asked, not quite willing to give it up.

He laughed again. "She'd been at one of the outside tables drinking her coffee. It was coincidence that she had gotten up just then. Coincidence that you and I had come through the door at that moment, that's all, Sammy." He had skipped the usual speech about his habit of 'just looking' and I silently thanked him for that.

He pulled into the garage and hit the garage door control on his visor. Then his hand slipped behind my neck and pulled me towards him. His lips touched mine and his tongue probed my mouth. I didn't resist. I was too tired and too hungry for him.

"I have a surprise for you," he said huskily as he pulled away slightly. "Remember I said I'd make it worth your while."

I was tired and creeped out by the continually running film in my head of Holly's dead body (and maybe a little more of Jack's dire prediction). I wanted a bath and bed and sleep.

Wayne kissed me again and I cursed center consoles everywhere. God, I was *so* easy!

"What's the surprise?" I asked.

He grinned and pushed open his door, trotting around to my side to open mine. He gathered me in his arms and we did some more tongue probing. I don't think we'd ever done it in a garage.

We heard the rapping on the glass of the garage door and looked towards the large round face of our neighbor Paul Wlodewsky. Wayne sighed and waved in his direction. Paul was a good neighbor if you didn't mind his meddling. He had been the first to introduce himself when we'd moved in. In fact, he had just walked in when we were unpacking boxes one day. He was short and stocky with thinning dark hair and tired looking blue eyes. In a matter of minutes of his barging in our home, we had learned that he and his wife of ten years had just separated (she had moved back to Virginia to be with her family), he had two massive dogs (a Doberman and a German Shepherd) they had rescued from the shelter. He had drainage problems, the former owner of our home and he had shared the cost of the fence, and a little bit about each and every one of our new neighbors before Wayne had succeeded in getting him back out the front door.

Paul came around to the side door of the garage and opened it by the time I slid from the car seat. "Couldn't figure out why you hadn't come out of the garage yet, wanted to make certain everything was okay."

"Thanks Paul," Wayne said clutching my hand.

"Did you hear about what happened to the Burgers?"

The Burgers lived two blocks away from what I could remember, they weren't immediate neighbors.

Wayne shook his head and squeezed my hand.

"They were broken into last night. The guy just walked right in the front door. I know that Samantha has the habit of leaving the front door unlocked so I thought I'd give you the heads up." He had probably tried the door himself.

"Thank you, Paul," I said hoping to be dismissive. Paul didn't talk to me, he was a man's man and directed all conversation towards Wayne.

"You should make certain that Samantha locks the doors. I saw a man go into your house last week; just walked right in the front door."

I looked up at Wayne. "Peter – when I was away."

He nodded and placed his hand on Paul's shoulder.

"She's hard to train, Paul, but I'm working on it. We're lucky to have such a watchful neighbor as yourself. Sam's been through a lot today and I'm taking her up to the house now."

He had piqued Paul's interest. I sighed. There would be no way of getting around telling him what had happened now.

But Wayne held up his hand and stopped Paul's question. "We're beat, Paul." Then he grinned and looked at me then back at Paul. "And I'm flying out again Saturday morning." Wink wink nod nod.

I bristled a bit until I saw that it was working. Paul was backing up and turning a deep shade of red.

"I'll just keep an eye out for you then – while you're gone," he said as he slipped out the door and hurried towards his yard.

"That's just great! He's going to keep an eye out for you. I won't have a moment's peace," I grumbled to Wayne.

"Maybe it will help you to remember to lock the doors at least," Wayne said as he slipped the hair behind my ear and bent to kiss me. "He has a good heart."

"He spies on people. I wouldn't be at all surprised if he was the one that was breaking into people's houses," I said as his hand slipped under my Wentworths shirt. My breath caught.

"We should probably go inside. I'm sure he's standing in his driveway waiting for us." Another deep, long kiss.

"Make sure you lock the doors," I said as I preceded him out of the garage and hurried up the lawn. I wanted to see my surprise.

CHAPTER 20

"I don't want you to go," I said as I watched Wayne fold laundry. He wore his robe tied loosely about his waist. I was in bed propped up on an elbow. I had awakened with the ringing of the telephone. Wayne had unsuccessfully tried to get it before I woke up. It had been Jessica telling me that the store would be closed for the morning and I was welcomed to stay home.

Wayne smiled indulgently and said nothing.

"Wayne?"

"I have to go, Sam, it's my job," he answered patiently. It wasn't as though I'd ever made the request before. I hadn't in the nearly ten years we'd been married. I'd never asked him. I knew he would go and that I'd let him, but right now I felt the need to put up a protest.

"You're away a lot these days," I commented. "Can I go with you?"

"Not this time."

"Why?" I persisted.

Wayne cocked his head and regarded me. "I asked you to go with me to Georgia," he stated.

"I had something else." I couldn't look at him, knowing I'd spill the beans about seeing Andrea and Greg – about actually *going* to Georgia. I hadn't told him because of his delay, because he'd ticked me off.

I'm an idiot.

Wayne settled the last piece of clothing into the clothes basket and slipped off his robe.

Hmmm.

He crawled the length of bed towards me, slipped under the blankets beside me, gathered me in his arms, and kissed me. Okay, so he had to go. So I'd make the best of it while he was here. Maybe we'd take another joint bubble bath as we had the night before, after we'd had the romantic dinner that we'd prepared together though I couldn't tell you a thing that I prepared or ate. I'd enjoyed that and I had nearly forgotten about Holly Bush.

Damn.

The tears came then – finally – and Wayne seemed to know enough not to say anything, to just hold me and let me cry. We stayed that way until the telephone rang again. I heard Peter ask how I was.

Wayne handed me the receiver and slid from under the covers. He went into the bathroom and closed the door. Double damn.

"Hello, Peter," I said.

"Sammy, how are you doing?"

"Okay, I guess." *For someone that discovered a dead body.*

"I was talking with Jack, he and I think you shouldn't go back to Wentworths."

That's nice. I'm sure Wayne agrees with you. "Oh, why?"

I heard a gurgling noise on the other end of the line. "We don't think it's wise for you to be in the middle of this. He's convinced that the other two accidents weren't accidents."

"That's what I told him." I smoothed out the quilt with my free hand. "Did Jack ask you to call me?"

Silence.

"I thought you said you weren't my nurse maid," I questioned.

"This is hardly the same thing as whether or not you go on a trip," Peter replied evenly.

"I'm getting background information at the same time I'm looking out for anything that may help Jack and I'm being careful. *And,*" I emphasized "I'm writing up a storm so you should be happy." I may have gone too far with that one. I waited for an inordinate amount of time before Peter finally spoke.

"I'm worried about you, Sammy, that's all, so's Jack."

"I'm a big girl, Peter."

I thought I detected a 'yeah, sure,' but I couldn't attest to it.

He changed course. "I'm setting up a meeting with Jake English for you, when are you free?"

"Who is Jake English?"

"He's the mythology expert you wanted. He's also an expert in the occult," he explained.

"I'm not working this weekend, Wayne leaves again Saturday morning."

"Good, he said weekends would be best for him," Peter paused. "I'll get back to you."

"The store is closed this morning, so I'll be here. I'm not sure about tomorrow, but if it's open, I'll be working."

Peter didn't comment.

Wayne stood in the doorway with his arms crossed over his chest. "He wants you to quit, too?" he asked.

I studied him trying to concentrate on his face and not below. "Yeah, he and Jack think my job is dangerous."

"And you don't?"

"No, not to me."

“I have to agree with them, Sam.”

“Noted,” I was too euphoric to rise to the bait of an argument.

He did some more staring, shook his head, turned back into the bathroom and closed the door. I heard the shower running and waited a few seconds before I quietly opened the door to join him.

Andrew’s call came about eleven thirty while I was trying to write at my computer.

“I thought certain I was going to suffer through a cavity search, that Detective Parnell was very snippety towards me. I suppose you told him I came from the store that night.”

“I had to, Andrew, but Fletcher was with you.”

“Yes, thank God, though *he’s* angry that I gave the police his address. He thinks they’ll harass him or something. Fletcher’s new at this,” he sniggered. “So what are you doing today? I’m completely at odds. It’s been a very long time since I’ve had a day off.”

“Wayne’s home,” I said.

“Oh,” he sighed. “I guess that means that you’re incommunicado today then. I was hoping we could snag lunch and gossip.”

“I’ll take a raincheck, he leaves Saturday on another trip.”

"Bad luck for you, good for me. I suppose you'll be bow-legged the next time I see you. Don't answer that, let me live in fantasy; it's unfortunate that he has no ass. I shall see you tomorrow then. Bye."

I recradled the receiver and stared once again at the computer screen. I was roughing up a story about murder at a china shop.

"Who was that on the telephone?" Wayne asked from his office. He had finished the vacuuming and laundry, giving me an hour or two at the computer.

"Andrew, the guy you met Wednesday." *Was it only yesterday?*

"The flamer?" he stood in the doorway.

"Wayne," I said warningly.

"Sorry, do you want to ride out to Great Falls and take a hike?"

I gave it a brief thought. I did want to do something.

"How about Mount Vernon instead? We could go to the Inn for lunch." I loved their peanut soup.

"Sounds good," he said and turned from the doorway. "I'll bring the car up."

We sat by the fireplace in one of the smaller rooms and ate peanut soup and homemade bread while we held hands. The sky was overcast and the air cool, but not cold.

"Where are you off to this time?" I asked sopping up the remaining soup with a corner piece of bread.

"Alaska – Fairbanks - for a couple days and then we fly to Adak Island, Guam, and end up on Johnston Atoll."

"The reason I can't go with you," I said matter-of-factly. They were all, save for Fairbanks, places that frowned upon visitors trailing along with the government worker.

Wayne nodded.

I pushed the plate away and lifted my coffee cup. "What do you guys do at these places?"

"We sit around in our underwear and grunt."

"Very funny."

He ran his finger up and down my cheek and smiled. "We miss our wives."

I grinned. "How much do you miss your wives?"

He snorted. "I have a feeling that up in Alaska, I'm going to miss you more than you could know."

The waitress came and cleared our plates; we opted for no dessert.

"The rain looks like it's going to hold off, do you want to walk along the river?" I asked as we waited for our check.

We walked towards Alexandria, the dull grey of the river to our right as we wound through the woods on the bike/hike path. Unfortunately, my prediction that the rain would hold off didn't come true. Although we had started back toward the parking lot well before it fell, we were soaked to the skin when we reached the car. I shivered from the dampness while Wayne fired up the car and heater and we headed for home.

I studied his profile as he drove and marveled once again at the fact that he had chosen me to marry him. Then I started the introspective on whether or not the little good in our marriage outweighed the fights and doubts that niggled occasionally. I shrugged. I guess it could be worse. I settled back against the seat and watched the sheets of rain cascade down the window.

CHAPTER 21

It took us a little longer to get home. The first wisps of rush hour had begun and, as always with the rain, drivers in the D.C. area grew cautious. They treated the rain as though we were in the clutches of a raging snowstorm, slowing to a crawl when they really didn't have to. Conversely, when it actually snowed, they bordered on maniacal and drove like race car drivers. Go figure.

As we turned onto our street, we slid past a dark blue Crown Victoria with fogged up windows parked in front of the house. Wayne looked my way with a grimace.

"It's probably your friend, Parnell, only police have Crown Vics these days."

"Let me out and I'll invite him inside," I said with my hand on the door.

I trotted to the driver's side window and Jack peered out from a slit. "I've been trying to get a hold of you all day."

"We went down to Mount Vernon. Come on inside. I have to get out of these wet clothes and then we can talk."

He nodded and pushed open the door following me up the lawn as Wayne came from the garage. They shook hands on the porch while my cold fingers fumbled with the key.

"Paul caught me and told me this strange car has been sitting out front for about an hour," Wayne said as they waited.

Jack snorted. "He called dispatch. Luckily, I caught the call before anyone was sent out to investigate. Neighbor?"

"Nosy neighbor," I said peeling off my wet coat and depositing it on the rug in the entry. Wayne tsked.

"Better a nosy neighbor than one who doesn't care," Jack commented and I rolled my eyes.

"You go ahead, Sammy, I'll make coffee," Wayne said as he picked up my coat. "Maybe make us something to eat."

"Don't go to any bother, Mr. Dunham," Jack said, shrugging off his jacket and hanging it neatly on a hanger.

I shook my head – men were obsessive. Me? I needed a hot shower.

Wayne had put on a spread of snacks when I emerged from the shower all warm and cozy. He and Jack were making small talk and I was pleased that they were getting along - after all, they agreed that I should leave Wentworths.

"What did you find out?" I asked as a preamble when I took the third seat at the counter.

Jack stopped mid-chew and looked my way. "About what?"

"About Holly's murder, from the employees after I left?"

"What makes you think it was murder?"

I sighed heavily. "I saw the body, Jack, I don't think she choked herself."

He grunted and helped himself to more shrimp and cocktail sauce.

"It was made to look as though she hung herself right down to the typed note." He wiped his mouth and pointed at me. "She was on the floor when you found her, right?"

"Right," I answered and then eyed him warily. "Why?"

"It was suggested that you may have cut her down and slipped off the rope she used."

"By whom?" It was Wayne that asked the question on my lips.

"A couple of them actually," he answered without revealing names. "You didn't think of anything else since you spoke with Gabe Johnson?"

I shook my head.

"Tell me again the order of their arrivals at the restaurant Tuesday night."

I closed my eyes. "Chris and Jessica were already there and I assume they came together, but I could be wrong. Gisele came in on the heels of Melanie and I, Andrew and his friend Fletcher came in maybe five minutes later. Jeffrey, Lisa, Tony and Betty Ann stated they wouldn't be coming."

Jack looked down at his notes, I hadn't seen him pull them out.

"I don't have those last few names – who are they?"

"Jeffrey is another sales supervisor like Holly. Betty Ann you should have, she was up front when I -" I waved a hand in the air. "No, I lie, she leaves at two every day, and she would have been gone. Louisa is another sales associate who usually works nights and Tony was hired with Melanie and me. He works at Barnes and Noble as well as Wentworths." I took a bite of a piece of cheese. "There are a couple others that only work weekends, I haven't met them yet, but their pictures are on the wall in the break room."

Jack nodded when he'd finished writing.

"Anyone leave the restaurant for an extended period of time?" he asked next.

"No one left the restaurant, but they did leave the table."

"Anyone receive any phone calls?"

I looked at him as though he was backward, this was the twenty-first century. "Everyone did; everyone has a cell phone," I answered. And everyone, but me actually has the damned thing on. He nodded as he took a sip of the beer Wayne had provided. He knew something, the corner of his mouth was quirky like he was smirking.

I sat there and stared and then smacked my head.

"Someone got a call from Holly," I said and Jack looked at me in surprise before he nodded.

"Who?"

He sighed. "Actually three of them did, Jessica Lupine, Gisele Fournier, and Nichols."

"Did they tell you that when you interviewed them?"

Jack smirked again. "They all seemed to forget that particular tidbit of information and all of them, when confronted, said it was commonplace and hadn't thought anything of it. She had a problem with the closing procedure and for some reason didn't know they were all together." He regarded me. "That's very perceptive of you, you know."

I shrugged nonchalantly. *Don't get me wrong, I was very proud.*

"Why wouldn't she know you all were together?" Jack asked next.

I mused over that one while Wayne poured me more coffee.

"I think she knew we were all going for drinks. Ask Andrew. He gave the impression she knew we were gathering and probably wouldn't show. I suppose it's possible she hadn't been invited and Andrew didn't know that."

Jack stared out the window thoughtfully as I watched him.

"Was Pete able to talk you out of working at Wentworths?" he asked as he sat back in his chair.

"Not really."

He glanced towards Wayne and nodded. "Okay then. Do you promise to be careful and report to me?"

"Of course, on both counts," I replied.

Wayne's chest puffed out, I don't think it was pride for me on his part. I leveled a look at him before he could voice his opinion. I had the distinct feeling we'd be discussing my new job at length when Jack left.

"You've hit it off with this Andrew. Will you ask him about whether or not Holly knew."

I nodded. "Anything else?"

Jack pursed his lips and looked as though he might revoke my assignment as he slid off the stool. "Yeah, be careful, you have my cell phone number?" He recited it for me and then jabbed a finger at the paper I'd written it on. "Do *you* have a cell phone?"

Wayne snorted then. "She does, but she never uses it."

"Get it out and have it with you at all times," Jack instructed.

When pigs fly –

"Understand?"

"Yes, boss," I answered and followed him to the door watching as he hunkered down against the rain. I turned back to Wayne who was cleaning up our detritus. He glimpsed my way with a look that said 'I really don't think this is a good idea' and that we'd be having quite a discussion. His eyes were very expressive.

"I'm going to do some more writing and charge my cell phone," I said and then escaped to my study before he could say anything.

CHAPTER 22

I drove to work the next afternoon very – how did I feel? Satisfied perhaps. By the time I'd emerged from my study the night before, Wayne had almost forgotten that he was perturbed with me. I had found him entrenched on the sectional before his massive television. He had on a Capitals/ Islanders game. I slid in next to him and things got better. There really is nothing I can think of more orgasm inducing than sitting close to my husband watching a hockey game. I mean if one doesn't get me, the other certainly will.

Wayne had risen at his usual early hour and gone running, taken a shower, (probably cleaned something) and started breakfast by the time I rolled out of bed around ten, bleary-eyed and ready for nothing more than my daily caffeine fix. I didn't have to be to work until two. Have I said how much of a morning person I'm not? He poured us both coffee and placed a plate of French toast before me along with a pitcher of warmed maple syrup. He sat down and started cutting his toast into evenly divided little squares before he poured the syrup over them. Anal.

"What are your plans today?" I asked as I forked up a piece of toast.

"I have to go into Bethesda for an hour or so," he was doing an intense study of his plate. "Maybe I'll stop off for your break?"

"I'd like that," I nudged him with my arm when he didn't say anything further. "What's wrong, Wayne?"

"I don't like what you're doing, Sam, and I especially don't like you doing it when I'm not here."

"Jack and Peter will watch out for me and I promise to be careful."

He looked my way long and hard. He wanted to argue, but had decided against it for right now. He smiled, his lips drawn tight. He wanted to say something along the lines of "you never found a dead body when you were writing fluff novels." Instead he asked, "Do you want me to drive you?"

"I got it," I said and swung my chair around, pecking him on the cheek before I headed for the study to get in another couple hours before I had to get ready for work.

It was still raining and cold. The weather forecasters were talking doom and gloom as they predicted by week's end (at best) we'd be buried in snow. It was February and we were in the D.C. area, of course it wouldn't snow again. Who were they trying to kid?

The store wasn't very busy. Not surprising really, but I think it had more to do with the fact that it was not prime buying time more than Wentworths' accident prone employees. If I had heard a murder had been committed here, I would have been curious enough to come have a look.

Andrew was busy in the stemware section filling in sections after he'd revamped the displays in each, freshening them up with Windex, dusting, and new flowers. Betty Ann smiled my way when I entered, but kept to her task. She wanted to finish what she was doing before she left. Louisa Perez was coming from the back, pinning on her name tag and smiling as she passed me on my way back to the warehouse.

Gisele was at customer service doing a return for our only customer. I nearly hit Chris with the door as I pushed it open to enter the warehouse. He was showing Tony how to do the shipping that had been neglected for too long. Tony was frantically taking notes and nodding a lot as Chris spoke.

I waved to them both and received a wave from Chris and a frightened look from Tony, even though Chris was doing his best to calm his fears.

"People will be so happy to get their shipments that they won't care how they're packed, Tony," Chris said as I reached my locker. The office door was closed so I couldn't see whether or not Jessica was in residence. I slid my bag in my locker and hung my wet coat on the rack emitting a curse when I realized I'd forgotten my name tag.

"Everything all right, Sam?" Chris called.

"I forgot my name tag."

"I don't think it will be a problem, but Gisele can make you a new one if she thinks it is. When you're ready and clocked in, come here and learn the finer points of shipping. I think Tony needs moral support and some computer savvy."

I was somewhat computer savvy. Well, I knew how to turn one on.

There was a nervous laugh from Tony as I rounded the corner. Chris was looking my way. "I heard you're an author," he said.

I hoped I hadn't missed a step as I nodded. "It doesn't pay much, thus the need for part time employment," I answered knowing I was turning red and he knew exactly *why* I had gotten a job here. "It gives me something to do when my husband is out of town."

"What does your husband do?" he asked conversationally.

"He's a government contractor," I stood with my hands on my hips resisting the urge to wipe my sweaty palms on my slacks. I thought of deflecting his questions with one of my own – namely, 'I thought you were in Virginia,' but figured he had been called back because of Holly's murder.

Chris smiled as we watched Tony wrap a delicate bone china tea pot in bubble wrap.

"We try to save the bubble wrap from shipments to cut down on the cost of buying it, but when we run low, you can ask Gisele to order more. You ask her or Jessica to order the tape and the packing paper as well. Make sure the item lives in 'suspended animation' for lack of a better description in the center of the box; there's less breakage that way. The Home Office gets a tad pissed when they have to replace a hundred and fifty dollar teapot."

Tony dropped the wrapped teapot on the floor and we all held our breath while he reopened and examined it for damage.

He laughed nervously when he found none. "I guess that's why we wrap it in this stuff." He looked at Chris. "Is this really a hundred and fifty dollars?"

Chris nodded. We all breathed a bit easier when it was safely tucked in the box. "All right then, Sam, you fire up the computer and Tony can take notes for labeling," he said, reaching for a notebook that was tucked on the shipping shelf. "Our codes are in the front of this and we ship UPS. We will do Fed-Ex if there's a specific request for it and all our shipping is domestic. If there's an overseas shipment, which is possible, but rare, we ship that via the post office and use money from petty cash."

He walked us both through the procedure explaining (and re-explaining when Tony needed it for his notes) until we had a printed shipping label.

"Normally you would pack up several and do the labels all at once. When all's said and done, you record the tracking number on the shipping request and file the white copy in the notebook along with the printed UPS receipt. If we have to research a shipment, we use these."

I looked at the UPS charge as opposed to what we had charged the customer for the service. "Why the discrepancy in shipping costs?"

Chris smiled. "We charge a flat rate based on cost of the item. Most of the time, the customer charge is under the actual shipping rate because of the weight of the dinnerware sets. For the few like this one, the cost to the customer may be a couple dollars more because it's light, but they don't mind because it's valuable. For a few customers and special circumstances, we won't charge any shipping, but that's all at the discretion of the manager on duty. The reasons should be written on the shipping request. If they aren't, then question the manager and make certain that reason given is recorded. For the most part, the cost evens itself out as far as our profits are concerned. Occasionally, the Home Office will look at our shipping records and take issue, that's why we keep the records." He took a breath, "Any questions?"

Tony and I looked at one another and shrugged; it seemed straightforward enough.

Chris rubbed his hands together and smiled. "Okay then, I'll let you have at it." He waved his arms at the two shelves chock full of items. "It's been a while. Hector used to keep up on it. I'd start with the earliest ones and work your way forward." With that declaration, he strode to his office.

I looked at Tony, and he at me. He grinned. "We'll each pack up a box to start with for practice, then you can print labels and file while I pack. Sound reasonable?"

I nodded. "Let's do it."

Two hours later, we had put a good dent in the process and had two dozen packed and labeled boxes to show for our efforts. I'd even persuaded Tony the computer wasn't really all that scary and we had switched off tasks so we could both claim expertise in the entire shipping process. When Chris came out of his lair, he commended us, declared us able, and told us to take a break. Tony held out his hand for a 'high-five'.

"You go ahead, Tony; I'm waiting on my husband."

Just about then, Andrew poked his head through the door and said Wayne was up front.

Tony smiled. "Go ahead, Sam, I'll do a couple more and go on break when you get back."

Wayne was talking with Chris when I came out with my purse over my shoulder. Chris gave it a cursory glance and shook Wayne's hand before we left.

"What were you two talking about?" I asked as we headed for Starbucks.

"The weather mostly," Wayne answered as he slipped his hand around mine. "And you; he wanted to know how successful you were."

"And you told him what?"

"That you felt the need to supplement your income and get yourself out of the house because I'm away a lot," he winked and then grew sober. "I don't like him by the way."

"Really?" Wayne rarely voiced his opinion of anyone. I was always the one to form them on first impressions. "Why's that?"

"The way he looks at you," Wayne said pushing open the door for me.

"You don't have to worry, Wayne," I left unsaid 'like I should'. I shivered some as we ordered and Wayne slipped his coat around my shoulders.

"They make jackets for this express reason, Sam."

I stuck out my tongue. "I didn't think it would be that bad." We chose a small table just vacated by three suits who had left their empty cups and plates for someone else to clean up.

Wayne touched my arm and shook his head when I turned to tell them they should. "It's not worth it, Sam."

"It's rude."

"It's okay," he tossed the mess in the trashcan (which was within arm's reach by the way) and took the seat next to me leaning in to kiss my cheek. "Did I do good by covering for you?"

"You did good," I said taking comfort in his close proximity. "Did you get done what you needed to?"

He nodded. "When do you get off?"

"The store closes at nine. I'm not sure how long I have to stay. I'll give you a call if you want."

He kissed my neck and I reddened; people were watching.

"Do you want supper?" he asked as his hot breath wafted along my neck sending chills down my spine – good chills.

I grinned. "Maybe you could prepare me another surprise," I whispered and kissed him.

There were a couple kids with their mothers next to us who emitted a disgusted "eww" as I did. I grinned and glanced their way winking at them. The little girl who looked to be about seven stuck her finger in her mouth like she was gagging.

This time, Wayne walked me back to the door and I watched as he went to his car and got inside. He waved as he passed. Louisa chuckled and Andrew whistled when I re-entered the store.

Andrew was ready to leave.

“I don’t know what you and Tony did, but Chris is singing your praises to Gisele as we speak. That will at least help make the evening go smoother.”

I raised a finger. “Speaking of the evening, when can I expect to get out of here?”

“With Gisele – around ten or so – she’s slow and methodical. You’ll spend the time straightening, sweeping, and emptying trashcans.” He waggled his fingers and kissed the air. “I’ll call this weekend if that’s okay.”

I nodded.

CHAPTER 23

By five thirty, Gisele, Louisa, and I were alone as far as employees went, surprisingly (to me) there were customers. By seven, Gisele pulled out a cart load of rag rugs that she wanted to put on a display Andrew had emptied out for her earlier near the clearance section. While Louisa priced them, Gisele and I set them out on the shelves she had somehow managed to adjust during the bit of busy time we'd had earlier. I ferried them from Louisa at register one to Gisele in the back.

"These are about as worthless as they come," she sputtered on one of my trips. "I'd like to know who the buyer is and what the hell they were thinking when they looked at these."

I chuckled at her.

"They're cheaply made with an expensive price tag. The only thing they'll be good for is use as a gurney or wrapping corpses."

There was a look of regret that clouded her face when she said it, but it passed. She was thinking of Holly -

I held up one of the rugs and studied it. "I'd have to agree with you, they certainly don't go with the other product we sell." I looked her way. "And why rugs?"

"God only knows. I can tell you one thing, when Corporate comes to visit, they'll want to see they're out and being sold. I may have to buy a couple myself," she mentioned as an afterthought. "I don't suppose I can interest you in one?"

I laughed then. "Wayne doesn't like throw rugs, but if it will help, I will." I glanced at the price tag and my eyebrows went up. "How much of a discount did you say we had?"

Gisele evidently thought the comment quite rich as she chuckled. I wasn't kidding.

We finished the display and she glanced at her watch. "We'll be closing soon, have Louisa walk you through my procedure."

When an opportunity presents itself –

"The procedure is different for each manager?" I asked innocently (hopefully).

She didn't seem to take exception. "The basics are all the same, but we have different quirks you should learn," she said with a smile. The smile faded quickly, I think she was thinking of Holly again.

I pointed towards the front. "I'll just go talk with Louisa then and get the skinny."

Gisele turned without another word and pushed through the side warehouse door.

"Gisele likes everything fronted and the place setting displays adjusted. We empty the trash and sweep up, the vacuuming gets done by Betty Ann every morning."

I knew that 'fronted' meant that stock got pulled forward to fill up empty spots from where customers had purchased. Adjustments to the place setting displays merely meant that the plate and soup bowl were on a stand, the salad plate, tea saucer and tea cup (with handle facing right) were stacked before them, and the stemware fanned from the top right of the salad plate in order of red wine, white wine and flute. It sounds picky, but it really gave some order to the displays and it was easy to maintain. In doing so, we also found odd items here and there that the customer had inadvertently – or not - left in the wrong spot.

"Gisele plays a canned announcement about five minutes before nine to say the store will be closing and purchases should be taken to the front. She then turns off all the lights in case the customers don't understand," she smiled. "It works for the most part. Gisele will page us when it's nine on the nose and we lock the doors. Customers that are in the store are serviced, but no one else gets in on pain of death. The only time all this is truly tested is when we're busy at holiday time."

The announcement came over the intercom and a few seconds later the lights started to go off. There were no customers in the store. Louisa glanced towards the back door.

"Gisele takes the longest closing, I have no idea why. If you want someone fast, pray you're with Jessica. And Gisele checks our work. If she doesn't approve, then we do it over."

"Is it all right to make telephone calls?" I asked as the pager rang and Louisa went for the door.

"Sure, just make them short and sweet and not too often."

I dialed our home number and frowned when Wayne didn't answer. I left a message that I probably wouldn't be home until ten.

Gisele came out and Lisa pointed to the trash cans. "You can do those while she counts out my drawer; I have to be there when she does it. Then you can start on the precious metals dinnerware. I'll sweep and start in the New Age and we'll meet in the middle. There are fresh trash bags underneath the full ones. Don't forget to do the waste cans around each register and the two bathrooms."

I nodded and went off to do my assigned tasks.

I tried home twice more with the same results in between trash pickup and straightening. Our efforts met with Gisele's approval. I had let Louisa out the front door and left it unlocked figuring Gisele and I would be leaving in her wake; not the thing that pleased Gisele. She delivered a ten minute lecture on the hazards of leaving the door open to predators who would take any chance to steal a place setting and try to return it for cash. In the short time I'd been there, I'd already seen that particular practice attempted and I knew with certainty it was successful any given hour of the day at least some of the time. I didn't really believe those few moments would have made a difference, but I dutifully listened and accepted the reprimand.

We passed through the doors and Gisele turned to lock them. "Do you have some place to be, Sam?"

I thought of my telephone calls to home and then of Jack's plea (my word, certainly not what he had done) to talk up the employees and figured this was as good a time as any. "Not really, what did you have in mind?"

"Maybe a bite to eat – and a drink? I really need a drink."

"Sure, sounds good. Let me call Wayne and at least leave a message so he won't worry." I pulled my cell phone from my purse (I had it in there!) and turned it on then dialed our number. Still no answer, so I left the message and turned it off again. *I didn't want to waste the battery, of course.* Gisele tapped her foot impatiently the whole time and smiled when I'd returned it to my purse.

"Use it often?"

"As little as possible, I hate the damned thing. Wayne is constantly yelling at me and leaving nasty messages." Which he has to retrieve because I haven't the foggiest notion how to do it.

"I'd be lost without mine," she commented as we walked toward the garage. The rain still fell, though not heavily and it was cold. We opted to drive the short distance up the Pike to Bennigan's.

The restaurant was crowded, then again it was Friday night and any place we ventured would have been. Our wait was five minutes tops and Gisele led the way ordering a Seven and Seven and a sampler appetizer platter before we even sat down. I asked for a Diet Pepsi and questioned my choice in coming with her. She looked tired. Where would I start my interrogation? *Mental rubbing together of hands –*

"You okay, Gisele?"

She plopped in the chair and sighed. “I will be as soon as I get that drink.”

If I’ve gleaned nothing else from my years on this earth, I’ve learned that if you want to find out something from someone – shut up and listen.

“It’s a mess, Sam,” she said after she took a long drink of her highball.

“What’s that?”

She stared at me for a few ticks as if to determine telepathically if I might be brain dead. “Wentworths,” she answered.

“In what way?” I fiddled with my straw and sipped absently at the soda.

She furrowed her brow and sighed again. “Holly’s murder for one. I can’t imagine why anyone would kill the girl.”

How about what it was like to discover her body? I shrugged. “Maybe she knew something.”

“About what though? If anything I would have said she had committed suicide. She was under suspicion -” Gisele stopped short and regarded me.

“The thefts? Andrew told me about them and of Holly’s troubles,” I said hoping to be nonchalant as well as encouraging. Maybe she should have another drink. “He said she called you the night she was killed. What was that about?”

"Closing procedure, she was never confident that she was doing everything. I'd get two or three calls every time she closed."

"She called Chris and Jessica, too. I guess she didn't know we were all together." I turned my glass slowly not looking up. If I looked up she'd know I was fishing for information. She'd ask me how I knew this stuff and I'd have to tell her I was in cahoots with the police.

"I don't think she'd been invited." She frowned. "Though Andrew seemed to think she'd been," she laughed. "Maybe that's why she called Chris; to complain that she'd been excluded. She was also never one to mind the chain of command."

"So she didn't mention it to you when she called?"

She shook her head. "She just asked me if she was doing everything right." Gisele fell into a funk and I searched for my next question; turns out I didn't have to bother.

"The accidents to Hector and Elaine certainly weigh heavily," Gisele said before she raised a hand to signal the waiter.

"So you still think they were accidents?" I asked and mentally kicked myself for doing so. Too soon. Maybe. And how about Holly's first accident? Did they all forget that?

She seemed to contemplate and then shook her head dismissively. “They have to be, I wouldn’t be able to handle it if you told me they weren’t.” Her words were slurred, evidently Gisele couldn’t hold her liquor any better than I could.

“How long have you worked at Wentworths?”

“Five years. I came as a second assistant manager for this store when Diane Harmon was manager. She and I had worked together at Hecht’s and she enticed me over here.” Gisele smiled at her glass fondly. “Anyway, she brought me over, trained me, and then promptly left. I believe she thought I would be made manager, but Chris hired Alphonse.” She screwed up her face in disgust. “Can you believe a name like that? He was all for show I can tell you.” This time she leaned my way in confidence. “Just like Jessica.” Her hand circled the air in a grand gesture. “Alphonse Pickering,” she recited with her mouth drawn tight and then she shook her head. “He was a good looking man, but no retail sense whatsoever.”

“So you carried the load,” I prodded.

“Then and ever since,” she finished off the second drink and I slid the platter of food towards her. She hadn’t yet indulged in any of it and I was starting to worry about her. So much for my killer instinct and grilling techniques.

Gisele stabbed the air. “I’ve been keeping records, too. Every time I have to do something *they* should do, I write it down – in detail.”

“Have you talked to Chris about it?” I asked innocently.

She snorted in disgust. “As if he would demote his precious Jessica.” She raised her hand once again to summon our waiter. I caught his eye and shook my head.

“Maybe I should drive you home Gisele. Where do you live?”

She rested her chin on her hand and stared into space stupidly, shaking her head. “I knew I was sunk the minute I saw her come in for her interview.” Her eyes moved to mine. “Do you think I’m an attractive woman, Sam?”

Oh great.

“I don’t think I’m bad looking.”

Evidently I didn’t need to answer.

“I could never understand why Chris just ignored me.” Her mouth went into a pout.

I pawed in my purse for my wallet and drew out a couple twenties, it would amply cover our tab.

“I’m not a flirt normally. I’ve devoted my life to being the best manager I can be and once in a while -” Again she stabbed the air. “Just *once,*” she emphasized. “I’d like some recognition, some affection.”

I stood and pulled on my coat and then slid hers from behind her. "Maybe you don't want that kind of recognition, Gisele." I thought of my first day and the half hour that was devoted to the employee hot-line that Wentworths had in place to anonymously report any odd behavior in fellow employees. Unless I was thoroughly off base, I think this qualified. "Maybe you should talk to someone at Corporate and tell them what's going on." I held her coat for her and she frowned up at me.

"Whatever do you mean?"

"You should tell someone at Corporate about Chris and Jessica. I can't imagine that type of fraternization is condoned."

"But that would break the chain of command."

I stared at her for a few ticks. "Huh?"

"I couldn't do that to Jessica or Chris - go over their heads like that." She seemed to be sobering fast. "And it would certainly kill my chances of advancement. No, I would never stoop that low. Why would you even suggest that?"

Shit, I don't know – maybe because their relationship is wrong.

"I guess I misunderstood you. I thought you implied that they were screwing around." I wasn't sure why I was getting angry and I tried to squelch it.

There were another few moments of staring and then she started to cry – and she wasn't quiet about it. The waiter approached and I asked him to call Gisele a cab. He nodded, looking almost relieved.

I placed my hand on her shoulder and bent low to her ear. "I'm sorry, Gisele, I know you work hard at your job." That statement seemed to calm her as she straightened and swiped at her wet cheeks.

"I've gotten a cab for you, you ready?"

She nodded and stood unsteadily, holding onto the table while I slipped on her coat and gathered up her briefcase and purse. The waiter returned and helped me guide her to the door where the taxi waited with his door opened. There were a few moments of protest on her part after we sat her in the back, but we prevailed and she finally gave the driver her address in Virginia. I slipped him forty dollars and watched as he pulled away. Gisele turned and waved to me out the back window.

"She was one wound up chick," the waiter said before he bid me goodnight and returned to his post.

I don't know how long I stood there – until my toes started to freeze I guess. I headed for my car and drove home. *She's one wound up chick* I repeated to myself. I wondered if she was wired for murder.

"Where have you been? And why the hell don't you leave your cell phone on?" had been my greeting from Wayne when I'd walked through the door. I stared at him with his hands on his hips and that stubborn look of his chin. *I have a few questions for you too, buddy.*

"Well?" he pressed.

"I went out with Gisele, she needed someone to talk to," I answered wearily.

"What about me?"

Ask him where he was now. "I called and left a message." I called several times.

"Sammy, I leave tomorrow – remember?"

"Wayne, I'm tired. I did what you always ask me to do and called. I'm sorry." I shrugged off my coat and looked towards the closet. Too far. I dropped it on the chair and Wayne immediately picked it up with a sigh. Jesus, maybe if he'd just left it there, I would have let go of the obstinance.

"I just don't think you're being very fair to me, Sammy."

Fair? He's the one that left all the time, how is that fair?

"It's my job, Sammy," he answered my unspoken question.

Damn, I'd done it again. I slumped off to the bathroom and closed and locked the door. It was as it always, a fight before he left on a trip. Why should this time be any different? He didn't try banging on the door or even just coming in when I got in the shower. Damn damn.

I went to bed and fell promptly asleep.

The next morning, he was gone.

Again.

CHAPTER 24

And the telephone was ringing and ringing and ringing.

"Hello," I spat out irritably.

"Is this Samantha Warren?" an unfamiliar voice asked.

"Yes." My irritation didn't subside. I figured if it was a telemarketer then it wouldn't be wasted.

"I'm Jake English, Peter said you wanted to talk with me and I was wondering if you were free for lunch."

I shook my head at my stupidity. "Of course, where would you like to meet?"

"Do you know Taglione's? In Friendship Heights?"

"I've heard of it, but I've never eaten there. Give me directions and what time you'd like to meet."

"It's right on the 355 or, if you're taking the Metro, it's the Friendship Heights stop and the restaurant is a block north on the opposite side of the street."

"I'll do the Metro, what time?"

"Let's shoot for eleven thirty. I'll call Peter and see if he can join us. See you then."

There were several men milling about the reception area of Taglione's when I arrived, Peter wasn't one of them. I attempted to pick out Jake English from a preconceived notion of what a full professor of mythology and the occult would look like and approached a gentleman roughly the age of my grandfather.

"Are you Mr. English?" I asked tentatively. He smiled and shook his head.

There was a tap on my shoulder and I turned to face a young man grinning from ear to ear. "That would be me, you must be Ms. Warren." He bowed slightly as he took up my hand and kissed the back of it. I blushed. I was in love. It may have been because Wayne was gone or even because we'd had yet another fight, but I fell and fell hard. He was about five foot eight with curly dark hair that framed his face and intense brown eyes. He sported a felt hat that he wore a little back on his head and a tweed brown and tan sports jacket with the suede elbow patch and evidence of fraying around the collar. A young, modern guy dressed in old professor garb save for the impeccable designer jeans that hugged his thin legs. I don't think there was a muscle on him. He was much too young looking to be a full professor.

He held his arm out for me and escorted me towards the hostess leaning in a bit with a smile. "I get that a lot, I'm not a child prodigy." He halted before the hostess and bowed again. "Maria, I think we'd like the corner booth today for a bit of privacy." He pronounced 'privacy' the British way and it rolled off his tongue nicely.

The restaurant was located in the middle of a busy block of Friendship Heights just across the street from a mall that housed Saks Fifth Avenue and Neiman Marcus. The front entrance was a café where patrons could buy pastries and bread and order coffee and biscotti while they took in the heavenly smells coming from the kitchen; even the coffee smelled good.

The reception was next with a dark Oriental rug centering dark paneled walls that sported murals of Italian villas surrounded by grape arbors and cupids. A staircase wound its way upward on the right. The dining room was fairly large, accommodating oversized booths on the perimeter and a sprinkling of tables for two among tables for twelve on the floor. It was a busy place. We passed by several tables celebrating birthday parties.

The walls had the same dark paneling as the reception area with mirrors in every other niche making the big room seem even larger and more spacious. The dark décor gave the illusion of being intimate when there was no earthly way it could be. Large vats of real ferns dotted the half walls hiding napkins and ice buckets for the servers' use.

"How can I be of service, Ms. Warren?" Jake crossed his arms on the table after we'd placed our orders.

I wondered how Peter knew him.

"Please call me Sam, sir," I opened. "Peter has picked me up as a client, I'm a writer."

"He said that and I cringe at the 'sir,' you must call me Jake."

I reddened and nodded, reluctant to take him up on the offer. "I have an idea for a story line involving mythology and romance. I like to provide a little truth to my fiction and want to learn what I could to help me do that."

"You do realize that mythology is fiction?" he said with a smile. "In twenty words or less?"

"Or more, I've no place to be."

"Perhaps you could give me some insight into your outline, you say it's a romance?"

I nodded. "My last required book before I branch out into mystery."

He reached into his briefcase and pulled out a yellow legal pad about the same time I pulled out my notebook. He turned pensive.

"Let's see, we should try someone that isn't normally romantically linked such as an ogre. Though we can't do the 'Beauty and the Beast' syndrome; been there, done that." He was looking ceilingward and stabbed his finger. "How about ugly female, handsome male, perhaps she could save him from fate worse than death." He scrunched his face and sucked in air through his teeth. "Maybe not," he regarded me. "You could probably make up anything you wanted and it would ring 'true,' Peter said you were good at making things up."

"He has a lot of misplaced confidence."

"Peter doesn't misplace anything, love. You're his client because he sought you out," he stated. "He says you're shadowing Jack Parnell."

I regarded him – it was as good a time as any to ask. "Just how do you know Peter and Jack?"

"My father was a policeman. He knew them both at the academy." The waiter deposited our entrees before us and offered fresh grated cheese. We both refused. "My Dad went into policing late in life," he explained further.

The conversation segued into Jack's current case at Wentworths and Jake grinned. "Peter said you couldn't meet until the weekend because you were working there. That's the china shop, isn't it?"

I nodded.

"So what is going on there? I ask Jack about his cases and he's very closed mouthed, hardly sporting of him I might add. I like a juicy story as much as the next guy. I mean what good is knowing a cop if you can't get the inside scoop?"

"He'd kill me if I told you," I said, grinning.

"Please, my love, I would never reveal to him my source. Never."

So over my mushroom ravioli and the most heavenly tiramisu, I filled Jake in on the goings-on at Wentworths.

After, we batted around our own theories. Jake held up his hand. "Jack wouldn't like all this speculation, he's a facts only man."

I laughed.

He glanced at his watch "Look at the time. This has been a true pleasure, Samantha, and I will put on my thinking cap to collaborate on this story with you. It will be superior when we are finished. I must hurry along now." He stopped me from paying and helped me on with my coat once again offering his arm and escorting me from the room.

We stepped outside into snow - and it wasn't snowing lightly either.

CHAPTER 25

I arrived home from the Metro parking lot in one piece. Remember I mentioned that drivers tend to the maniacal when it snows? I was lucky to survive with my life let alone without a dent in my van. The telephone was ringing when I unlocked the door – it's like it knows when I'm home and when I'm not. I did my usual cavalier, 'I'll let the machine get it this time,' before I snatched up the receiver and said "Hello."

"Hi sweetheart," Wayne answered. He tends to call me sweetheart when he hasn't quite forgotten that we were fighting when he left (or not talking as the case may be).

I stared out at the snow falling, it was getting even heavier. "It's snowing," I said, searching for neutral ground.

"I know, we ran through the storm over the Mid-West. Now I'm stuck in Seattle because of it. You'd think that Alaska would be used to it and have the runways cleared."

I found myself wondering if the delay in Seattle had been planned into his trip and shook my head angrily at the thought. I guess I was silent long enough that he began to worry some.

"Sam?"

"Yeah?"

"I miss you."

Sure you do. I kept silent knowing I'd cave and tell him I missed him, too. "I met with this professor from AU for lunch, interesting guy." See Wayne. I can have liaisons too.

"What for?" He couldn't quite keep the anger out of his voice. I think he thought I'd do the caving by now, maybe I'd done it one too many times.

"A story idea I had. Peter set it up for me," I grinned at the receiver – *take that.*

"Oh," he sighed "I should go."

"Okay."

He waited for a few moments and then hung up. I hadn't said I was sorry and I hadn't said I missed him. I was and I did. And I hadn't said for him to call when he reached Fairbanks – and I hadn't said I loved him. Damn.

I slid into the kitchen chair and pulled out my notebook making notes from Jake's and my conversation. I jotted down some ideas I wanted to bounce off him when we met or talked again. I was working up a good depression, too. It happens, what can I say –

I was just about to head to the computer with a couple of workable scenarios when the telephone rang again. I stared at it determined that *this* time I'd let the machine – *oh hell.*

"Hello?"

"Sam?"

My anger subsided. "Peter; I thought I'd see you at lunch."

"Couldn't make lunch. How did it go?" I heard papers shuffling in the background and realized I didn't know where his office was. Did he know it was snowing?

"Pretty well. I decided to have his babies."

Peter chuckled. "Did Wayne get off all right?"

Wrong topic. "Yeah, this morning, and he just called." And I didn't tell him I missed him and that I was sorry and that I loved him and that I thought he was cheating on me and had been since Day One (or maybe Day Four at the earliest).

"Sam? Everything all right?"

It took a few moments to answer and then I didn't really answer – I nodded my head. Peter waited patiently.

"Did you know it was snowing?" I asked.

"Yeah I can see that, what are you doing for dinner? We have things to discuss."

"I'm sure there are leftovers."

"You like Chinese?"

Again I nodded and could feel him smiling over the phone.

"Sammy?"

I started. "Yes, I do."

"Anything in particular?"

"I like everything," I sighed.

"I'll be there in a half an hour."

"It's snowing."

"I know how to drive in the snow, Sammy."

I sat at the table with the receiver in my hand wondering what the hell was wrong with me. It wasn't as though Wayne didn't leave *all* the time for God's sake. I saw a car turn the corner from Dowlais Drive and pull into the driveway behind my van surprised Peter was here so soon and then realizing I'd been sitting motionless for a half hour.

I turned on the burner under the teakettle before I went to open the door for Peter. He carried two huge bags that smelled wonderful and placed them on the counter before he went back to stomp the snow off his shoes and hang up his coat. It must be a man thing.

"Jack said he was here Thursday afternoon."

I nodded and smiled. "He gave me permission to stay at Wentworths and be his mole," I answered as I pulled two plates from the hutch.

"That isn't exactly what he said."

I waved a hand of dismissal. "Close enough, let's eat in the dining room."

Peter laughed as he carried the bags to the table. "I have fried rice, lo mein, garlic beef, spring rolls, General Tsao's chicken, moo shoo pork, and hot and sour soup."

"I'm making tea," I said as I poured the hot water over the loose tea. Big effing deal. I grabbed silverware and two soup bowls before joining him at the table.

There were placemats and napkins under the plates and two cups just waiting for my contribution and, at some point, he had gotten serving spoons for all the containers. *Had I been in the same room*? I brought the teapot to the table.

The next few minutes were taken up with the passing and ladling of the little cardboard containers, transferring food to our plates and bowls.

"You have a book signing scheduled the end of the month for 'Lakeside Passions," he opened.

"Where?"

"Boston, New York, and back here. I thought I could schedule a couple of interviews with publishers while we're in New York."

"You're going with me?"

"Of course," he said, and then paused. "I take it Harry didn't."

"Harry didn't," I answered.

"You should buy a dress or a nice suit."

The fork I'd loaded paused halfway to my mouth. "What makes you think I don't have a dress?" *I have one – I think.*

He took in my sweatpants and oversized sweater; I knew he was wondering if I'd worn them to my meeting with Jake. He smiled.

"I own a dress," I said disgusted. "I own a lot of clothes." Wayne buys them for me all the time.

"Do you own something that doesn't hide your figure? Did you wear this today?"

Bingo!

I didn't answer him. I didn't really know for certain about the dress, but I'd check when we were finished eating – and I'd check to see if I had a figure, too. I hadn't thought so up until then.

"Tell me what Jake said."

I launched into a blow by blow account of our lunch including the information Jake had given me on how he knew Jack and Peter. Then I segued into my late night conversation with Gisele which brought me to my arrival home. I stopped talking.

"What's wrong, Sam?" Peter asked placing his hand on my arm.

I bit back tears. "Where's Moira tonight?" I asked lightly.

"Sam?"

I cried, not really sure why, but guessing I really needed it. Peter's hand reached out and touched my back in comfort and I was glad for that.

"Want to go for a walk?" he asked when I'd managed to get myself under control.

I snorted. "In the snow?"

Peter shrugged. "Why not?"

I frowned. "I don't need a babysitter you know."

He snorted as he cleared the table and went to put the dishes in the dishwasher. I hopped up and snatched the plate from his hand.

"I don't want you to go on another drinking binge," he explained as he rinsed the second plate and handed it to me.

"Ha, ha. Which brings me back to my question of where's Moira?"

Peter grimaced. "She's otherwise occupied."

"That's not an answer, did you two break up?"

"We weren't together long enough to get that far."

Ah, something to pursue.

"Get your coat," Peter instructed as he pulled his own from the closet. "Do you have boots?"

"Yes, father."

"Hat and mittens?"

"You know I could learn to dislike you if you keep this up."

He wrapped his arm around my neck and pulled me to him. "No, you wouldn't, I'm a nice guy."

We stepped off the porch into a good three, maybe four inches of snow, the light fluffy stuff with a thin layer of ice underneath. Perfect walking weather if you wanted to slip and slide your way along. The moment I hit pavement, I slipped and Peter caught me. We struck off across the lawn and I turned to him walking backwards before him.

"So tell me about Peter Frost's love life."

"No."

"Ah come on, I may be able to use it."

"No," he stated a little more emphatically.

"Where'd you meet this Moira? What does she do?"

He pursed his lips and frowned. "She's an interpreter for the State Department."

"Interesting, and you met where?"

"At a state dinner at Christmas time at the White House."

"Cool. How many times have you been out with her?"

"Once."

I groaned. "That night?"

He nodded.

"Ouch, she didn't take kindly to having to clean up after me, did she."

"Actually, that was the high point of the evening."

I waved a hand. "It must have been her fault, she works for the government after all."

Peter chuckled. That was good.

"Who else?"

"Well, there was the woman I was with at the state dinner."

I reared back in surprise. "You're kidding; wow. What did she do?"

"We're not discussing this any more," Peter averred. "What happened between you and Wayne?"

"Nothing unusual, we always manage a fight when he leaves." I sighed as we trudged along. "Lately, we fight more than not." I kept trying to focus on the good times and found myself losing them more quickly as time went on. "Tell me about your daughter," I said next.

Peter looked my way with a grin. "She's the light of my life."

"How did she take the divorce?"

"As good as any child caught in the middle, I suppose. Tracy and I try to keep our differences to a minimum."

"And the reason for the divorce?"

Peter snorted. "Tracy told me she was pregnant, so we married."

"I take it she wasn't."

"Not pregnant when we married, but soon after." He looked off in the distance. "I had been angry with Tracy for deceiving me and vowed to myself I'd never love Lisa after she was born. I was so wrong. The moment I saw her, I was in love."

As we came up Shippers Lane towards the house, a figure approached from the direction of our house. Paul Wlodewsky.

"Everything all right, Mrs. Dunham?" He fell all over himself emphasizing the 'Mrs.'

"It's not Mrs. Dunham, Paul. I'd like you to meet my publicist and lawyer, Peter Frost."

Paul looked Peter's way warily and nodded. "Wayne asked me to keep an eye out on the house and his wife."

"Neighbor of Sam's?" Peter asked him.

"Paul takes his job seriously, Peter," I interjected. "He called the cops on Jack when he came over the other night." I said it hoping to make Paul squirm – I doubt if it worked.

"Sammy needs looking after," Peter said and I could have hit him. Paul, up to that point had been at odds how to proceed – now he laughed and shook Peter's hand.

"That's what I do best," Paul declared and then started to do the other thing he does best; talk your ear off.

I started towards the house. Peter was on his own.

I had deposited my coat and boots in the hallway (for the record, no, I did not hang it up) and was making a pot of coffee by the time Peter showed at the door.

"Nice guy," he said leaning against the kitchen doorjamb. "I should head home I guess."

I nodded.

"You should call Jack and tell him what Gisele Fournier said and did last night."

"You think so?"

"I think so. You should tell him anything you see and hear no matter how trivial you may think it."

"Okay," I stood with my arms hugging my body. "Thank you, Peter - for dinner and the rescue."

"No problem, Sam," he pushed off the doorjamb and leaned over to kiss my cheek. "What are your plans tomorrow?"

"I plan to veg in front of the computer. I've been neglecting it."

He smiled. "Call Jack." He had that look about him that said 'call Wayne' too.

I nodded. "What are your theories about the Wentworths crimes?"

"I have no theories."

"Like Jack."

Peter sighed. "A cop can't afford theories. You get facts and process them and come up with a conclusion. That process keeps you alive."

I cocked my head. "Were you ever shot?"

"Grazed once, a superficial wound. Some guy went berserk when we answered a domestic disturbance call." He shrugged as though it was nothing.

"How about Jack?"

"Jack has never been shot," Peter stated and took hold of the door handle.

"Thanks again," I said holding the door open and watching him to his car. As he slewed up the slope of the street towards Dowlais, I closed and locked the door. Peter was a nice guy I thought as I padded towards the bedroom.

Chapter 26

Sunday was a day of introspection and writing. Luckily, I absolved myself of much introspection after the first ten minutes I was up. Introspection usually turned to depression and I didn't want to mope around the whole day. I got down to the writing.

Jake called sometime in the early afternoon and we chatted on the telephone for close to two hours talking about using some characters from Norse mythology for my book. We decided on connecting Loki, the God of mischief and evil, and Freya, the Goddess of beauty, as a sub-plot to the main theme of a heaving bosomed woman captured by an enemy of the Vikings. He dragged her off to his cave and enslaved her; they fall in love. Sounds boring (and short), but you'd be amazed at how many pages I can fill with heaving bosoms and pulsating members and the like.

We worked up a scenario where Loki saves Freya from the clutches of Hel, Loki's daughter and the queen of the underworld. Hel doesn't like Freya because of her beauty and plots to disfigure her, inviting her father along for the sport. Loki likes what he sees and double-crosses his daughter and Freya feels an obligation to him. Freya is very absent-minded and self-centered and spends a lot of time looking at herself and ignoring him. Eventually, Loki realizes the error of his ways (in hooking up with Freya, not being evil) and goes back to his lair a wiser man. While all this transpires, they mess around with the fates of the Viking woman and her captor – as gods sometime do for fun.

Andrew called almost as soon as Jake hung up. I hardly had time to go to the bathroom.

"Sam, thank God you're home, I am bored to tears."

"Where are you?"

"At work. Can you believe the store is even open? We have no customers."

"Why you?" I asked as I padded to the kitchen to get a Diet Pepsi.

"Gisele couldn't make it in, her neighborhood isn't plowed. Since I live across the Pike, she asked if I'd mind coming over. She said she'd make it up to me and believe you me, she will."

Gisele probably couldn't make it because she's hung-over. Then I realized she didn't have her car either.

"I didn't know you knew how to do manager stuff. Who's with you?"

"Brooke Wentworth, no relation by the way. I don't think you two have met yet. And, yes, I do manager stuff. In fact I was a sales supervisor at Leesburg and an assistant at Fairfax. "

"I haven't met Brooke."

"The God-awful thing is we're not supposed to do displays on the weekends, but I had to so I wouldn't go stir crazy. I don't think anyone will tell."

"Gisele was worried about the corporate visit that's coming up. She probably will be happy."

"Gisele's always worried about corporate visits."

"So there isn't one coming up?"

"Not any that I know of, but she could have set one up. She's always trying to trip up Jessica."

Was that noteworthy? Would Andrew know if any were imminent?

"Are we detecting today?" Andrew asked and I could almost see him rub his hands together at the thought.

"No, I'm just telling you what she said Friday night, nothing more."

"I heard there was more," he said and then fell silent.

"What did you hear?"

"That you had to call her a cab."

"She wasn't in any shape to drive." I wasn't sure I was in any shape to gossip. And how had he heard? "Where did you hear this?"

"A friend of mine that lives in my apartment complex works at Bennigan's. He said she was crying and carrying on something fierce."

"It wasn't quite that dramatic," I commented.

"That's not what Bruno said."

"Bruno? You actually know someone named Bruno?"

"An absolutely delicious creature, too, but he isn't persuaded in my direction. He's the bartender by the way; I know you're trying to place him. He likes your books and wants me to get one signed for him."

I ran through Friday night in my mind's eye and remembered the bartender being very large and scary looking. "Is Bruno large for his age?"

Andrew chuckled. "You got him; large and hairy, that's Bruno."

I just couldn't wrap myself around the fact the man I remembered likes romance novels.

"Do you think you can make it in tomorrow if it's still snowing?" Andrew broke my train of thought.

"Probably; if I can't drive then I can bus it to the Metro and come up that way. Why?" The Twinbrook Metro stop was a couple blocks from the store, it would be a round-about trip, but it would save me from competing with the crazies.

"Gisele is stressing about the store and doesn't think she's getting out and she's no where near a Metro station. She wants to be able to tell Chris that someone will be here and the store will be open despite the fact that no self respecting shopper will be out. He's over in the Virginia area until the end of the week."

"And Jessica?"

"No one ever knows about Jessica, if she's here she's not *here*," he laughed at his own joke. "Good then, I shall tell Gisele we're covered and she can rest easy and I will see you tomorrow. Maybe we can do something after, your husband is out of town, isn't he?"

"Doing something after sounds good," I answered. I could always get a taxi home. I had avoided answering about Wayne deftly I thought. I hung up the telephone and went to the front door and flipped on the outside light. It was snowing again. The whole day had passed me by and I hadn't noticed. That made it a good day. I went to take a shower.

I don't know what I was dreaming, but I woke from it in a sweat. I tried to dredge up the particulars, you never know when a good weird dream can be incorporated into a story – and couldn't. I sat up in the bed and rubbed my face and the telephone rang making me jump about a mile vertically.

I snatched the phone from the cradle and growled a hello.

"Sweetheart, did I wake you?" Wayne sounded bemused.

The bedside clock registered nine-forty two and I scrunched my eyes closed trying to ward off a headache.

"I was taking a nap - talk, I'll be fine." I hated to take naps for this very reason. The waking up process from them really sucked. My mind was muddled, my sinuses were usually clogged, and my head usually managed to work up a good ache. I wasn't real pleasant either. My brows were furrowed in a permanent scowl.

I tuned back into what Wayne was saying and had to admit he sounded like a frigging travel brochure. He'd been to the North Pole and took pictures of Santa's house blah, blah, blah.

We'd had a discussion once about Santa, one of the many times we'd talked about the possibility of kids. Wayne said if we'd ever had kids (which would be a cold day in hell), he wouldn't propagate the myth that was Santa

Claus. We had disagreed vehemently. Some of my fondest memories were of Christmas and how long my parents were able to keep me believing in Santa Claus. I was thirteen the year the truth came to light. I can honestly say the fact my parents had "lied" to me didn't send me in search of an analyst. Oh well.

"I thought you didn't believe in that," I said to Wayne when he took a breath from his dissertation. I was still groggy. I was trying my damnedest to un-furrow my brow and un-narrow my eyes.

He snorted. "I thought you'd want to hear about it that's all."

I rolled my eyes. My thoughts lay somewhere in the vicinity of 'where are you really, Wayne?' I wondered who I could call to find out.

"Sam? Are you there?"

"Are you, Wayne?" I asked back, biting my tongue for voicing my thoughts and hoping he was innocent enough not to pick up the double entendre.

"What the hell is that supposed to mean?" he asked angrily – certainly not innocently. *Jesus, what was I doing!* I shouldn't read anything into a, most likely, innocent conversation.

There was a long silence where I dredged up and discarded several retorts that were inappropriate. *Did I really want to fight long distance?*

"So you made it to Fairbanks all right then?" I tried.

"Yes – obviously. We fly out to Adak tomorrow morning. I won't be able to call for a couple days."

"Okay," I rubbed my head. "We ended up getting a good seven inches of snow," I estimated.

"Did you use the snow blower?" he asked.

Are you kidding? "No, we're supposed to get more tomorrow, I thought I'd wait."

"If you use it, make sure you read the instructions first, or ask Paul to help out." Yeah right.

"Okay," I could have sworn I heard the strains of tropical music in the background. "Are you staying warm?"

"Sitting around the stove in our underwear, gotta go. I love you, Sam."

I know I should have said it, a marriage counselor would have me for lunch praising Wayne for his effort and damning me for my non-effort.

"Before I forget, I have a trip coming up with Peter. We're going to Boston and New York for a book signing."

Silence. Had I forgotten something?

"When's that?"

"I don't know the exact dates." Why?

"Let me know when you do. Bye, Sam," he said and hung up.

Hmmm - sounded terribly dismissive. Why shouldn't he be? I certainly wasn't making any effort.

CHAPTER 27

Getting to work on Monday morning wasn't as bad an adventure as I thought it would be. It was snowing again as predicted, very light, but steady. I trudged through the accumulated inches of snow to the bus stop on Bauer Road. The main roads were clear aided by lots of passes with the plows as well as the sand and salt trucks. The side streets would be ignored for a few days. The bus stayed on those main thoroughfares until it reached the Metro station. There was no thought of them venturing into the neighborhoods. Besides the streets not being plowed, the haphazard parking by residents would have made the streets doubly impassable.

I rode the Metro from Rockville station to the Twinbrook station, then walked the two and a half blocks to the store where Andrew waited just inside with two large cups of steaming coffee. I stomped off the snow on the patch of rug at the door and took a long sip of the brew. I really needed it.

"You won't believe who is here," Andrew said in a stage whisper they could have heard in Virginia.

I sloughed off my coat and stuffed the hat and mittens in the pockets. "Who?"

"Jessica herself," he chortled. "The queen bee, she was here waiting when I arrived. Nearly scared the hell out of me," he waved a hand in the air. "I thought I'd forgotten to set the alarm last night."

"Where does she live?"

He shrugged. "Search me, she's never said and I've never asked." He paused. "I think Chris persuaded her to show and she's holed up in the office with the door locked."

I took another grateful sip of the coffee surprised I still needed it. I'd spent most of the night at the computer with a pot at my beck and call.

"Let me put my things away, what are we doing today?"

Andrew glanced out the window at the snow. "Twiddle our thumbs as far as customers are concerned. I've a few things on my agenda, projects we can legally work on and I mentioned to Jessica what you told me about Gisele's declaration of a corporate visit. I think she's back there trying to find out whether or not it's true."

I nodded and went to take care of my stuff. Andrew switched the lights on and then we loaded up a cart with dinnerware and stemware to use for a display and restocking. He outlined all the things he wanted to do. I was pretty sure we wouldn't get it all done, customers or not.

We were well into our projects when Andrew dipped his head down to look at me. "How are things on the home front?"

I looked up at him – my facial expression must have spoken volumes.

His mouth formed an 'O'. "More trouble in paradise?"

"Lately, there's always trouble in paradise. We had a little fight."

"About the job?" I wonder which one he meant.

"Sort of."

"How does that compute? Sort of?"

I shrugged. "I guess he sort of wants me available when he is." I said it without really thinking about it and was surprised at how accurate the statement seemed.

"All this just begs the question, darling, does your Wayne feel as bad about the fights as you do?"

I narrowed my eyes at him. "What makes you think I feel bad about the fights?"

"It's classic this look you have; your posturing, the defensive nature when I mention the home front. Classic."

"I'll bet you take bubble baths," I snorted.

"It gets me in touch with my feminine side," he giggled. "I have a plan," he leaned toward me after he glanced back toward the warehouse door and then to the front door to make sure no one was within hearing range.

"For what?"

"How to flush out the Wentworths' strangler."

"What do you mean?"

"It's like the game of 'Clue.' I absolutely love that game," he declared. "You go around accusing everyone and watch their reaction. I've already started, it's absolutely hilarious."

I knew my mouth dropped as I watched him and, for a moment, I couldn't think of anything to say.

"Andrew, this isn't a game, two people are dead and one is close. If you have suspicions about anyone, let me hook you up with Detective Parnell." I wondered if Jack would slap Andrew in jail for stupidity. I remembered Jack's speech about not jumping to conclusions and Peter's about how important it is to stay away from theory. What would they think of this?

Andrew grunted and waved his hand before my face. "Sammy, darling, don't be so serious. I don't *know* who, but you should see people squirm when I sidle up to them and mention the stolen merchandise. Then I place my finger on my face and speculate perhaps Hector's death wasn't accidental, perhaps Elaine was pushed, and how we just know Holly would never in a million years kill herself. It is delightfully delicious."

"It's dangerous, Andrew, think of Holly. She did the same thing and look where it got her." I paused. "You did tell Detective Parnell about that, didn't you?" I would have to remember to tell him myself. I had forgotten that. Perhaps I should call him now.

Andrew waved a hand of dismissal. "Holly was paranoid. She would accuse anyone to get the suspicion off of her."

"What if there's truth to it?" I asked, wondering what I could say to him that would make him realize his intentions were a bad idea. "It has to be someone who works here."

"Obviously, darling, and it has to be someone who has a key," he stated further. "And it has to be someone who has a security code."

"So you've been going around accusing management then?"

"I can't think of any of our employees that would think of making they're own key and getting a code. You've closed with Gisele, everyone has to come up front while she puts in her code. We all do that to assure no one takes note of our particular selection." Andrew had startled and I frowned his way – I think he'd thought of something.

"What?" I asked.

He leveled his gaze at me and slowly shook his head. He'd definitely thought of something.

"Andrew?"

He flung his hands about. "Nothing. Let me get you started on this wall. I just realized I haven't confronted old Jess as yet."

I didn't think I'd done a very good job of dissuading him, but at least I'd tried. He would have nothing to do with it.

Andrew set me up with my project and sauntered toward the back through the main warehouse door. I debated heavily with myself knowing I would be leaving the front unprotected, but I had to hear what he was going to say to her. I had my promise to Jack to think of and some misguided loyalty to Andrew to keep him from doing something foolish. Well, not actually *keeping* him from it – I had failed to do that.

I felt like Holly hiding in the dinnerware to spy on people as I stood by the lockers and strained to hear. I had no idea what I'd do if either of them caught me. At least they had left the door opened.

I heard Andrew's preamble of. "I'm surprised to see you here today, Jess."

Her reply was soft and inaudible. I couldn't get closer. I wished either Melanie or Betty Ann had managed to come in, I would have at least had the right to be back here.

"Yes, that's what I heard." Andrew said next. "Sammy told me. Did you hear about Gissy's night out Friday?"

Gissy? I'm sure Gisele loved that. Jessica's reply was lost in the wind.

"You think?" Andrew said surprised. "Well, I think …" what Andrew thought was lost. Damn him. "Call and find out what the procedure would be," he said next. "It couldn't hurt."

Murmur from Jessica.

"I'm revamping the stemware and the New Age stuff. It's very tried looking. Fortunately, days like this are helpful towards that end even if it does mean we've no customers. Look at the bright side, you don't have to pay anyone that doesn't work."

I heard a strangled noise from Jessica and decided I'd better hightail it back to the sales floor. I figured Andrew's conversation was going to be done very soon. I made a mad dash to the door and nearly plowed into a customer who was heading for the bathroom. I smiled meekly and waved as I headed for the front. There were two more milling about looking a bit perturbed no employees had been front and center. My hand went to the left side of my shirt and I smiled inwardly. Oh damn, I'd forgotten my name tag.

"Sorry I wasn't here, what can I do for you?" I asked the tiny Asian woman who looked the angriest. She narrowed her eyes and launched into a tirade about poor customer service and how she should speak to a manager. Somewhere in the midst of the diatribe, she inserted her desire to purchase twenty-four place settings of *Platinum Pleasure* for a dinner party she was hosting that night. Okay.

I was thankful we actually had twenty-four place settings in stock and on the sales floor. "Let me see if I can garner you some sort of discount."

"Garner? What does this garner mean?" she asked, her beady little eyes still shooting daggers towards me.

"I'm going to ask the manager if you can have a discount – if for nothing more than the fact you came out on such a lousy day to shop at our store." I smiled at her; beamed. I'm helping you out, you old bat, so you won't complain to anyone – namely the manager – about my not being out front when you arrived.

The woman's eyes turned from deadly to suspicious.

"You think I cannot afford to purchase these dishes?"

Sigh.

"No ma'am, not at all." I'd never run across anyone who would pass up a discount in my life. "Would you like any serving pieces to go with the dishes? We have a full complement of accessories in this pattern." *Because it's gaudy and ugly and has to be hand-washed and - did I mention gaudy?* It was too, a bright white plate with an inch wide band of platinum around the edge and an elaborate curlicue of a raised pattern in the center.

She narrowed her eyes again. "And I will get discount for these, also?"

I laughed and nodded. She smiled then - a wide, toothy grin. Now we were on the same page. Now we understood one another perfectly.

"Let me show you what we have; will you need any stemware or cutlery?" I asked as I led her back to the precious metals. Andrew pushed through the door and I turned to him. "This lady would like twenty-four place setting of *Platinum Pleasure*. Would you mind getting those and checking them for damage for me? And do you think we could give her a discount?"

He raised his eyebrows and smiled. "I think we could do that, we won't bother Jess," he said as he ducked back in the warehouse and brought out a cart. "We have the perfect stem to go with them, ma'am. I'll get them and set it up with a place setting so you can see for yourself."

"That will be good," the woman said. "I would be pleased to see that."

An hour later, the coffers of Wentworths Rockville were five thousand two hundred and eighty-two dollars richer despite the thirty percent discount for my new friend - no necessity for complaint to the management for my dereliction of duty. The warehouse was also a lot lighter in inventory of *Platinum Pleasure*. I didn't get any kudos, but that was fine with me because she hadn't complained. It gave me a whole new prospective of little old Japanese women, although I was beginning to think she might have planned it all from the outset.

CHAPTER 28

We were back to being by ourselves, the snow was coming down heavier, and Jessica had ventured over to Fridays for lunch.

I started straightening the register area, smoothing out unused pieces of newsprint in which we'd been wrapping stemware. Andrew stood before me.

"So how much did you hear?"

"Huh?"

"Don't be coy, Sammy, I know you were listening. How much did you hear?"

I sighed. "Not much and only a little of your end of the conversation," I frowned at him. "How did you know?"

"One of the other customers mentioned that no one was out here and he thought that was bad for business. You're lucky Jessica wasn't the one he told."

"I guess I should say thanks then."

"Damned right you should." Andrew leaned on the counter.

"So what was said?" I asked. "Keeping in mind that I still think this game is a bad idea and I will tell Jack Parnell."

I heard something that sounded like a tire losing air coming from his lips. "I can tell you one thing; Chris will have my ass for upsetting Jessica," Andrew commented. It didn't look as though the prospect upset him too much.

"What did you say to her?" I reiterated

"We talked about the supposed visit and it turns out that Gisele had set one up for the end of the month on the QT."

"Speaking of Gisele, where did you come up with the nickname of 'Gissy'?"

"Oh she hates it."

"That's a surprise," I said dryly.

Andrew chuckled. "We came up with that, Jessica and I, on one of Jessica's first nights here. Jessica caught on that Gisele didn't like her much. She's pretty astute despite her looks. Anyway, Jess is upset about the visit and reamed the powers that be at corporate for not letting her know, considering she is the manager." He paused for a breath and ran his finger along the edge of the register. "Then I just happened to mention that I may have heard a rumor that Jessica was involved somehow in the thefts, or at least under someone's suspicion."

"Andrew," I said warningly. "How did she react?" I wasn't any better than he.

"She wasn't happy, I can say that. She came to us from the Coach Factory Store and doesn't really know the intricacies of Wentworths' rumor mills, but I think she's catching on now. Suffice it to say, Jessica is on the warpath."

I eyed him suspiciously. "And who did you hint around may have been behind that rumor?"

He tossed his head to the side. "Oh, I didn't mention anyone in particular, but I didn't let anyone off the hook either. I think dear old Jess suspects both Chris and Gisele equally," he shrugged. "It will raise havoc with Jess' love life, I suppose, but she'll be better off. I haven't been very charitable where she is concerned."

I shook my head. "So, they're really – you know." I waved my hands. "The two of them?"

"Judging from what I've read in your books darling, you seem to be at an unusual loss for descriptive words. Yes, that's what I understand and Gisele isn't happy."

"That's what Gisele intimated the other night. She asked me if I thought she was attractive." I shook my head.

Andrew laughed. "Chris would never give Gisele the time of day, that way or any other. Did you know he's married?"

"Chris? No he hadn't mentioned that."

"No reason he should. His wife and family are safely ensconced in Northern Pennsylvania. He doesn't see them often." Andrew leaned his chin on his hand. "I guess I don't blame him for seeking shelter elsewhere."

I bristled. Suspecting I was on the wrong end of that stick certainly gave me the opposite opinion and I started to say something to that effect when Jessica returned and effectively tabled any further discussion.

She had bought us each a sandwich and handed them to us absently while she stared out at the snow contemplating some deep thought for a while before she spoke.

"I'm calling it a day and I'm closing the store. It isn't fit for anyone to be out in this weather and I don't care who thinks otherwise," she declared with a firm shake of her head. "Andrew, could you close out the drawers and bring them back to me? I'll file the reports when you're finished. Sam, you can lock the doors and post a sign that we will be closed due to the weather."

I nodded and pulled out a sheet of paper from the fax machine.

"I have a couple of phone calls to make," she said before she started back.

Andrew stopped her. "Is it all right if Sam and I keep on working, Jess? I do have a lot to do and I do my best work when no one's around."

She regarded him and then nodded her head. "I suppose that would be all right. No, I know it will be. I said you could and *I'm* the manager here," she avowed and then strode purposely towards the back.

Andrew watched her in awe. "I think she's got it," he said as she disappeared through the double doors. "I think she's finally got it."

We had a very productive day after we packed Jessica off fresh from her first major managerial decision for Wentworths. It didn't hurt our day's total in only a sparse three sales exceeded last year's by three thousand dollars. The store was allowed to close with the Home Office's blessing, gratitude, and assurances that if it was necessary, it would be all right not to open tomorrow.

I helped Andrew empty out several fixtures and readied the new product for the shelves and, while he did his thing with those, I packed up more of the shipping requests in the back. While I packed, I thought about Wayne and really tried to fathom what the latest wrinkle in our relationship could possibly mean. At some point during the afternoon, I vowed I would try to get in touch with him when I got home. It wouldn't matter that Andrew and I had plans for dinner after work, Wayne was four or five hours behind me in time difference. I wouldn't be waking him no matter when I called.

Let me say this, I wasn't absolving myself from any blame here. Perhaps I wasn't working hard enough on the marriage. Maybe Andrew was right in saying that distance justified infidelity? Naw, I didn't believe it any more now than I ever did before.

The telephone rang a few dozen times as well and we managed to take in a few more sales. That would only help if we did actually stayed closed Tuesday as those sales would be counted when the store was reopened and we could enter them into the computers.

I also took a few moments to call Jack Parnell and fill him in. I didn't think I was telling him much, but he sounded appreciative and asked a couple of questions about Gisele. I answered as best I could and hung up with a feeling of uselessness. I'd been at Wentworths for a week and I didn't have much to show for it.

The weather looked as though it would break – well, maybe – when we actually left that evening. The snow had stopped, but weather reports promised more before morning. At least the school age kids would be happy.

We opted to eat at the new steakhouse that had recently opened in Congressional Plaza slipping our way up the sidewalks with the knowledge we had done a good days work and should reward ourselves for it. Eating out also served a dual purpose in keeping me from bare cupboards at home. They probably weren't actually bare, but I had no desire to cook for one – I could cook for twenty yes, but one didn't excite me.

Stan's (the steakhouse) had opened just before Christmas and the appeal hadn't waned. We waited for nearly a half hour for a table. People in the area just liked to eat out, weather conditions notwithstanding.

It was bright with pine walls and floors, not rough hewn like the Lodge in Gaithersburg, but smooth with multiple coats of clear varnish. There were two large dining rooms to the left of an ample reception area which provided plenty of room to sit comfortably while you waited. I thought that a smart decision on someone's part. There was also a bar to the right if you were so inclined. Andrew was, so we gave our names and took a seat at one of the high tables that had just been vacated by a waiting foursome.

"I hope this is worth the wait," Andrew said after he'd ordered a whiskey and water for himself and a Bailey's for me. "Fletcher had heard good things about it, but we haven't had the chance to come."

"Will he mind that you didn't wait for him?"

Andrew laughed. "I asked permission before I suggested it to you and even invited him along. He'd have my balls in a sling if I hadn't."

"He couldn't come?"

"He's a homebody in weather like this – when he isn't in class."

I smiled and rested an elbow on the table. "Where did you two meet?"

"In college, we went to Frostburg State."

"Where's that?"

"Western Maryland, up beyond Cumberland. It's a good school if you take advantage of it. I didn't."

"What does Fletcher do? I never got the chance to talk with him when we went for drinks."

"He's a paralegal striving to be a lawyer. He takes courses at University of D.C. at night," Andrew smiled as the waitress brought our drinks.

"How about you and your husband, where did you meet?" he asked.

"We were on vacation in Bermuda. I'd given myself the trip for graduation and he was there." I paused – I didn't know or didn't remember why Wayne was there. "Anyway, I had a near disaster with a moped and he came to my rescue and we hooked up."

Andrew regarded me. "That's an odd way of putting it, darling."

I snorted. "It's what happened."

"I'll bet you got married right off."

I nodded. "Two weeks later, before we could think about it or come to our senses."

"And it's been how long?"

"Nearly ten years now – long time." I did an intense study of the table and Andrew dipped his head so that I'd look his way.

"Do you love him, Sam?"

"I do, I certainly don't tell him enough. In fact, I had an epiphany to that effect this afternoon and I will call him when I get home."

"Have you been faithful?"

"Me? Yes, *I* have."

Andrew sighed. "But he hasn't," he stated.

"I don't believe he has, but I don't know – and I don't want to know."

Andrew shook his head and tsked.

I laughed. "You react like my friend Andrea. You and she would get along real well"

"Abuse is abuse, darling," he said, as our name was called and we were shown to the table.

"I can't really be accused of working at our relationship either. I have thoughts of when Wayne retires and is home all the time, we just won't have anything to talk about. I think that would be sad."

Andrew leaned on the table. “You sound as though you’re ready to move on.”

I shook my head. “Being alone scares me too much. I like the couple part even though we’re not together all that much.” I bit my lip. “I’d like to change the conversation now, I think,” I said, as the waiter hovered above us.

Andrew considered my request as he ordered. Evidently he agreed to change the subject as he rubbed his face wearily. “I do hope the store is closed tomorrow, I’m exhausted. I shall stay home and do nothing if it doesn’t open.”

“Do you think Jessica will prevail?” I asked.

“You mean between her and Gisele? Yes, I think Jessica will prevail. Even given her relationship with Chris, he doesn’t just hire people for their looks. She must have shown some spark of intelligence to him. She is a smart cookie. Also, she is the manager; the home office doesn’t take that lightly.”

I debated long and hard about pursuing a line of questions about Wentworths’ workings. I could ask him more about the thefts and how they were discovered and then decided I wouldn’t. Andrew was becoming too much of a good friend to me.

“You mentioned your Mom and Dad are in West Virginia, do you have any other family?”

His eyes softened (and glistened some) when he spoke of his mother and father. There hadn't been a lot of drama when he'd announced to them he was gay at the ripe age of fifteen. They'd not tried to talk him out of it, nor even attempted to therapy it away. They accepted their only son's assessment of his sexual persuasion and moved on, meeting and greeting his boyfriends with equal grace and joy – something I'm not certain I would have been able to do myself had I been faced with the same situation. Perhaps now, having known Andrew, I could manage.

Now on neutral ground, we discussed family, childhoods and friendships past for the duration of the evening.

CHAPTER 29

I paid the taxi and had my doubts that he would be able to navigate Dowlais to get back on the cleared paths that served as our main roads. He plowed through resolutely and disappeared around the corner. I shuffled around the driveway searching for my buried newspaper before I slipped into the four walls that served as my haven.

I started a pot of coffee and a bath before I retrieved the portable telephone and dialed Wayne's cell. I'd start there and then try the duty officer on the base if Wayne didn't answer. His cell went right to his answering machine, so I searched through the papers on my desk for the phone roster Wayne had given me. I dialed the number and identified myself asking for the best method of contacting Wayne.

"Is it an emergency, ma'am?" the duty sergeant asked. It was exactly the question I knew he would inquire.

I sighed. "I can't lie to you, sir, it isn't an emergency, but I'd really like to talk with him."

"I'll see what I can do, ma'am, I promise. Let me have your number."

I recited it for him and broke the connection. I poured a mug of coffee and sifted through my mail. I'd won money – yay! All I had to do was order some magazines and I'd be put into the running for millions.

There were a couple bills for Wayne which I placed on his desk as well as the water bill for the house. I'd give that to Peter the next time I saw him as he now kept my bills paid for me. *I am useless*. I added some bath oil to the steaming water, spread out the towels on the floor before I stripped off my clothes, and carefully lowered myself in the water. I think I needed a restorative bath. I had worked really hard.

The telephone rang and I plucked it from the floor.

"Sammy, everything all right?" Wayne asked worriedly.

I had decided to open with, "I love you." I think it surprised him as much as it did me.

"I love you, too, Sammy. What's wrong?"

"I've been kicking myself all day for being such a bitch when you called and wanted to make amends."

"That's a relief."

I frowned. "What do you mean?"

"I mean, Sammy that you never call me - particularly when you have to go through the duty sergeant. I thought something had happened to you."

"Oh, no, I'm fine. I'm taking a bath, it's heavenly."

It took a few ticks before he replied. "I wish I was there."

"I wish you were, too. You should have seen me today, I was a super salesman."

"You worked then?" An icy chill raced over the wires and I hunkered down a little lower in the hot water to ward it off.

"Yeah, there were only three of us and the manager closed the store early because of the weather."

"So no new murders?"

"No, Andrew and I did a lot of merchandising and then tried that new steakhouse on the Pike. It's good."

"Andrew?"

"The one that thinks *you're* sexy, darling," I said as I told him about Stan's. "What did you do today?"

"The usual, no visits to Santa."

I laughed and so did he.

"You leave for Adak tomorrow?"

"If the weather holds, they don't have much hope."

"Hmmm," I stared at the bathroom wall sadly. I'd actually run out of things to say to my husband and it *was* extremely sad. “I guess I’ll let you go then. I love you, Wayne.”

“Me, too, Sam.”

I tossed and turned most of the night. I couldn’t rid myself of the thought of us running out of things to say, then couldn’t figure why I was focusing on it. I wondered again what we’d ever do if he left his job and was home all the time. Do we fight because we know he’ll be gone or is it because we’ve been together for two or three days running and we tire of one another? It wasn’t something I really wanted to consider. I wish I wouldn’t obsess so about it.

I woke up bummed.

I looked out at the falling snow and wondered if Wentworths would even try to open. As if on cue, the telephone rang at my side and I picked it up.

“Hello?”

“Sam, Gisele here, just letting you know we won’t be opening today – weather again,” she sounded horrible.

“Are you all right, Gisele?”

“Exhausted, but all right. The snowstorm just compounds the problems. We have that scheduled visit from corporate coming up and we can’t afford to have these delays.”

Should I ask her when the visit was? Or tell her Jessica knew? Had Jack talked with her about what I'd reported to him? I tried to think of something soothing to say and came up empty. It didn't seem to faze her any.

"I can't seem to impress upon Jess the importance of getting all our ducks in a row, and I can't do it all myself."

"You do a lot," I stifled a yawn. *And* just wait until you get a load of the new Jessica.

"Thank you for noticing. Too bad Chris didn't when it came to hiring another manager after Alphonse quit."

"Maybe you do your job too well," I offered. "You're too efficient."

"It's just that I've been doing it for so long. It's easier than training the managers who never seem to stick around."

I made some appropriate ruffled feather soothing sounds.

"Do you think you could make it in early tomorrow? I'm coming to stay in town as soon as I can convince a taxi to take me and I've asked Andrew to come in, too. We really have to prepare and the place is going to hell. Having Andrew managing by himself is a near disaster."

I bridled at that comment. After all, I had been with Andrew the day before. I voiced it. “I thought we did a lot yesterday. I even did some more shipping.”

Gisele laughed. “I didn’t mean to be critical, Sam. Yes, you did get a lot done. It’s just that Andrew tends not to *sell.* He just isn’t conditioned that way. He’d rather display – always has.”

I guess it didn’t matter that we didn’t have any customers for most of the day. “We had one big sale and there were a lot of calls in the afternoon that Jessica said would go on the next day’s receipts. We did a lot of telephone sales.” I tried to assess why I was being so defensive.

“Jessica was in yesterday?” The words seemed to stick in her throat.

“Yes, she was. She authorized our closing early, but Andrew and I stayed on to do some displays,” I reiterated.

“She shouldn’t have done that.”

Why not? She is the manager. “There weren’t any customers and it really got nasty out. I don’t think anyone will fault us.” Besides, she received the blessings of the Home Office, I didn’t add.

“Again, I’m not being critical of you,” she sighed heavily and I found my lip curling into a pout once again blessing the powers that be for not going forward with video phones. “Anyway, do you think you can come in?” she repeated.

"Yeah, I can," I hesitated for a brief – very brief – moment before I asked. "Has Jack Parnell gotten a hold of you yet?"

There was silence on the line – the dead kind – and I thought she'd hung up on me. It happens to me a lot – thinking people hang up on me.

Her voice came back strained and a bit angry. "That's the reason I have to be in town actually. He wants to talk with me, I wonder what he heard?"

Okay then, now's a good time to play dumb. I searched for a reply and then she sighed again.

"It serves my purposes, I talk to him and then I'll be in the area so I can go to the store. Chris has even authorized me a hotel room so it's not an out-of-pocket expense. I guess it could be worse, huh?"

I think I answered her – I know I was happy to be off the phone when I finally hung up. I have a feeling we weren't going to be going out on the town together again any time soon.

I stepped out onto the porch to assess how much snow we'd received; another eight inches at least. It wasn't light and fluffy powder either and I didn't relish the thought of having a heart attack as a result of shoveling the stuff. Okay. It was either leave it alone and let it melt (a distinct possibility sometime in the next month), or try out the new snow blower we'd purchased for this very reason. How difficult could it be to operate?

I read the instruction manual (there was no way in hell that I was going to go ask Paul for help). I located each knob and button and pull string as I read along and then read it through once more before I opened the garage door and pushed it to the edge of the snow. Fortunately, Wayne had thought to have a full tank of gas available.

It took three tries and Paul appearing in his door before I got it fired up. There were a couple of anxious moments when I couldn't figure out how to direct the shoot. Then I was home free and blowing snow like a professional. Other than the fact that I managed a face full of snow once, it was kind of cool.

I had the driveway in front of the garage nearly done and was considering doing Paul's two driveways when he showed up at my side. He scared the crap out of me. He was talking - or trying to talk - above the roar of the machine. His arms waved and gesticulated about as his mouth flapped. It was great, I couldn't hear a thing. I finally turned off the machine - bad move on my part.

"I wish you wouldn't throw the snow in my driveway, Samantha," he said – *and* he was serious.

"Huh?"

"When you were doing that side; you threw some snow in my driveway," he said again. *I think the wind blew it, jackass.*

I looked over at his driveway, there was maybe a cup of powder on top of the twelve inches that hadn't been touched. "Yeah?"

"I wish you hadn't done that," he said, watching me.

"I directed it over here, Paul," I pointed to the left. "Not toward your driveway."

"Well, some of it got over there," he whined. "Wayne wouldn't have blown it in that direction."

I raised my eyebrows. "Wayne's not here, Paul," I said evenly.

"He would have made certain that nothing got over on my driveway," he continued as though I'd said nothing.

"It's not that much, Paul. When you shovel it, you'll hardly notice."

He reared back a little in surprise. "Wayne would use the machine on my driveway."

"Like I said, Wayne's not here, Paul. I was thinking about doing it for you, but it will be a cold day in hell before I'll do it now."

"That's not very neighborly. I'll tell Wayne."

"Have at it, Paul," I said before I fired up the machine and moved off around the corner so I could clean out our upper driveway. If I could have figured out a way to blow it down here onto his, I would have. What a jerk.

Chapter 30

After another restless night, I trudged the final fifty feet of my journey coming up the garage side of the store and noticed right off there were no lights on. Either Gisele or Andrew was in the back room and hadn't started to work or neither one of them was here. I dreaded the second option, but somehow knew that was the reality. A whole hour and a half wasted getting here -

I glanced in the garage and saw no familiar cars and then scanned the lot to find none there either. Of course, Gisele didn't have hers and Andrew probably walked. I shaded my eyes and peered in the doors trying to see some signs of life. Nothing.

I started rapping on the window with one hand while I searched for my cell phone with the other as the wind whipped about me. Neither the knocking nor the calling produced favorable results. I stomped my feet trying to get some life back into them as I hunched down against the wind. Where the hell were they? Had I struck out from the warm confines of my home and bed in vain?

My eyes began to water from the cold and the gentle tendrils of coffee aroma emanating from Starbucks beckoned me towards the shop. I decided I deserved a cappuccino and could watch for them from there. I pushed my way into Starbucks and saw Gisele in the corner eating a pastry and drinking tea with her cell phone to her ear. She saw me at the same time and managed to look somewhat apologetic.

Somewhat.

I ordered a large coffee and cooled my heels as it was made before I joined her at the table.

“Have you seen Andrew?” she asked as I put my coffee down.

“Good morning to you, too, Gisele,” I unzipped my coat and hung it on the back of the chair.

She snorted. “He’s not here and he’s not home. I’ve been trying both the store and his number for half an hour. Did he say whether he’d be at Fletcher’s last night?”

I tried to remember if he’d mentioned going there after we parted company after dinner at Stan’s. I’m pretty sure he was headed home.

"Doesn't Fletcher live in D.C.?" I asked as she punched the redial button and held the phone to her ear again.

I wasn't sure why we were waiting to go in the store, so I asked.

She leveled a look my way. "We're not supposed to go into the store alone – *any* of us," she emphasized giving the impression that she felt *she* should be trusted if no one else was.

I nodded. "A good policy, saves you from having to cover your ass should something go wrong. Is that another policy that's only been enforced since the thefts?" I guess I was still sore from having to wait outside in the cold. Besides, there were two of us now.

Gisele frowned, but didn't answer; rather she tried 'redial' again. No answer.

"We can go in I suppose," she said gathering her coat and briefcase.

"I haven't finished my coffee." I eyed the pastries. I could use one of them, too. "Can I get you another tea? I'm going to have something to eat," I said and rose.

"We should go."

"A few more minutes aren't going to matter much. Did you want anything?" I asked her again.

She shook her head. The scones looked good. I knew Gisele was doing a slow boil at the table and frankly

I didn't care. I had gotten out of a nice warm bed this morning to come here to help out and for nothing as noble as to spy on the employees of Wentworths. Oh no, it was because I worked here now and had some misplaced loyalty I should give them a hundred and ten percent. *And* – perhaps – a little because Wayne didn't want me to.

A hand touched my shoulder and I turned to face a matronly looking black woman dressed in a business suit of grey flannel with a frilly creamed colored blouse and a ruby the size of Rhode Island on her right hand. She had glasses that hung from a gold chain that rested on her ample bosom - reminded me of a teacher I had in fourth grade.

I can't recall where we lived at the time, but I'll never forget Miss Thompson. I broke out into a cold sweat.

"Excuse me, I am sorry to bother you at such an early hour, but I have a bet going with my friend over there," she pointed towards a thin woman sitting in one of the easy chairs at the window, a cup of coffee at her lips. The friend waggled her fingers at me and smiled tentatively. I waved back.

"What's the bet?" I asked.

"Tamara says that you're the romance author, Samantha Warren. I say you're not."

She gave me that look that Miss Thompson gave me when she'd asked a question of the class and then called on me to answer because I'd unsuccessfully morphed myself into the desk. Any minute now, she would place her hands on her hips and start tapping her foot, calling me lazy.

I smiled at the thin woman and nodded. "What does she get if she's right?"

The woman reared back a little. "Dinner."

"I'm Samantha Warren," I said, holding out my hand.

The woman took it and frowned. "I don't suppose you have any proof."

I laughed then. Miss Thompson hadn't believed anything I'd said either.

"What would you like to see?" I reached for my purse and caught sight of Gisele sitting there taking this all in with her chin resting on her hand. I shrugged at her.

By then, the thin woman had arrived. "Hildy, for God's sake, what are you doing?" She held out her hand to me and covered my offered hand with her other. "I'm so sorry to bother you, Ms. Warren. I can't believe she's being so rude."

"It's not a problem really, I mean dinner is at stake here," I answered with a wink towards Hildy. The woman nodded empathically.

"Well, it's rude anyway. Your next book comes out the end of the month, will you be signing around here?"

I nodded. "I'm not sure where in the area. We start in Boston, then New York, but we'll end up here. Give me your name and phone number and I'll have my agent contact you with the information."

"You don't have to do that," Tamara said as she searched through her bag for a paper and pencil. "Maybe we could get special passes?"

I chuckled. "I think that could be arranged." I took the paper from her. "We could go out to dinner." I looked from Hildy to Tamara. "The three of us; my treat."

They seemed to think that a good idea, though I'd left them speechless as they backed up to their table. I turned to Gisele.

"You left that off your application," she said wryly after I'd explained the encounter.

I shrugged. "I didn't really, I'm self-employed. That was on the application."

She seemed perturbed and I wondered if I really cared one way or the other. I suppose I did. "Look Gisele, there's no ulterior motive here, nothing sinister. I just wanted a part time job."

She pursed her lips and reached for her briefcase. "If you're done schmoozing with your fans, we should get to work. Maybe Andrew has shown by now." She was out the door before I had a chance to move.

Whatever.

Andrew wasn't waiting at the door, he wouldn't have anyway. He would have gone inside, alone or not.

When Gisele opened the door, I think she expected the alarm to be on and she hurried to punch in her code before it went off. But it wasn't on, there was no telltale beeping in the distance. I followed her at a more leisurely pace and pushed through the back to find her once again agitated. I guess it was better she was agitated with Andrew rather than with me.

"I can't imagine where he could be," she said absently pulling out her cell phone once again and punching the redial as she'd done so many times already.

I'm not sure what made the bells ring in my brain. It could have been the new display in the stemware section that I'd seen, but hadn't registered it until then. I know it hadn't been done when Andrew and I were here – and we had been the last ones here. I guess it could have merely been the fact that I'd found Holly's body last week and something to do with Andrew's declarations of wanting to play detective.

I looked at her hard. "Has Andrew ever been late?"

"Never; especially for something like this. He thrives on coming early or staying late to finish." Confirmed – that's what Andrew had said.

My feet were rooted to the spot on the warehouse floor. Then I noticed that the packages I'd packed up

Monday morning were missing. "Did you come into the store yesterday?" I asked.

She looked at me as though I was from outer space. "No," she answered.

"Did anyone?"

"Not that I know of."

Someone had to have.

"Can you find out who came in?" I asked over my shoulder as I pushed through the door and went onto the sales floor.

Gisele followed me. "Sam? What are you trying to get at?"

I looked back at her irritably. "The codes; is it possible to find out who last entered a code?"

"Of course, the alarm company has records."

A thought raced through my brain and was lost before I could snatch it.

I stood among the crystal vases and looked left and right, dreading whatever decision I made. I went left first trotting through the stoneware through the round room and back out to the center. The white section was next, then I veered left and faced the clearance and the back hallway. It was dark in the corner. It shouldn't have been - there should have been emergency lights back here. Another fact that had registered from the night I'd closed.

"Gisele, go turn on these lights," I said from my position.

"They should be on," she answered as she started towards me verifying that I hadn't been mistaken.

"Go turn on the lights," I said a little more emphatically.

She stopped her forward progress and I could hear her heavy breathing. She wasn't happy with me ordering her around. I didn't much care.

I sniffed the air and felt sick, literally and figuratively.

"The lights, Gisele!"

She moved then. I guess if she hadn't, I would have flipped them on myself – all of them. She must know which switches would light up this particular section. After all, she was the queen of conservation. The lights started to come on and I advanced slowly towards the woodware looking ceilingward first and noticing the smashed lights before my gaze traveled downward and I saw the foot.

I knew that foot.

I tried to step forward and couldn't. I knew what I'd see and I didn't want to see it.

I had no earthly clue –

He was there in the corner tucked into the now bare fixture he and I had emptied before we left on Monday. The one fixture in the whole store that was all glass shelves. His body was splayed, his butt resting on the base and his arms flung back over his head. His face looked calm and serene as though he was happy that this had happened to him.

I didn't think that was true.

Three large jagged pieces of glass shelving protruded from his body. I think someone wanted to make it look as though it had been accidental. That Andrew had been positioning a shelf above and it had fallen and broken and speared him. It was too neat, too staged.

I don't know how long I stood there looking at him. I know the tears fell for my friend. I had touched my hand to my mouth to stifle a scream and to keep from vomiting, but I didn't move. I knew there was nothing I could do for him. No amount of CPR would have saved him. He was too pale, there was too much blood that had flowed from his body.

It was Gisele's scream that brought me back to reality and spurred me into action.

After I threw up, I called Jack Parnell.

CHAPTER 31

After a momentary lapse of all reason when I'd knelt over Andrew and felt his carotid artery, I took Gisele's arm and we waited by the front door. Gisele stood by the telephone in the confines – and comfort? – of the register area. I leaned against the cold glass of the front door, hugging my arms to my body and waiting for the first of the police cars to arrive. Jack Parnell strode purposely towards the door and I turned the lock and let him inside.

He looked angry until he stood before me and saw the blood on my hands and then the anger turned to concern.

"Sam?" he leaned down and held my shoulders in his hands. "Can you show me?"

I swallowed hard and glanced toward the back corner and nodded, starting to move. When I wretched, Jack stopped me.

"It's back here?" he asked as he pointed to the left.

"It's Andrew, the body, you know Andrew Barker. He's not an 'it', Jack."

Jack pursed his lips and nodded grimly. "Sorry," he said as he looked significantly towards two of the uniforms that had followed him inside. One of them stayed with us and the other went with Jack.

I heard the officer's sharp intake of breath and Jack cursing and leaned against the window again for support. All I could see was Andrew and those pieces of glass sticking out from his body, it wasn't any prettier the second time around. Even the whirling about didn't help erase that memory – I fainted.

I regained consciousness in confusion. There was an oxygen mask over my mouth and nose and I was inside an ambulance. Someone was taking my blood pressure and another my pulse. A face appeared above me and smiled.

"Hi, I'm Cameron, you passed out in there. How are you feeling?"

The memory of Andrew came flooding through my brain.

"Whoa! Don't answer that, I think I know," he declared as he grabbed an emesis basin and had it at the ready. "It wasn't a pretty site," he said in a soothing calm voice that seemed to work on my churning stomach. He sat back. "There's someone waiting outside to see you. Do you want to sit up?"

I nodded and he helped me to a sitting position as Peter hopped up into the ambulance and sat where Cameron and the other EMT had vacated.

Peter didn't ask me how I was, thank God.

He placed a protective hand on my neck. "Jack is questioning Gisele right now. He said I could take you home if you want."

I didn't know what I wanted. I glanced out the back of the ambulance and saw a crowd milling about the sidewalk in front of the store. I guess guts and blood take precedence over any inclement weather and poor driving conditions. I turned a confused expression towards Peter. "Where did they come from?"

He shook his head. "It happens. Most of them probably live in the area, some are employees of the mall. Jack had an officer interview Mrs. Mitchell, Tony Yang, and the young girl when they arrived." His mouth was set tight. "There are reporters there, too."

"I guess they figure this is front page news," I said absently as I thought of something. "Someone should call Fletcher before he hears it on the news."

"Fletcher?"

"Andrew's boyfriend, I don't know his last name, and Andrew's parents, they live in West Virginia."

"I'm sure that will be taken care of, Sammy, nothing for you to be concerned with."

My gaze met his and for the first time there was a moment of – doubt, I guess – it was certainly not dislike towards Peter. He didn't know me very well if he thought it wouldn't concern me.

Peter smiled and touched my cheek lightly. "Sorry, I didn't mean that the way you took it. My concerns are for you, Sammy, and I want to protect you."

"I don't seem to be the one needing protection. I should have tried harder to talk him out of it, Peter."

"Let's get out of here before the reporters realize who you are," Peter said stepping down from the ambulance and turning to shield me from the crowd. Something kept their collective attention inside the store and we walked unimpeded to Peter's car. He opened the door for me and waited until I was buckled in before he went to the driver's side.

"Talk him out of what, Sam?" he asked as he pulled out onto Rockville Pike.

"He was accusing everyone of the thefts. It was a stupid thing to do," I said before my voice caught. We drove in silence. Peter stopped at a deli in Twinbrook Shopping Center, bought subs and chips, and then we continued on to my house. The side roads still weren't plowed, but there had been so many cars over them the snow had been packed down.

Peter helped me inside the house and took my coat. "Go take a shower Sammy, put on something warm. I'll make coffee and we'll wait for Jack."

I nodded. I guess I hadn't realized it until I saw myself in the mirror, but I had blood all over my shirt and pants. Andrew's blood. I stripped naked and stepped under the piercing jet of water and cried again. I did everything automatically - soaped up, shampooed, cream-rinsed (there's a throwback to my youth, I guess it's conditioner now) and then let the water wash it all away before I stepped out again and wrapped myself in a towel. The clothes were gone from the floor. Peter must have taken care of them, I was glad Peter was there. I dressed.

He handed me coffee and tried to persuade me to eat. I didn't think I could. Not yet. We waited for Jack to show, both shuffling our feet in the kitchen while the snow once again came down in earnest. It didn't seem long before Jack pulled up behind Peter's car.

Peter let him in and I squared off before him. "You shouldn't have let me leave the store," I said before he had a chance to remove his jacket. "I shouldn't get special treatment, it's a murder investigation."

Jack looked beyond me to Peter and then back at me. "It's not as though they don't know who you are, Sam, and I'm pretty sure you didn't do it. How are you feeling?"

"I just found my friend gutted by three huge chunks of glass shelf. How do you think I feel?" I was angry, angry enough that I felt comfortable lashing out at my friends.

"I'm not the enemy here, Sam," Jack said calmly. He draped his coat over a chair and accepted the cup of coffee Peter offered.

"Do you want my statement now?"

He sighed and shook his head. "Look, Sam, I understand what you're going through. I even understand why you're angry, but right now I'm hungry and I'm going to eat." He brushed past me and went to the dining room table where Peter had set up our lunch. Peter waited for me to follow and when I made no move to do so he held out his arm.

"Come on, Sam, you need to eat."

I bit back a retort and jumped violently when the phone rang by my ear.

"You want me to get that?" Peter asked. I snatched the receiver from its cradle and cast him a black look as I said, "Hello."

"Sammy, are you all right?"

"Andrea," I managed before the tears flowed again. How did she know? I caught Peter's gaze and knew he must have called her when I was in the shower.

"You listen, honey, and I'll talk. Your friend Peter called and said it would be a good idea for us to chat. I know you're not up to it just now, but I wanted you to know I'm available. Do you need me to come there? I can hop on a plane and be there by nightfall."

"No," I sniffled and then swiped at the wet on my cheeks. "I'm good Andrea."

"Do you want to tell me what happened?"

"Not yet, but I promise to call you later. Will you be around?"

"You bet. If I don't hear from you by evening, I'll call back."

"Thanks, Andrea."

"That Peter's a gem, honey, don't lose him."

I smiled at the phone after she'd broken the connection and took a deep breath. Time to make amends again. I went to the sink and sluiced water over my eyes and face and dabbed them dry with a towel before I slumped to the table.

"I'm an ass, I'm sorry."

Jack grinned. "You're not an ass, Sammy, you were right. Sit and eat."

Peter laughed and placed a sandwich on a plate for me. "You'd better appreciate that, Sam, he doesn't say people are right very often."

My stomach churned, whether from hunger or revulsion to the morning's events, I wasn't certain. I tried a bite of sandwich and chewed thoughtfully. When nothing regurgitated, I tried a little more. My head was a mess still, but the food seemed to provide comfort and the sustenance it was meant to.

Jack retrieved the coffee pot and poured us all more, then slopped some cream into his before he leaned back in his chair.

"You ready?"

I looked his way and nodded.

"Walk me through this morning and then we'll rehash the last few days."

I swallowed hard wondering where to begin. "Did Gisele tell you she asked Andrew and me to come in early today?"

Jack nodded. "She mentioned that yesterday in our interview and this morning. When did you last see Barker?"

"We parted company about nine-thirty Monday night, maybe closer to ten. He called me a taxi and waited with me until it came."

"Where?" he asked, with his notebook at the ready.

"We were at Stan's, the new steakhouse on the Pike at Congressional Plaza."

"Did he go home?"

"I assume he did. He was tired and knew he would be up early if no one else could get in to open the store."

"So he had a key?"

I nodded. "He lives just across the street in the apartments there. He has a key and a security code. He was a keyholder in two other stores in the area."

"So he could have gone to Wentworths any time."

I nodded trying not to speculate why he was asking these questions. Obviously Andrew had gone in yesterday –

I asked. "Have you checked the security company's logs? Every time some one activates or deactivates the alarm, it's recorded. Everyone that has a key has a code."

Jack wrote. "If anyone were to find themselves in possession of a key; would they know any codes?"

"Since I've been here, I'd say no. When we close, everyone but the manager on duty is sent up front to wait by the front door. I can't vouch for anything before that, but it seems to have been common practice. It's fairly easy to tell when they've been following company policy and when they haven't." I told him about the bag checks and the procedure for the counting of registers.

"How about yesterday, did you talk with Barker?"

"No, he said Monday night if the store didn't open then he was going to take advantage and not go in for a change. When I talked to Gisele yesterday morning, she gave me the impression no one was going to work until today."

He regarded me. "And you know for a fact someone was in the store since then?"

I felt the tears well up and forced them back. "Aside from the obvious that Andrew had done some merchandising, the packages that I had packed up Monday afternoon were gone. UPS can't get in on their own."

"Ms. Fournier said you seemed to know something wasn't right when you two got in this morning, almost as though you knew he was there."

My eyes flashed angrily and Jack held up a hand to ward off the daggers. I backed off when I saw his level gaze. He wasn't accusatory. Gisele probably had been.

"There were several signs I didn't register right off. There was a display up front in the stemware section he must have finished. We had emptied the fixture in preparation for the new exhibit on Monday. The security system wasn't on and that surprised Gisele." I shifted in my seat. "No one, at least since the thefts discovery, is supposed to enter the store alone including management, although I'm sure Andrew didn't hold hard and fast to that rule." I pointed at his notebook. "The packages were missing and Gisele said Andrew was never late. Never."

I leaned forward and grasped the mug with both hands. "Andrew was going around accusing people of the thefts."

Jack nodded. "He told me, he called after you because you told him it was important. I don't think he knew you called me Monday," Jack finished off his coffee and set the mug down carefully. "Gisele said you and Andrew were working in that corner Monday afternoon."

My gaze met his. "I wonder how she knew that," I said. "We emptied it Monday along with several other sections like the one up front that he'd filled. We set the glass shelves where they needed to be so all he'd have to do is fill them the next time he went in."

I shuddered.

"It was just you and he there Monday?"

"No, Jessica was there until about two. She was in the store before Andrew in fact. She also authorized the closing before she left and Andrew got permission from her for us to stay. We left around six."

"Were you scheduled yesterday?"

I nodded. "Gisele called to say we wouldn't open."

"From the store?"

I started to answer no, but stopped, I didn't know for certain. I went to retrieve my phone and scrolled down for the number. “It’s a listing under Matt Fournier and it’s a Virginia exchange.” I held it out to him so he could record the number. “Could it be a cell phone?”

Jack grinned. “I can certainly find out.” He looked up at me. “What else did Gisele tell you?”

“That she was getting a taxi and coming into town to talk with you. Chris Nichols authorized a hotel room for her.”

“And Chris Nichols was where?”

“He’s been at the stores in Virginia this week.”

“So you haven’t seen him?” Jack asked as he scribbled another note.

“No.”

Jack stared at the table. “You’ve been there a week, Sam. You’ve made some astute observations. Any theories on how someone would go about,” he waved his hand and searched the air above his head for the proper word, “smuggling merchandise from the store?”

I frowned. “Since the thefts?”

His eyes meant mine. “Any time.”

I shrugged and then grinned. “I thought you didn’t deal in theories.”

Jack slouched in the chair. “Perhaps I should have said observations. If you wanted to get merchandise out of the store, how could you do it?”

“Without detection or does that matter?”

He shrugged.

"You should talk with Tony Yang about the truck receiving and check-in process. Ask him how easy would it be to slip a few boxes aside and deal with them when no one is looking. There is conjecture that the merchandise was handed off to customers at the register, stuff was just bagged and not rung through the registers. I would think this time of year that wouldn't be as easy as when the store is busy during the holidays. I assume that's when most of this happened." I shrugged. "Although there is less staff now," I added thoughtfully, "so a little more opportunity to hand it off. I was alone on the floor Monday morning."

Jack nodded and waited for me to continue. When I didn't he prodded. "How about the packages you shipped?"

I blew air through my lips "Each item has a shipping request attached which is generated through the register. The packages are shipped through UPS and there's a shipping statement filed for each one."

"So you would know where they went?"

I nodded and cocked my head. "Why?"

Jack grinned. "I can't imagine all of a sudden these people realized there was stuff going missing, certainly not upwards of fifty thousand dollars worth."

A thought flashed through my head. "The warehouse manager – what was his name?" Why did I have such a mental block with his name?

"Hector Rodriquez."

"Hector, he must have seen some discrepancies. And the woman that fell from the top of the storage fixture -" I nodded my head vigorously. "That has to be something. When Gisele was giving us the tour of the warehouse, Melanie asked her what was up on top. Gisele told us overstock. Maybe the girl found something, like items the thief was squirreling away. I could check."

Peter had been quiet until then. "No, I don't think so, Sam."

I think he surprised Jack as much as me.

It was Jack that said, "Why not?"

"Sam's not going back there," he stated. "Sam shouldn't have been there in the first place, even you said that, Jack."

"He's changed his mind," I answered evenly. I sat forward. "Someone killed a friend of mine, Peter, and I'm going to find out whom." I seemed to have forgotten the mess that had once been that friend – I think Peter wanted to say that just then. There was no need, Andrew was front and center.

Jack held up a hand. "We'll discuss this later. The store is not going to open for a day or so anyway. In the meantime, let me talk with this Yang and have another go-around with Gisele Fournier and the rest of the gang." He looked from one to the other of us. "Okay?"

Peter nodded reluctantly and I followed suit.

"Where are those shipping forms kept, Sam?"

"There are two notebooks by the shelves just as you enter the warehouse. One has the register generated forms and the other the UPS information. They're fairly thin and go by month, I'm sure last year's are packed away."

"You wouldn't know where, would you?"

"Sorry," I hung my head. "Has anyone contacted Andrew's friend, Fletcher, and his parents?"

"We've sent someone over to both places so they wouldn't hear it on the news first."

"Good."

Jack rose and ran his hand through his hair. "I'd better be off, I'll be in touch."

"You obviously think the thefts are the key here," I said as he sauntered through the kitchen.

He turned and regarded me. "Yes, I do, I think the thefts are everything."

CHAPTER 32

It was on Thursday when Jack called with an update. Peter answered.

Peter had stayed the night, sleeping in the rarely used guest room downstairs. I had to search for sheets and blankets that would fit the double bed, having to pull them from boxes we hadn't yet unpacked. I had tried to dissuade Peter from staying, voicing that it wasn't necessary, but was relieved when he insisted.

Peter had let me sleep in. I wouldn't tell him that I had stayed up the better part of the night typing up an outline chronicling the Wentworths' slayings - for a story as much as to order things in my head. The story outline fared far better –

I also spent a late night hour and a half on the phone with Andrea and Greg. She provided sympathy for everything from my discovery of Andrew's body to my marriage (Did I mention that Andrea didn't care for Wayne?) and he mulling over theories of murder and mayhem.

I had heard the telephone and roused myself from bed noting that it was almost eleven as I slipped on a bathrobe and followed the scent toward the kitchen. I don't know what he had made, but it smelled good. Of course, I would have eaten dirt at that point, I was starved.

Peter stared at me his mouth set tight as I took a mug off the tree and poured coffee listening to his side of the conversation, but gleaning nothing from it. He hung up and told me Elaine Newcomb had died and never regained consciousness as I filled a plate with hash browns and scrambled eggs.

I nodded between bites (okay, shovelfuls). "Jack was hoping she'd wake up and tell them who pushed her."

Peter sighed deeply. "Who said she was pushed?"

"No one, but it doesn't take a rocket scientist to figure it out given what else has happened." I took up the coffee mug and drank half.

"You were busy last night," Peter said as he picked up the coffee pot and refilled our cups.

I regarded him. "You read it?"

He nodded.

"How did you get into my computer?" I asked a little irritated, but not angry.

"Your password is your birthday," he answered dryly.

I frowned. *How did he know when my birthday was? What do I know*? "So you think it will pass muster?"

"I think it will," Peter answered staring at the floor. "You really liked Andrew. You really got to know him in a short time," he said quietly.

Tears welled in my eyes as I nodded. I raised my gaze to his. "Maybe he was unconscious when he was … when the glass …" I swallowed hard. "You don't think he was aware of what was going on, do you?"

"I don't know, Sam. It's a little too soon for Jack to have anything there."

"He looked so serene. I've never quite known the real meaning of that word until I saw him … there, you know… in that state." I started crying in earnest. "He was peaceful, like he knew he was going to die and there was nothing he could do to stop it. He had to have been unconscious. Andrew would have put up a fight."

Peter leaned against the counter and stuffed his hands in his pockets. "It's important for you, isn't it?"

I nodded as I sniffled.

"I'll find out for you, Sam," Peter said and then leaned forward and placed his hand on my back. "I'll find out for you, I promise."

"Thank you, Peter."

He snorted. "For what?"

"For all you've done for me."

"I'm protecting my client."

I smiled and jabbed him gently in the stomach. "Sure you are, and your client appreciates it."

"When is Wayne due back?" Peter asked and I shrugged.

"I'm not really sure, he's on Adak, I think."

Peter leveled his gaze at me and I frowned. He looked as though he knew something.

"Peter?"

"Yes, Sam?"

"He *is* in Alaska, isn't he?"

"He's in Alaska," Peter pushed off the bench and started to clean up the mess. I let him.

I have a feeling Peter was keeping tabs on Wayne.

We heard from Jack again that evening. Peter had asked him over for dinner and he declined the invitation. He did verify Andrew had been drugged and he was, most likely, unaware of his fate. I liked the way he had put it and I wrote it down in my notes.

Peter and I had gone to the Safeway and bought the fixings for spaghetti. Wayne didn't like pasta much. I guess maybe it wasn't exotic enough for him. No, I shouldn't say that, it's not fair.

We talked about Lisa as we warmed the sauce and toasted the garlic bread.

"I told Lisa about you," Peter said as he stirred the sauce absently. "How pig-headed you are."

"I'm not pig-headed," I said testing the pasta for doneness.

Peter's answer was another snort.

"What's that supposed to mean?"

"That you're pig-headed and are too pig-headed to admit it."

I had no answer – so I stuck out my tongue at him. We carried the full plates to the table.

"When do you think the store will open again?" I asked as we settled down to eating.

Peter looked up at me. "You're not going back."

"Sure I am, it will be the safest place in the country to work, the world even. Gisele says that Chris is bringing in management from other stores so there's at least two at all times."

"When did you talk with Gisele?"

"This afternoon, when you were out shoveling and bonding with Paul."

Peter just stared. "Did you call her?"

"Of course, I had to see if I was on schedule," I said innocently enough (I thought).

Peter laughed. "As well as to see how her interview with Jack went, I suppose."

"She called it a grilling, nothing short of an inquisition. She said she was near to confessing, he was so persistent."

"I don't think you should go back, Sam."

"Jack doesn't agree – remember? There's something he's missing, Peter. Gisele said he was all over the warehouse, asking about shipping procedures and the like. He was in the office with Tony, Jessica, and Chris for an hour talking about truck check-in. She was furious because she couldn't go in." I looked up at him with a grin. "I think she forgets sometimes she's the *assistant* manager."

"I read what you wrote, Sam. If the killer has any inkling you know that much, he or she is going to come after you."

"That's just it, I don't know enough."

"Sam, you told Andrew this wasn't a game, don't you go and treat it as such."

"I promise to be careful."

"That's not enough."

"It will have to be." I touched his arm. "Peter, I'm not going to be as careless as Andrew – or Holly for that matter. I won't go around accusing anyone. I'm just an observer now. Trust me, I do not have a death wish. I'm as chicken as they come."

He held my gaze and then finally broke off and shook his head. My attention was caught by a figure coming up the walkway and I swore. Peter followed my gaze and grinned.

"He's mad about you not snow blowing his driveway," Peter commented as he went for the door.

I headed for my study. "You're on your own, Peter."

I heard him open the door and greet Paul as I closed the door to my study. I leaned against it and closed my eyes. *What was I missing*? *Who* would have done that to Andrew?

CHAPTER 33

It turns out Wentworths *was* a pretty safe place to work – and a busy one as well. My first day back on Saturday, as well as the first day it opened after Andrew's murder, the place was packed. There wasn't a chance in hell that any self respecting murderer would attempt to snuff anyone with that crowd.

They were buying, too. That pleased Jessica and, in turn, Chris to no end.

Betty Ann had been asked to come in and refused, it was Saturday after all. Jeff suspected she'd had about enough and was going to quit. Brooke Wentworth came in reluctantly, so I was finally able to meet her. She was tall with blonde hair that hung down clear to her butt and turquoise colored eyes that I was pretty sure were natural. She and Melanie drew a lot of attention from the male customers, so I relegated myself to being their dogsbody. Anything they needed from the warehouse, I retrieved.

Jeff and Jessica opened and Gisele and a manager from the Fairfax store would close along with Louisa and Tony. Chris was there, too, spending most of the time in his office and coming out when needed. I overheard Jessica insisting he pitch in when the throngs started. It was a testament to the 'new' and authoritative Jessica Lupine. It was kind of cool.

As I said, I was the fetcher. I was nearly run ragged finding dinnerware sets, place settings, tea pots, champagne flutes and vases. I avoided the back corner where Andrew had met his demise. Rumor had it that the fixture had been scrubbed and bleached – and stocked. I didn't bother to verify the rumor. Brooke had gone on and on about how it didn't look at all like anyone had died there. A little macabre, but I guess that's a good thing. I still wasn't going anywhere near it.

Brooke was standing at the customer service desk computer checking stock with her latest customer when I came out from the back from a short break. She turned a smile toward me and I sighed inwardly.

"Sam, it says we have a couple vegetable bowls of *Midnight Madness* in the back, could you go look for me?"

I nodded, and then hesitated. "Would they be up top?"

"They should be on the middle shelf or on top of the third unit adjacent to the flatware. Do you mind ladders?"

I smiled. That was the first time she'd even thought of it – whether or not I liked climbing ladders. I had been doing it all morning.

"What's the number again?"

She recited it and I went in search of *Midnight Madness*. I steered the ladder into the aisle between the two shelves. It was one of those large metal jobs on wheels so that most of the stock on top I'd be able to reach from the top step. Not that I minded climbing up into the shelf, it's just I wanted to avoid having to – thoughts of Elaine Newcomb flashed through my mind. I checked and rechecked the lower shelves before I trotted up the steps probably a bit too cavalierly.

I scanned the nearest boxes, hoping there'd be some sort of order up there and found there wasn't. If it had been me - *yes, me* - I would have at least put things alphabetically. The only 'order' was the accessories corresponded with the dinnerware in the two shelves below. It was evident early on, I would have to climb up and sift through the boxes. I cleared myself a path and slipped up on top pausing long enough to determine that the shelving was indeed solid and steady. I began to wonder if this was the one that Elaine Newcomb had fallen from and quickly dispelled those thoughts. There was no need adding to my anxiety level. I truly hadn't been aware I was afraid of heights until I was up there.

I started from the left and checked each box, stacking them to my left when it wasn't the correct one. There were a lot of boxes and I was deep into my task when I picked up an empty one. This ordinarily isn't such a big deal, except when you're expecting it to be full. It sort of throws you off balance. I managed to steady myself and not pitch off the shelf. I was sweating like a pig. I waited for my heart to stop racing and went back to my task conscious now of what I was picking up when it happened again. In fact, I managed to find a couple of dozen more empties before I noticed Jeff standing on the ladder and offering his help. I hadn't heard him. He should have said something.

I screeched and nearly plummeted downward. He caught me and I sat down hard on one of the boxes. Another empty. It buckled beneath me.

"You all right, Sam?" he asked as he kept a hand on my shoulder.

"You scared the crap out of me, Jeff."

"Sorry, I thought you may need help, any luck?"

"Only in finding empties I'm afraid – so far." There was no way I was moving any time soon.

He frowned. “Let me help you down onto the ladder,” his voice was in actuality very calm and soothing, but I was hearing sinister undertones – quite clearly.

“I’ll be all right,” my voice squeaked like the pig I was sweating like.

“I insist. You look as though you’re going to faint and I’m not getting down until you’re safely ensconced at the least on the ladder platform.”

I looked around me. “I have to find this stuff for Brooke.”

His eyes flitted among the remaining boxes and then he grinned. “Here it is right here,” he said. I was sitting next to it. I moved it toward Jeff and he reached in the box and pulled out one of the two vegetable bowls. He grinned again (evilly?). The pattern was an ugly black on black in a paisley design with one line of red running through it diagonally. The designer must have been a vampire.

“I’ll take both of them. If Brooke can convince the guy to buy one, she could probably talk him into another, they’re abominable.”

He took the box and trotted down the steps frontward and then came back up for me. I was really grateful he was helping me, but I was still scared. He saw my hesitation – and fear. We both heard the swish of the back door and I was galvanized into action. I scooted forward and was on the top of the ladder before he had a chance to hold out his hand in support.

He smiled tightly and sprinted back down the stairs grabbing the box and heading back onto the sales floor. I tried to breathe and to fit Jeff into the mold of a killer. I couldn't do it – the making him into a killer part. Of course, I had a hard time doing that to any of them.

"You all right, Samantha?" Chris Nichols was leaning over me. I had slumped down into the bottom step of the ladder.

I nodded.

"You're flushed, don't care for high places?" he asked. Yes, I heard sinister in his voice, too.

"I nearly fell – or thought I was going to – Jeff kept me from it."

"Good, we can't afford to lose anyone else," he said and moved off to the next fixture.

I bristled and then realized he was probably right.

"Could you get me a dolley, Sam? I have to retrieve twenty place settings of *Summertime* for Jessica."

Okay, back to business.

The rest of the day went without further incident – and I deftly avoided having to go up on the ladder again as well.

Fine by me.

I think I was hoping that Peter would be waiting in the parking lot for me when I got out of work that night. I had been scheduled until six, but didn't end up leaving until nearly seven-thirty. When he wasn't there, I hoped he was home with dinner ready. He wasn't there either.

I stood in the hallway as depression washed over me. I was in over my head. It was something that happened on occasion and I'd not found a way to deal with it yet in my life. It had been that way when my parents died, when I'd gained and lost my first job, when I'd married and Wayne left two days later for one of his inevitable trips. Tears flowed silently, my shoulders sagged, and the telephone rang. I gave up all pretext telling myself to let the machine pick it up and went to answer it.

"Hi babe," Wayne said as a prelude. I hated that particular salutation and bit back the retort that formed on my lips.

"Hey."

"You sound tired."

"Guilty. I did a marathon stretch today."

"At Wentworths or writing?" he asked.

"Wentworths," I hadn't spoken with him since Andrew died and I told him about finding him.

"And you went back to work there?" It was his turn to bristle.

"Yes," I said not able to say anything further. Wayne took my hesitation as a challenge rather than the grief for Andrew that it was. "Why would your hump let you go back?" he asked angrily.

"Peter is not a hump, Wayne," I said evenly.

"He is in my book, but that doesn't answer my question."

"He didn't have a say in it," I replied. There were several moments of silence and I tried a different tack. "I used the snow blower, we got about twelve inches all tolled."

It was effective. "Did you read the manual?" *Anal.*

"Twice."

"Did you do Paul's yard?"

"No, he pissed me off because the wind blew the snow his way and he blamed it on me. I told him happy shoveling."

"That's my girl," Wayne said with a hint of amusement. I suppose he was trying.

"Where are you?" I asked innocently enough I thought.

"I gave you my itinerary, Sam," was his answer; he wasn't trying any more. "Look it up."

I was at a loss for words. I tried to think of another neutral topic and frankly couldn't come up with one. It took me a few moments to realize that he had hung up on me.

Too bad, I was going to do it to him. I replaced the receiver carefully and cursed him. Then I started wondering why he wouldn't tell me, to the point where I picked it up again and started dialing the duty sergeant. I stopped mid-dial, hit the disconnect button, and dialed Peter.

"You busy?"

"Hello to you, too, Sam," he said dryly.

"How would I find out where Wayne called me from?" I ignored his retort.

"When?"

"Just now."

"Where's he supposed to be?"

"Hold on, I'll check," I padded into the study and sifted through the papers on my desk looking for his neatly typed itinerary. "Guam, he's headed for Johnston Atoll tomorrow."

"I take it he wouldn't tell you where he was."

"No, he just said I should check his itinerary."

There was no questioning me as to why I wanted to know and why I wanted him to check for me. I guess that was good.

"I'll call back," Peter said and broke the connection. I waited there in my study for his call back twenty minutes later.

"Well?"

"He didn't call from Guam, it was a Hawaiian exchange," Peter answered. "But I was told that military flights go out of Hawaii to Johnston Atoll. Wayne would have to catch a flight there."

You're defending him? I thought and then bit my lip waiting for Peter's rejoinder in case I'd voiced it. Evidently I hadn't.

"What do you want me to do, Sam?" he asked finally.

I didn't know. I grinned at the phone. "You mean like break his legs?"

"Do you want me to?"

I think he was serious. "Not really, maybe he'll call back."

"Everything else all right?"

"Yeah, it was a long day, we were very busy."

"I know, I was there. Don't do any drinking," Peter advised (wisely) and then hung up once again.

I snorted and replaced the receiver. I will if I want.

Wait – he was there? I hit the redial button and barely gave him time to answer.

"You were at Wentworths?"

"Yes."

"Where?" *I looked for you.*

"I sat in the parking lot most of the day."

It must have been cold. "Why?"

"To keep an eye on you," he answered bluntly.

I thought it was kind of sweet. "I could have used you in the warehouse."

"How so?"

"Well, for one thing, I wouldn't have had to use a ladder with you there."

"Very funny. What would you say if I told you I was sensitive about my height?"

"Too bad. Anyway, I nearly fell off the top of one of those fixtures."

There was a stretch of silence on his end before he asked what had happened. I told him.

"You say you *read* the sinister part into his behavior?"

"Pretty sure I did, I don't think Jeff would hurt a fly. I'd been wondering to myself if that was the shelf Elaine Newcomb fell off when he appeared. I was spooked."

"And Jack has spoken with this guy?"

"I think so."

"How about the night Holly was murdered? Where was he?"

"Studying, he takes a course at University of D. C., at least I think that's the one."

More silence.

"What are you thinking?" I asked.

"I'm thinking you should call Jack with this."

"But Jeff didn't do anything, Peter."

"You don't know that for certain, Sam, and this is something Jack should know. Are you going to call or do you want me to?"

Now he was scaring me again. "I'll call."

"Are you on schedule tomorrow?"

"They need the bodies – and it's busy." Now *bodies* was a double entendre if I ever heard one.

Peter sighed, but didn't try to talk me out of going. "Do you want to go out to dinner tomorrow night or shall we eat in at your place?"

I laughed. "We'll see tomorrow. Goodnight, Peter."

"Call Jack."

"I'm doing it right now," I said feigning irritation.

I did - prefacing the call with Peter's urging me to report before I told Jack the story. The third time around it sounded pretty harmless to me. Of course, men stick together and Jack told me how important it was to tell him everything.

I hung up the phone, locked the door, and shed my clothes on the way to the shower. I'd forgotten to tell Jack about the empty boxes. I stared at the stream of water and debated calling him back deciding I would tell him tomorrow.

I let the hot water work its restorative powers on my back and neck and then fell into bed waking up well beyond the ten o'clock hour I was supposed to show up at Wentworths.

CHAPTER 34

I groaned and threw off the covers and grabbed the telephone. Maybe by the grace of God they wouldn't need me today.

No luck.

Jessica was at least nice about it, but said it would be helpful if I came in. She continued by explaining it was only eleven-thirty and it was busy already. I chuckled, Andrew would be proud to know his grisly death was making money for Wentworths.

I opted out of a shower, grabbed a clean set of underwear and shirt, and reused the slacks and socks I'd shed in the hallway the night before. I'd get coffee at Starbucks and was on the road fifteen minutes after I'd awakened. Sometimes I hated that I was so dedicated.

Louisa and Jeff were manning the front registers when I pushed through the door. I looked left and Melanie was running the rarely used register four. Jessica and Brooke were neck deep in customers at the customer service desk. As I passed, I saw that look Brooke had and knew she was looking to saddle me with another fetching job. Tony and Chris were checking in a truck. I frowned in Tony's direction. It was Sunday, wasn't it? I hadn't slept through it, had I?

"They've been trying to deliver this for a week, between the weather and the …" he stopped and reddened. "Sorry, Sam."

"No need, should I help here or out there?"

Chris looked up then and shrugged. "Better ask Jessica."

Wow – she'd even tamed Chris Nichols! Truth was, I wanted to help with the truck because I wanted to see first hand if and how anyone could make merchandise disappear fresh off the truck. I wondered if I could convince Jessica to let me.

I stuffed my purse into my locker and pinned on my name tag, and jumped sky high when Gisele appeared around the corner. She didn't look at all happy as she hurried past towards the bathrooms without a word in my direction. I watched her disappear and turned, coming face to face with Jessica - a smiling Jessica.

"I'm glad you came in, Sam," she said as she noted the exit Gisele had taken. "I need you to help with the truck if you don't mind. We have enough associates on the sales floor and there are things we need for customers." She handed me a list. "As they finish checking them in, could you haul these aside and put them in the shipping area?"

"Sure thing," I was scanning the list when Chris approached.

"I have a big order for a transfer, Jess," he said wiping his brow.

She nodded. "I want my orders filled first, Chris, and you can have what's left over," she said turning and heading back to the sales floor. Chris had that same look as Gisele had. I was doubly proud of Jessica.

I couldn't help smiling. "Show me what you've cleared already," I said. Chris wasn't listening. "Chris? Everything all right?"

He shook his head and turned his gaze on me. "What?"

"Everything all right?" I asked again.

"Yes," he replied with pursed lips. "Everything is great."

"Could you show me what you've cleared then?" I repeated and followed him.

He pointed to a pile of boxes down the first aisle. "These are for a transfer I need for another store. Try to fill those orders from stock we already have, then use what's here."

I scanned the first three requests and matched eight boxes to it. I would have pointed that out to Chris had he not stormed off towards his office. I shrugged and followed Jessica's orders, she was the force to be reckoned with, not Chris or Gisele.

Tony whistled while he worked and it made the time go fast. There was a point when Gisele came back and requested one of us to the floor so breaks could be taken, but Jessica had come in right on her heels and countermanded her. I had a truly hard time not grinning then – but I managed. Gisele made a half-hearted effort to get Chris involved, but he either refused to rise to the bait or didn't because he knew he'd lose. I didn't think he and Jessica were an item any longer. Gisele seemed to be buoyed by that observation even though she was seething at Jessica's treatment of her.

Jessica waited for Gisele to leave the warehouse and then broke into a grin. "How is everything going here?"

"Very well, there're only a couple items from the list that didn't come in. Do you want me to pack these up?"

She glanced towards Chris' office and then nodded. "Let me get you the packing slips and after everyone's breaks, I'll help you," she started back out onto the floor. "You'll have to teach me, Sam, this is another thing I wasn't taught and need to learn."

"We can do that, Tony and I are experts."

"Good."

I looked toward Tony who had stopped mid-whistle when Gisele and Jessica had had their confrontation. He still looked a little shocked.

"I think our boss had finally got it," I said, echoing Andrew. The thought made me miss him even more.

After schooling Jessica on the finer points of shipping packages, she asked, "So your husband won't mind you staying then?"

"He's out of town until …" I grunted. "You know, I don't know when he's due back. I didn't look at the itinerary this morning."

My expression must have amused her; she laughed. "I have a feeling there's a story there."

I laughed with her. "Not a very good one."

"You could make it a good one," she said.

I regarded her. "You know about my writing then?"

"Gisele thought it worthy of note – and not in a nice way." Jessica sorted through the papers we would use for shipping. "I'd be mindful of Gisele," she added.

I thought I read something in her voice, but wasn't sure enough to question it. I waved a hand of dismissal.

"*Are* you going to write this up then? Will there be an exposé on the Wentworths' murders?" she asked curiously.

I shrugged and then grinned. "I've already started it."

"Maybe you'll let me read it," she looked beyond me with a far-off look. A few moments later Chris passed us with a nod to both of us as he left with his briefcase and coat in hand. I wanted to say something to her, but telling her she was better off without him didn't seem to be the right thing just then.

Jessica sighed. "Maybe we can go to eat after?" she asked.

I looked at her, considered and nodded. "Is it all right if my publicist joins us?"

"Of course, the more the merrier," she commented.

"I'll just go tell him."

"He's here waiting?"

"He thinks I need watching, given what's happened."

She thought that funny and smiled. "He's welcome to come in and wait."

As I walked the length of the sales floor toward the front door, I thought Peter could do worse than Jessica. I had never tried match-making, maybe just maybe, I was good at it.

I think Peter was suspicious from the moment I rapped on his car window. He had to be cold sitting there, even in the warmer temperatures. They hovered around forty in daylight and were already starting to plummet now that the sun was going down.

We solicited Peter's help in our endeavors to box up all that I'd accumulated that day. Jessica had spent the rest of the afternoon searching other store coffers for the items we had been missing and I noted long before we started packing Chris' transfer pile had diminished considerably.

"How are transfers handled?" I asked Jessica as I watched her enter a shipping order into the computer.

"There's a form that's filled out stating what's going from this store to another," she answered as she weighed the box she'd just packed and entered the weight. "Chris tends to take everything and I don't see why our own customers shouldn't get the advantage before his other stores," she added absently.

Peter was taping down a box he had carefully packed and glanced my way. "Have there been any discrepancies in what's been transferred and what stock you owned?" he asked.

Jessica stopped what she was doing and looked from one to the other of us thoughtfully. "The thefts – you want to know if that's one way the merchandise was removed."

Jessica was climbing the respect scale fast. Peter nodded.

She pondered the question for some time and finally nodded her head. "I suppose that would be one way."

"There are others?" Peter asked.

"Detective Parnell asked me that, too, you know. I didn't give it as much thought as I should have," she fell silent and entered a couple more boxes. She glanced my way. "Did Andrew tell you he thought I might be stealing from the company?"

"He told me he mentioned that. He was just trying to bait you, Jessica."

"I was so angry at him, I was spitting nails. I wanted to fire him on the spot, but Chris convinced me I would regret it."

I felt a little guilty tag-teaming her. "You didn't have anything to do with the thefts, I know that." I couldn't look towards Peter.

"Of course I didn't. I've been kept in the dark since I started," she snorted. "Let me tell you now *that* is changing. I'm getting a crash course in Wentworths' management and I'm taking no prisoners." She looked my way. "How's that?" she asked in reference to the shipping request she'd just finished.

"You forgot the phone number and the dimensions on that one."

"Damn," she answered.

"Not to worry, the computer would have told you before it let you print anything."

"Damn machines, they know everything," she said grinning. "So how long have you been working with Detective Parnell, Sam?"

I raised my eyebrows at her in surprise. "What makes you think I'm working with him?"

"Oh, I don't know, maybe because he lets you go home after you discover a dead body – or at least the second dead body. That's a clue," she said dryly, "though you did leave the building after finding Holly,"

I tsked. "I told him he shouldn't have let me go."

We finished up the rest of the packages and Peter occupied his time with stacking them neatly by the back door for the UPS man the following morning. Jessica locked up the office while I retrieved my purse from the locker and held it out for her inspection.

She smiled as she peeked inside. "No dinnerware sets that I can see, now you have to check mine." So I did.

"Where are we going, ladies?" Peter asked as we headed for the parking lot after the door was locked and Wentworths was once again safely alarmed.

"I love the Cheesecake Factory," Jessica said, beeping open her door.

Peter nodded. "I'll drive." We piled into his car and headed south on the Pike.

I thought of a million questions to ask her, but absolutely none of them were any of my business. None of them.

Chapter 35

"Where do you live, Jessica?" Peter asked as he waited for the light to turn into White Flint Mall.

"Gaithersburg, I have a condo up in Rio."

"Family?" he parked the car and pushed open his door.

"My folks live in Baltimore County," she answered as we fell in step together.

"Not married then?"

She sighed. "No I'm not." She snorted. "I thought I had a prospect and it turns out he was stringing me along."

I looked at her then. "You didn't know Chris was married?"

"No I didn't," she stated evenly. "I found out that little tidbit of information from Gissy as well."

Peter held the door for us. It was not something he had to do since they were automatic. I guess it was inbred.

"Who's Gissy?" he asked after he gave our names to the hostess.

"Gisele, Gissy is her pet name from Jessica and Andrew. Cute, huh."

He nodded and smiled.

"Peter has a daughter, Jessica," I said as we leaned against the wall.

"You do, how old?" Jessica bit and I nudged Peter to talk. He didn't give me the evil eye or anything. To tell you the truth, I don't remember much that happened that night. One good thing is I didn't have to carry on a conversation; Peter and Jessica took care of that all by themselves. It was just as well - despite my waking up late that morning, I was exhausted.

And I was frustrated. Why I thought I had a brain smart enough to figure out mysteries was beyond me. *I was missing something, some little tidbit of information that would crack open Jack's case.* I ran my hand through my hair - that was it, of course, this was Jack's case and not anywhere near mine. I was *not* a police detective.

I had lost a good friend in Andrew and still had the thought far back in my brain that I was at fault for his death. I contended that if I hadn't gone to work for Wentworths then maybe he wouldn't have been compelled to try his hand at detecting. I absently stirred at my soup and thought back to last Monday when he and I had worked together.

He and I and Jessica –

"Hey, Jessica, did you go into work on Wednesday when the store was closed?"

She looked at me blankly. "What do you mean?"

"Wednesday, did you go to work?" I think I must have interrupted their solving of the world's problems the way that Peter and she were looking at me. She finally shook her head no.

"Was Gisele there?" Had I asked that of Jack? I'd have to remember to ask him whether or not he'd solved the mystery of the missing UPS boxes.

"I don't know, Sam. Why?"

"UPS picked up the boxes I packed on Tuesday, they can't get in unless someone is there right?"

"Right," she answered. "Detective Parnell had me get a list of code entries for the last six months. Do you suppose that's what he was looking for – who was there?"

I studied her. I didn't think she was really acting dumb. I believe at that moment I was sure she hadn't anything to do with the thefts or deaths. But, I'm an idiot –

"Will he be able to tell?" I asked next.

"We all have our own codes."

"Andrew mentioned there was a universal code, too."

Jessica regarded me and then nodded. "He didn't tell it to you, did he?"

"No, he mentioned it existed though." *When he was thinking of ways that a thief could get around the system the night we ate at Stan's.* "Is there any way to tell what door someone used when?" I asked next.

"No, the code shuts down the security system, you'd only need a key to get at any of the doors." She shifted in her chair suddenly interested in where I may be going with this line of questioning. Great! I was roping her in, too. I didn't dare look at Peter.

"Could anyone make a key?"

"No again, we have them changed yearly and it's done through the Home Office," she sat back. "A fact I also recently learned by the way. They have a warning not to duplicate on them and most key places won't do it. Why, Sam?"

"I think the two of you should stop speculating," Peter said before I had a chance to answer. When he said it my reason flew out the small window of my brain.

We ordered dessert and coffee even though I hadn't touched a single bite of my hamburger. I think I wanted a piece of cheesecake all along. We each ordered a different flavor with the stipulation that we'd get to sample them all.

Yes, I had the hamburger packaged up to take home. I wasn't wasteful, even though I knew I'd be tossing it into the trash in a week's time.

The waitress brought coffee and our cheesecakes – a Snickers bar cheesecake, Dulce de leche caramel, and a white chocolate raspberry truffle - and extra plates about the time I remembered why I was asking Jessica those questions.

"How exactly were the thefts discovered, Jessica?"

"You know the door at the end of the hall where the bathrooms are?"

I nodded.

"Stock had been stacked there. There's a stairway and a substantial sized hallway. The outside door which isn't on any alarm showed evidence of having been taped, apparently so that the thief or thieves could come back later and retrieve the boxes. On one of those occasions – we assume there was more than one - an employee from Barnes and Noble was tossing trash and saw whoever it was and told Chris and I the following day." She shook her head. "It was my first day there, too, what a welcome."

"I take it the Barnes and Noble employee didn't recognize anyone."

"He says he didn't. He looked over the pictures on the wall of fame and couldn't pick anyone out. That's why we're convinced whoever it was had outside help." She sipped her coffee. "Up until then I guess, Chris thought that the stuff was going out the front door."

"So he knew about it?"

"He had an inkling, particularly after inventory came up with major discrepancy. I have a theory that Hector and he had conferred."

She fell silent and I cocked my head. "You have a theory?" I asked her.

"I think Alphonse Pickering was behind the thefts, he quit right after Christmas."

"He was questioned by the police?"

Peter snorted and sat forward. "Enough you two," he stated. "You're going around in circles and you've no business there." He waved to the waitress for our check and pulled out his wallet holding a restraining hand to Jessica when she went for her purse. "It's my treat, Jess."

Jessica and I went to the ladies room while he took care of the bill and waited for him at the outside door. "What was the name of the Barnes and Noble employee?"

"Beats me. Chris would know though, he filled out the report," she sighed and leaned against the wall. "I'm exhausted."

"Do you work tomorrow?"

"Not until late, you have the day off by the way. You've gone over and above the call of duty and I have taken you off the roster." We were sailing along the road back to our cars.

"It's all right," I said half heartedly.

Jessica laughed. "Don't sound so enthused, Sam. No, you deserve a day off and I'm sure there are things you have to do," she winked at me.

Peter pulled up beside my car and turned off the engine and slid from his seat with every intention of opening Jessica's door for her. He wasn't in time.

I took my time getting into my car while Peter walked Jessica to hers.

He held my door open when he returned. "You don't have to play match-maker with me, Sam, I'm quite capable of finding a date on my own."

"Sometimes people need a nudge," I said as I slid behind the wheel. I looked back as Jessica drove by and waved. "She's nice."

Peter nodded. "Yes, she is."

"You should ask her out."

"Goodnight, Sammy."

"Goodnight, and thanks for dinner."

CHAPTER 36

Did I have the good sense to go to bed when I finally got home that night? Of course not. I sat before the blue screen of my computer and thought about Wentworths. I did manage to type out a few things; notes of what I thought I should do the following day. On the top of it was to find the employee from Barnes and Noble and ask him about the thief he saw outside Wentworths. I also had to tell Jack about the empty boxes. If I'd had his email, I would have sent the information to him then.

I think I managed to crawl between the sheets around four a.m. I do know I was very irritable when the telephone rang at eight thirty the following morning and Gisele was harping about Jessica changing the schedule. So irritable that I hung up on her.

It didn't do any good, she called right back.

"We were cut off, Sam," she said as a prelude. "I can tell you I'm so mad I could spit nails. Jessica has taken one step too far. I have half a mind to retrieve some of the items she took from Chris' list."

I sighed and lay back against the pillows. Were all retail establishments like this? One big soap opera? "She *is* the manager, Gisele," I said calmly. "I wouldn't unpack those boxes we packaged either." *I'd be as upset as Jessica.*

There was a moment of silence on her end. "But I make the schedules, I always have. What did she tell you about me?"

"She didn't tell me anything about you," I searched for the right words. "She just feels it's time she started to be the manager, that's all. I guess she feels no one taught her properly." I winced at my own words and waited for her reaction.

"Well, I agree with her there, Chris should have sent her to another store for training."

"He probably thought that you would take care of it," I ventured.

"What did she say to you, Sam? Did she say something about my lack of cooperation?"

"Like I said, Gisele, she didn't say anything about you." I was beginning to feel as though I was a mother placating a child.

"Are you coming in today then?" she asked.

"No, Jessica gave me the day off and I'm taking it. I think I've done quite a bit for Wentworths this week." Not to mention finding all their dead bodies. "Did you go into work last Wednesday?" I asked before I could stop myself.

My question was met with another pause. "Why?" she asked guardedly.

"No big reason, no hidden agenda, Gisele. I was wondering what happened to all the boxes I'd gotten ready for shipment on Tuesday."

"The guy comes every day, Andrew probably let him in."

There it was - the simple explanation. I sighed.

"I was up most of the night, Gisele, I'm going back to sleep. Are you free for dinner?" Perhaps I could pump her for more information. I'd have to keep her sober though.

"I'm at work until six," she replied without answering the question. I guess she didn't want to go out with me. I looked at the CID readout and saw she was calling from work. Then I wondered if she was there alone. I bit back the obvious question and said goodbye. I'd ask Betty Ann when I casually visited later that day after going to Barnes and Noble.

I fully expected to drift back to sleep, but it wasn't meant to be. I stayed in bed staring at the ceiling until nearly ten and then tossed off the covers and padded to the kitchen to make coffee.

I walked into Barnes and Noble around noon and stood at the base of the stairs still wondering how I could find the witness when I remembered that Tony had, or perhaps still did, worked here. I went to the customer service desk and asked for him.

The woman there was in her late fifties, early sixties, a thin, spindly woman that reminded me of a typical librarian replete with the tattered cardigan and the glasses that sported the chain supporting them when she didn't have them on her face. I have a vague memory of my grandmother using one of those. When they hung down over my grandmother's ample chest, they served as a catch-all for everything she ate. I remember she used to lick off the glasses each and every time she'd finished eating to retrieve the residual food that had fallen there.

"Can I help you, ma'am?" she asked looking at me through washed out hazel eyes.

I shook myself mentally and smiled tentatively. "Is Tony Yang working today?"

She nodded and reached for the telephone. "May I say who's asking for him?"

"Samantha Warren," I replied and caught a quick smile of recognition.

“I thought so, but I wasn’t certain,” she replied as she spoke into the receiver. She hung it up seconds later and said he’d be right out. I moved away and stared at the rack of discounted books until I felt a tap on my shoulder and turned to Tony’s smiling face.

“Sam, how are you?” he asked.

“Good, do you have a minute?”

“I have all the time you need, it’s a slow day – coffee?”

I’d had a full quota of coffee already. “Can you walk to the Giant?”

He nodded and turned to the woman that had summoned him. “Marty, I’ll be going to the grocery store. I’ll be back in a half hour. Could you tell Dick for me?”

She nodded and picked up the telephone – evidently to relay Tony’s message to Dick.

It was a relatively warm day considering what we’d been up against the past week and a half so he opted out of going for his coat. It wasn’t far anyway and we stuck to the sunny side of the walkway.

“What is it you wanted, Sam?”

I chuckled. I guess I’d already gained a reputation for my nosiness and wouldn’t be seeking him out just for a lunch. “What makes you think I want something, Tony?”

It was his turn to laugh. “Maybe after all this mess is cleared up, you’ll come by without an ulterior motive.”

He stepped aside as the automatic door swung open and let me precede him into the store. “I think I’ll have a sandwich, do you want anything?” he asked as we headed towards the deli in the back.

“I’d go for a salad,” I replied and circled the salad bar while he ordered his sandwich.

“Now, what is it you wanted?” he asked as he watched me pile cottage cheese and mushrooms over the lettuce.

“Did you hear about the guy that witnessed someone loading stuff from Wentworths’ back door?”

He studied me for some time and then nodded.

“Can you put me in touch with him?” I added after a second.

“I would if that was possible, Sam. Philip Watkins died in a car wreck about a month ago,” Tony said as the woman behind the counter handed him a wrapped sandwich.

“Oh?”

He nodded and went to the cooler selecting a quart of milk before we returned to the registers up front. “Philip worked with receiving. He was a teacher attending the University of Maryland part time for his Masters. He helped us out when it was busy – holidays and such.” Tony paid for his lunch and we started back towards Barnes and Noble.

"Where did the accident happen?" I asked all the while thinking perhaps I should be calling Jack now. Did he know?

Tony shrugged. "I didn't hear details, just that Philip had been killed." We sat at one of the Starbucks tables in the sun while we ate in a now awkward silence.

He slapped the table. "I have to be getting back, Sam." He stood and looked down at me. "You ask too many questions, Sam, I hope you don't end up the same way as Andrew." With that he walked away.

CHAPTER 37

I don't know how long I sat there. The sun ducked behind a cloud and a chill went through my body before I finally rose and headed for my car. I passed by Wentworths without a second thought and was more than a little alarmed when the door opened and Betty Ann burst through, giving me an effusive greeting. To say I was startled was an understatement.

"Jesus, Betty Ann, you scared me."

She chuckled. "Just couldn't stay away, I see. Where have you been?"

"At the bookstore, I can't stay away from them," I stressed. "Are you done for the day?"

She nodded. "I'm thinking about leaving for good. I spoke with Gisele this morning before we opened. Of course, she's trying to dissuade me."

"You shouldn't leave," I said, not really knowing why.

"To be frank, I'm afraid."

I laughed half-heartedly. "I don't think you have anything to worry about, Betty Ann." I looked up at the sun that had burst forth from behind a cloud and squinted. "So was Gisele here when you arrived then?"

Betty Ann nodded. "She's in a state over Jessica, muttering and cursing as though everything is a personal affront to the queen she's worked herself into."

I was surprised at her vehemence, she was usually a Gisele advocate. "Anyone else around?"

Betty Ann looked at me then and shook her head. "I don't mind saying you'd best keep your questions to yourself, Sam. I'd hate to be attending your funeral next."

I chuckled. "I'll try to be careful, Betty Ann. Anyone else here when you arrived?"

"No, there wasn't, just Gisele," she answered with a sigh and a shake of her head. "Do you work tomorrow?"

"I'm not sure, I guess I should check the schedule." I said waving to her as she crossed to her car. I waited until she was out of the lot before I retraced my steps to Wentworths. Melanie was busy straightening the front register area when I walked in.

"Hey, Sam, what are you doing here?"

"Betty Ann said that the schedule's been changed and I came to see when I work next. Anything happening?"

"Other than Gisele's warpath – no. She's discussing things with Chris Nichols. I'm to call her if the need arises."

"When is Jessica due in?"

"Soon, she called to say she's on her way." Melanie glanced toward the back and returned her gaze to me. "What do you think will happen here?"

"Happen? What do you mean?"

"I'm just wondering if I should be looking for another job."

I shrugged. "I have a feeling that Wentworths will weather the storm, Melanie. They'll bring in managers from other stores to fill in until people are hired."

She nodded. I'm not sure if I'd set her mind at ease or not. A customer walked in and I continued on toward the back. The schedule was posted on the bulletin board in the break room. I checked it and jotted down my new hours.

I walked out into the warehouse and stopped, the urge to go listen at Chris Nichols' door was great – enormous. I spoke with my inner self and tried to justify doing it. My inner self reasoned that there would be no explanation that could cover being discovered by either Chris or Gisele if the door suddenly opened. *How about the storage room next door then?* I asked myself.

"Hi, Sam, I thought I said you were off today," Jessica said as she came through the doors. I think I jumped a mile straight up. Trailing behind her was a woman, tall and black with tight cornrows that hugged her hairline.

"I was just checking the schedule, not working."

"Good, I was hoping I wouldn't have to ream Gisele for calling you in. This is Charisse Young. Charisse, Samantha Warren."

I took the woman's strong handshake.

"I'm trying to entice Charisse over to Wentworths. She works at Crate and Barrel as a visual merchandiser," Jessica explained.

"You'll like it here, Charisse."

"I do already, ma'am, it's a beautiful store."

"Andrew did good work."

Charisse glanced at Jessica with a questioning look.

"Andrew was the man I told you about," Jessica explained. She smiled at me. "Go home and enjoy your day off. Charisse, if you'd come this way, we'll have that chat and then I'll show you around."

"Nice meeting you, Charisse," I said shaking her hand once again. I glanced towards Chris' office and nixed once and for all the thought of eavesdropping. With Jessica taking Charisse on a tour, I didn't want to risk being caught lurking.

With the sun sinking in the west, the day was taking on a chill and I hunched into my coat for warmth. What to do now? I should do that dress shopping thing. I truly hated shopping unless I was in the mood - that happened about once a millennium.

I headed for my car and it magically headed for the public library. I'd be better able to search for an accident that happened last month there than on my home computer. Besides, I really didn't want to go home and be alone again.

I waited for the librarian – at least the person that currently manned the desk – to be free before I made my approach and requested newspapers for January. He directed me to the reference room in the back corner.

The papers were chronologically filed from the current day backwards. I imagine occasionally (perhaps quarterly) they were taken from the files and placed in an archive somewhere else. I took the papers from the first of January through the fifteenth to a reading table by the only window in the relatively small room and started leafing through them. I suppose somewhere articles were catalogued in preparation for when they'd been consigned to microfiche or disks or whatever they did with them now.

I was amazed at how much information had passed me by over the past month and a half. I wasn't much for actually reading newspapers. We received one daily at the end of our driveway and I have to admit when Wayne wasn't home, they mostly went from driveway to the recycling bin. I did the occasional crossword puzzle, but that was about all. Wayne? He read them from cover to cover.

I didn't imagine the news of Philip Watkins accident would make any more than a blurb in the police notes so I scanned those sections and finally happened into the information on January sixth. It was no more than a report of a fatal accident on Route 270 late one rainy night on a slick highway surface. He had been traveling home to Gaithersburg and slid off the road, first hitting a jersey wall by the Montgomery Village exit and then a tree and fence. End of story. Ouch.

I read two or three more papers and caught his obituary next. He'd been twenty-four years old, his parents lived in Cumberland, Maryland. He'd been attending the University after transferring from Frostburg State University so he could be closer to the Middle School in which he taught. Nothing about his working at Barnes and Noble, it was a part time job not worth mentioning. I closed the newspapers and sat back dissatisfied. I wasn't sure why I thought there'd be more – maybe to make his short life worthy of note.

I carefully put back the papers and left the library taking out my cell phone and turning it on. I had three messages which I didn't know how to retrieve. I confess I don't really listen when Wayne goes into his tirade and shows me how to pick them up. I punched in Jack Parnell's number and held the phone to my ear as I unlocked my car door.

"Parnell."

"Hi, Jack, its Sam, is this a bad time?"

"No, what can I do for you?"

"I've heard more about the thefts at Wentworths …" I started and he interrupted.

"Pete told me. He said you and Jessica Lupine were hypothesizing last night. You shouldn't do that."

"Yeah, yeah, I know. The guy that witnessed the late night transfer of goods when the thefts were uncovered is dead."

"I know."

I guess I thought he'd be more curious.

"You don't find that odd?"

"Not now, I don't."

"So you don't think it was any more than an accident?" I ventured.

"As I've said countless times, Sam, I don't *think* anything, I go on evidence. His accident is being investigated."

"You mean re-investigated," I said grinning. I then told him about the empty boxes I'd discovered in my search for *Midnight Madness.*

He hmmed and then said, "Sam, go home."

"What makes you think I'm not home?"

"Because you're on your cell phone, I have caller ID," he replied sardonically.

"Who at Wentworths knew about Philip Watkins?" I asked as I started my car to warm it.

"It hasn't come up in conversations," Jack answered.

"Don't you think it should?"

Jack sighed and I could hear a steady tap, tap, tapping through the phone line. "Let me do the asking, Sam," he finally said.

Okay fine. "You're welcome, Jack," I said before I signed off.

I'd asked Gisele about dinner and scrolled through the phone calls received to see if one of them had been her; perhaps she'd changed her mind. They were all from an unknown exchange so they were most likely Wayne.

I debated returning to Wentworths to ask her again. No sense pushing her. I went home.

CHAPTER 38

To my surprise, she did call me around eleven that evening and sounded quite drunk, but happy. It seemed that Chris and she had made a night of it.

"Oh, Sam, it was amazing, we just clicked."

"You do remember he's married, Gisele," I said through clenched teeth – I think it was that shoe being on the other foot thing again. And, come to think of it, wasn't she? Perhaps she was divorced, I'd never been told or thought to ask.

"Minor detail, we'll get through that."

"There's nothing to get through, Gisele, the man is scum. He's stringing you along just like he was Jessica."

"It's nothing like it was with him and Jessica," she replied with intensity.

I loved denial. I knew it well as I was in it constantly. "Gisele, you have to look at him objectively."

"Pish, Sam, be happy for me."

Oh God. "Is Chris there now?"

"He's gone to get us a snack, I just had to call someone. See you tomorrow."

She hung up before I could say any more to her. I should have checked Star 69 and called her back. I should have pressed. I ran my hand through my hair and marveled at her idiocy.

Then I marveled at my own –

I went to bed disgusted with females in general.

The following day at work was uneventful and devoid of mystery clues. Another shipment arrived and I ferried boxes between Tony and Betty Ann for pricing. Gisele wasn't in residence that day so I couldn't be indignant towards her for her stupidity. I couldn't take her aside and say what I'd wanted to say on the telephone.

Chris wasn't there either – not an alarming fact if you were going around with the information I had. I kept picturing them in bed and shuddered each and every time.

Jessica had a steady stream of applicants in for interviews and she seemed emboldened by the fact she was taking over the reins she'd been entrusted by Wentworths. Customers trickled in and out, Betty Ann left, and Louisa and Jeff came to start their closing shifts at two. Before long it was time for me to go.

As I mentioned, an uneventful day.

I didn't want to go home.

There was still that dress I had to buy. I searched the parking lot for signs of Peter and didn't see his car anywhere. I didn't want to do this thing alone. For the first time in a couple days, I thought of Wayne and I thought it horrible I hadn't thought of him more often. It didn't take much more to work me into a good depressed state. Maybe a nice drink would be the answer.

Oh my God, woman, just go shopping!

Having suitably admonished myself for even considering drinking, I strode purposely to my car. In Rockville, there are no less than four major malls within a five mile radius and that doesn't even take into consideration the couple dozen or so strip malls like the one Wentworths occupied. I sat at the wheel of my van and considered which one I would go to – evidently for a long time.

Peter's knuckles rapped on my window and I hit the roof of my car. I was far too jumpy these days. I depressed the window button, swore at him, then asked. "Where were you?"

He grinned. "Am I at your beck and call?"

"I have to get a dress and I don't know where to start and if I venture out on my own I'll end up at some bar," I replied trying all the while to un-knit my eyebrows. Don't ask me why I was so cross.

He laughed, then rounded the front of my car and slid into the passenger seat. "We can't have you do that, can we? Where to?"

"That's what I was trying to figure out when you scared the crap out of me."

"Tracy shops in Tyson's Corner," he answered, still smiling.

"Too far and we'd hit rush hour traffic."

Peter mused a bit and then pulled out his cell phone and punched in a number.

"If I were looking for a cocktail dress and a suit, where would I go in Rockville?" he asked the person on the other end. He listened for a few moments and then cut the connection. "She says White Flint Mall or Montgomery Mall."

"Who says?"

"My secretary."

"She's still at work?"

"Nope, home with her family. Shall we?"

I started the car and put it into reverse. "You weren't supposed to be with Lisa were you?"

"Not tonight," Peter looked my way. "Why are you so pissed?"

"Nothing happened today," I answered.

He chuckled. “You mean you didn’t find any bodies?”

I snorted.

“That’s very unbecoming.”

I did it again as I pulled out onto the Pike and headed south. “I looked for you in the parking lot.” I was easing myself out of the funk I’d worked myself into.

“Jack called me.”

“Jack was there?”

“No, but his guy was.”

I grinned then. “Have you called Jessica?”

“Called her for what?”

“A date.”

“We wouldn’t get along,” he answered.

“How do you know that?” I drew into the left turn lane and signaled for the White Flint Mall entrance.

“I’m not as convinced as you are she hasn’t anything to do with the thefts and murders,” he answered finally. “It’s best not to involve yourself with someone who’s being investigated.”

I raised my eyebrows. “So no gut feelings then, just incontrovertible truth.”

Peter kept silent.

“What about after Jack solves this?” I asked.

“Stop trying to be matchmaker, Sam,” Peter said evenly.

I laughed. "I just don't want you to be as miserable as I am, I guess."

"If you're miserable in your relationship, then you should get out," he replied.

"Run you mean? Because I can't hold my marriage together, I should run away?"

"You deserve better, Sam."

"Wayne's a good guy," I pulled into a space and cut the engine. "We probably shouldn't talk about him," I concluded.

"When's he due back?"

I shrugged. "I keep forgetting to check his itinerary." We sat there for some time in silence. I finally hit the steering wheel and pushed open my door. "We'd better get this thing over with."

It turns out that it was kind of fun shopping with Peter. He gave a man's perspective and didn't make me too uncomfortable as I paraded in and out of various dressing rooms with countless dresses and suits a very persistent and enterprising saleswoman thrust in my direction.

We settled on a black cocktail dress and a charcoal grey suit with three blouses in white, green, and a pale pink. I endured trying on shoes next and managed to survive despite my bitching. The saleswoman seemed grateful, but I think she was thankful to be rid of us even though the commission she earned financed her child's education.

We opted to eat at Hudson's Restaurant and it was a wise decision. Hudson's was well established in a business center opposite TGI Fridays. It was small, the kitchen on a raised platform in the back. The décor was dark paneling as a backdrop to stark white table linens and a few oil paintings by local artists that patrons could purchase if they felt so inclined.

The service, as much as the food, made it well worth the wait of a half hour. We stayed away from chat about Wentworths and murder – and even my husband for a while. Peter had been busy setting up interviews with publishing firms for us when we were in New York and I waxed poetic about things I wanted to see while we were in Boston.

"We lived in the Northeast for a while and I always wanted to go to Boston and never made it."

"You and Wayne?"

"No, my parents and I, we were stationed at the Naval Air Station in Brunswick. My grandparents lived in Maine somewhere, I don't remember where exactly."

Peter smiled. "You look as though your memories of there are good ones."

I nodded. "I guess it was my age as much as anything. I wasn't quite to my rebellious teenage years." I smiled. “We left there for Florida, I finished high school and went on to college. Then my parents died one after the other.” I paid silent homage to them as I said it.

“No other family then?”

I shook my head.

“Where did you meet Wayne?”

I thought of the day I’d told Andrew the story and fought the sadness that ensued. “We were both on vacation in Bermuda. I’d just come off a particularly nasty breakup and we hooked up the first day,” I explained, retelling the tale of my unfortunate attempts on a moped.

My hands enveloped my coffee cup and we sat in companionable silence while our plates were cleared. My fondness for Peter grew tenfold – and it wasn’t what you’re all thinking. I was not romantically drawn to him. I guess I liked the fact that he was watching out for me – like a surrogate dad.

I felt his hand on my arm and looked at him through a film of teary eyes. He was smiling indulgently.

“We’ll go wherever you want in Boston, Sam, and if we don’t see everything you want the first time, we’ll go back.”

I nodded, not able to do any more just then.

I dropped him at his car and he offered to follow me home. I refused. I was going straight to bed.

“Thanks again, Peter.”

He leaned down through the open car door. “You’re welcome, Sam.”

CHAPTER 39

Walking into the house that night was lonesome. I hauled my new clothes inside and laid them across the couch still in their traveling bags. I stood in the living room for a long time listening to the silence. I wanted – no needed – to talk with Wayne. I knew I couldn't.

Yes, I could have called the duty sergeant and he would have started the process and eventually Wayne would have called back if he could have. I didn't think my reason of wanting to hear the sound of his voice was a valid enough one for everyone to go through all the trouble. We'd probably end up fighting anyway.

I wanted to tell him about my boring day at Wentworths and my shopping trip and the dinner. He would have been proud of the shopping trip part. Maybe it was a need to confirm he was still alive, that he hadn't been caught in some dreadful form of death like Andrew.

No, don't think about that. I told myself.

Maybe I wanted to ask him why we always seemed to be at odds with one another. I wanted to know why ninety-five percent of the time we were in a brooding silence in one another's company. It couldn't be normal marital procedure.

I plodded into my study and checked the answering machine. No blinking lights to indicate that someone – anyone – had called me.

Shit.

I'm sure there's something psychological here, some deep-seeded – what? Fear perhaps? Fear I didn't want to be alone even though I was quite capable of existing that way. Sometimes I was even better off –

This is not getting you anywhere, Babe – all this self pity and lonely crap!

I could hear my mother say that I should make of my marriage what it is – even though she'd never met Wayne. I'd heard her say that once about a friend of hers who had gotten divorced. My mother had shaken her head and tsked that women should do better at working at their marriages. My father had smiled tolerantly and not replied.

I laughed and shook my own head in hopes of ridding my mind of those thoughts. *Maybe when Wayne gets back, you'll remember this and not pick a fight with him.*

When pigs fly –

I shed my clothes and took a long hot shower, sinking into bed and my dreams with equal fervor.

If I'd never experienced the 'sleep of the just', I did that night. It was as though someone had given me a lobotomy and erased all memory. I awoke well rested and resolved. I didn't have to be at Wentworths until afternoon so I did some much needed picking up of the house. I actually hung things up and *thought* about vacuuming and making the bed.

I ventured into Wayne's study and sought out his neatly typed itinerary. It showed him due home that day and I immediately dispelled the thoughts of whether this particular homecoming would be delayed like all the others.

Next to his schedule was mine, or least the one Harry had sent me. I was supposed to be in Nashville for a four day conference for Romance writers. Right then as a matter of fact – until Saturday. I smiled, certain that Peter had cancelled it just as he had the Chicago thing.

I sat in Wayne's desk chair and spun around to look at this room and how he had arranged it. Even when he was away, there didn't seem to be any accumulated dust. He had a grouping of pictures on the wall of places we'd lived. That was his reminder of them - oil paintings and watercolors of scenic views. Nothing of us. My head swiveled and I took in his oak desk and the three file cabinets and the angled bookshelves. No personal pictures anywhere.

Then I stood in the doorway of my study and looked about, none there either. Had we taken pictures? Had anything of our nearly ten years together been chronicled by Kodak? I could picture us in our dotage arguing over whether or not we'd seen the Eiffel Tower or the London Bridges - the actual one in London *and* the transplanted one in Lake Havusu City, Arizona.

Forever arguing – at least I was picturing us in our dotage.

Well, it's as much your fault as Wayne's. You could have taken pictures, no one said you couldn't have a camera.

I guess I made my first resolution then, that I would take up the sword and rectify that particular lapse of recording our history for whoever may be interested a thousand years down the road. There had to be some measure of our existence.

Did we even own a camera? Maybe I'd buy one for Wayne's birthday in April.

I did some laundry as I needed a clean shirt for work and loaded the dishwasher with the several coffee cups I'd dirtied over the course of the past few days. It wasn't full, but I put it through its paces.

It had rained some during the night and I noticed it was warming up when I went for the paper. A lot of the snow we'd gotten was now gone and we were back to nearly springlike weather. I thought of renewal and crap like that as I shuffled back to the house reading the headlines. The headlines were depressing, so I tossed the paper in the recycling bin outside the front door.

Renewal. We could renew our marriage vows on our tenth anniversary and take pictures. Was Wayne ever going to be surprised when he came home!

I settled in front of my computer and rattled off a few hundred words before my thoughts returned to my introspection. It was as much my fault as Wayne's – probably more. I knew I loved him as much as I knew I didn't trust him. But wasn't this all due to my own imagination? I hadn't ever actually seen him with someone else. Of course, he had shown interest of a carnal nature toward Andrea, but perhaps that had been only in jest.

Well, maybe not, there was the fact of Andrea's hatred toward him.

There was all the talk and innuendo, people trying nicely, but firmly, to tell me he was unfaithful. Maybe I hadn't listened to them because deep down I wanted our marriage to work? What better basis could I ask for? If I wanted it to work and Wayne wanted it to work, then nothing and no one else mattered.

As I stared at the words on the computer screen that I had written, I vowed that when Wayne returned I would work harder at our relationship. I would give him the benefit of my doubts (until proven otherwise). Bottom line, the man was my husband. I also thought seeing a counselor couldn't do as much damage as Wayne may think. It could only help us. I shall insist on it.

I checked the clock on the computer and deemed it time to get ready for work. I was beginning to like this particular routine, at least when I was well rested and I wasn't doomed to finding dead bodies. I was almost to the point where I was considering staying on at Wentworths even after this mess was all cleared up if they'd have me. That thought segued into what Peter had said about Jessica and I, once again, tried to place her in the role of murderer and thief. I couldn't do either. That means nothing of course, I'd been bilked by the best of them over the years. If I liked someone, I can easily turn a blind eye – which brought me back to my relationship. Sigh.

CHAPTER 40

There was a skeleton crew at work. Betty Ann was in a sour mood and flashed me a discouraged look when I entered. Two unknowns to me were dismantling a display at the front and I bristled. Andrew had worked hard on that. Then again, Andrew was dead and Wentworths had to move forward. The two turned out to be our new visual merchandiser, Maria Starosta, and an assistant manager from the Hagerstown store whose name was Debbie Clinton. Debbie was tall and thin with mousy brown hair and a pinched face. Maria was short in stature with smooth light brown skin and large brown eyes. Her hair, though it was the same color as Debbie's, didn't have the same unkempt, plain look. It hung down her back and was pulled back loosely with a pale blue scarf that matched her sweater.

I introduced myself to them and we chatted inanely for a couple minutes. I found myself searching the parking lot and then smiled to myself. It was daylight, there would be no need for my watchdogs until after dark.

Jessica greeted me at my locker with a tight smile.

"What's up with Betty Ann? She looks as though she could kill." I regretted the analogy almost as soon as I voiced it.

"She wanted to quit, I asked her to think it over. We really need her," Jessica left volumes unsaid and I cocked my head.

"What's wrong?"

"No one seems to like the fact I'm taking over the controls, certainly not Betty Ann. I tried to extend her hours some, adjust them so they're more suitable for Wentworths rather than catering to her whimsy. She went into quite a tirade about how badly I was treating Gisele. I think she's Gisele's only champion."

"She hasn't been her champion in the past."

"No kidding," Jessica replied.

"Andrew told me once that Betty Ann was a mercy hiring under the first manager when Gisele came in as an assistant. He said there were some creative working hours when a manager would start at six a.m. so more merchandising could get done before opening."

"The problem with that is no one's around to do customer service later in the day. That was one of the first practices I changed," Jessica sighed.

"I think, too, Betty Ann knows Gisele is seeing Chris and thinks you're doing all this out of spite," I said wondering whether or not Jessica knew about Gisele and Chris.

"I suppose that's part of it as well. I tried to talk with Gisele about all the things wrong with her and Chris, but she wouldn't listen."

"Same here, she said their relationship isn't the same as yours and his. She's a fool."

She chuckled and seemed to relax. "I hope to be out of here before she gets in today. Debbie said she'd stay on. Talk about not wanting a confrontation. Besides, I have errands to run." She leaned against the lockers and smiled. "I had this idea I ran across the visual merchandising guru at the Home Office."

"Oh?" I replied as I pinned on my name tag.

"I've called Bertram's Furniture to see if they want to display some of our dinnerware. We'd loan them the patterns and people can see what it all looks in an actual dining room setting. Then when we need furniture, like for the bridal show coming up, they'd loan us some pieces. Items such as tables and chairs so it would give the couples a better idea what they were looking for. We both could include some coupon or something to be given away."

I grinned. "Sounds like a managerial decision to me."

"They liked it at Bertram's, too. I'm going over this afternoon." She looked at me thoughtfully. "Maybe you could go over with me? In fact, I'll take you along anyway. It's just up the street and we wouldn't be gone all that long. You could help me decide what patterns to take and jot down notes."

"I'd like that."

"Well then, that's what we'll do. Let me count out Betty Ann's till and we'll go over. Did you meet Maria?"

"On the way through, yes, what happened to Charisse?"

"I found out she stretched the limits of Crate and Barrel's medical leave policies, they are deep into litigation. She injured her back, but still had the capacity to lift things when she thought no one was around to see it. That isn't something I want this company to get saddled with if I can help it." I walked with her to the front and went to Tony who waved to me from the stemware.

"Sammy, I haven't seen you for a bit, are we closing together tonight?"

"Looks that way."

"How are you? I mean since you found – since that thing that happened?" Tony reddened.

"I'm fine, Tony."

"Have you heard if there's a service?"

I hadn't. I hadn't even thought to ask Jack if the body had been released. What a friend I was.

"I haven't heard, maybe Jessica knows, I'll ask her. We're supposed to go over to Bertram's for a meeting when she's done with Betty Ann."

"Go to Bertram's for what?" Gisele asked behind me. Jessica's aspiration to get out of Wentworths before Gisele's arrival was unsuccessful.

I wondered if it was my place to tell Gisele. "She's set up a program with them to have them display Wentworths' dinnerware exclusively in exchange for furniture loans when we need them."

"Whatever for?"

"So people can see what we have in the proper setting." *You dolt.* I think Gisele has lost sight of the purpose of retail.

"Chris won't like it," she declared. "I'll see that he hears about this immediately." She turned to go and then turned back. "And why are you going?"

"Because Jessica asked me along," I said with a smile.

"Who do I have working with me today?"

“Tony’s here,” I stabbed a finger towards the front window. “Debbie from Hagerstown is helping Maria get acclimated.”

“Maria?”

“The new visual manager, Jessica hired her.”

She stood there and her facial expression took on a life of its own. There were a million questions. I think at some point during her inner tirade, she realized she was talking to a lackey and she spun on her heels and headed for the back. Gisele Fournier did not like being put in her place. I returned my attention to Tony. Gisele Fournier should get a frigging life.

CHAPTER 41

"That was interesting; talk about blatantly ignoring me," Jessica said as we walked up Chapman towards Bertram's. She sniggered with delight. I kept silent. "I left Gissy dialing the telephone to talk to Chris."

"Do you think he'll side with her?"

"I don't care. I have the blessings of the Home Office on this. Chris Nichols and Gisele can go to hell."

I chuckled. "I think I'm liking you more and more every day, Jess."

"God knows I can use the support, all I can say again and again is that it's about time."

The snow pack was nearly gone on the grassy surfaces leaving only an edge of dirty snow lining the sidewalks. Before the day was out, I would guess that most of that would be liquid as well. Hard to believe just a week ago there was so much snow.

"Have you heard about a service for Andrew?" I asked.

"Not yet, his parents weren't certain they'd have one. Fletcher said Andrew wanted to be cremated without a fuss. The last I heard they were scrambling around searching for something he may have written down for confirmation."

I nodded. I'd really dropped the ball there. I should have at least called Fletcher by now.

We passed through the doors of the furniture store and approached the front desk where Jessica asked for Shannon Ryan. The receptionist was the epitome of a ditzy blonde, about my height, shoulder length pouffy hair, vacant blue eyes. She was smacking on a wad of gum and snacking on a bowl of Skittles. Smacking loudly, I might add, with mouth revealing every bit of chewed candy. I would hate to have to be in the same county with her when she ate a meal. She stared blankly at Jessica and Jessica leaned over the counter and repeated her request slowly.

"We're here to see Shannon Ryan, could you page her for us?"

"Shannon?" the woman said and I glanced at her name plate. Colleen Vega was four hundred and ninety-nine pages short of a ream, a hundred forty three short of a gross, a – well, I guess you get the picture. For blondes everywhere, and I'm not saying you're all ditzy, but this woman was the poster child.

Jessica nodded encouragement as the woman's mouth worked the gum and Skittles alternately; stuffing one in one cheek as she chewed the other. It must have tasted awful.

Jessica was far more patient than I was. Finally the woman took up the telephone and punched in a two digit number. "Do we have a Shannon working here?"

I could hear the voice on the other end of the line and grinned. I think it may have been Shannon herself and Shannon was angry. Colleen hung up the receiver and nodded, evidently she was processing whatever the person on the other end had said. She picked out two green Skittles and placed them carefully in her mouth before she looked up to us.

"May I help you?"

Maybe she was the full ream and a gross short.

"We're waiting for Shannon, thank you," Jessica said and turned away before the grin broke through. We wandered into the first room which that was set up with mahogany furniture, big, thick stuff with lots of curlicues and intricate carvings and etched glass doors on the hutch.

"Have you seen the new square pattern with the pink and gold paisley print?" Jessica asked as she ran a hand along the table.

I searched the air for the name. "*Cecilia*?"

Jessica nodded. "Wouldn't that fit here? With the pale rose colored placemats and the gold-rimmed stemware?"

"I'd have to see it," I answered as diplomatically as I could muster. *Cecilia* was ugly. I didn't think it would fit in anyone's outhouse let alone in a formal dining room. Jessica laughed. "Exactly the purpose of this exercise, Sam."

A small, black haired woman entered and strode forward with her hand outstretched towards me. "Hi, sorry to keep you waiting, I'm Shannon."

"I'm Sam, this is Jessica, Wentworths' manager. She's the one you want." I pointed and Shannon took up Jessica's hand.

"Sorry," she declared. "We're very excited about this. I can't tell you how much this will help our visual budget."

Jessica smiled. "I think this could work out well for both of us. How do you want to do this?"

I half listened as they hammered out details. How many place settings would work, it was decided on at least four of each pattern along with the same number in stemware and flatware. Whether or not we'd provide placemats, napkins, napkin rings, vases and the like…

I followed and took vague notes, better notes when Jessica turned and cast me a significant look that asked *why aren't you writing this down?* Andrew would have liked this idea. He had tried his best with what Wentworths had given him to work with in the store and would have loved the variety of woods and 'themes' from here. Damn. I wondered if I'd ever be able to think of Andrew and not tear up.

"You okay, Sam?" Jessica asked with her hand on my shoulder.

"Yeah, I'm good. I was thinking how much Andrew would love this."

She smiled and nodded. "It was his idea. I figured it was the least I could do for him," she said and turned back to Shannon. Jessica Lupine went up another notch in my book and down another in the suspicious character roster. I'd have to remember to tell Peter and Jack.

We finished up, and Jessica bubbled over with enthusiasm on our trip back, rattling off patterns to fit each area that we'd seen. I glanced at my notes and saw that I'd labeled each section with headings of 'country', 'English', 'French Provincial', 'modern', etc., jotting down names of patterns Jessica had thrown out as we'd entered each room. I hadn't remembered doing that.

She wanted to start immediately when we walked through the doors, but Maria was standing there red-faced and angry.

Jessica emitted an audible sigh and asked her what was wrong.

"It's Ms. Fournier," Maria said and I was certain I heard Jessica reply 'no shit' as she gently guided Maria toward the back. I looked towards Tony who seemed stunned by whatever had transpired before our arrival.

"What happened?" I asked.

He shook his head as if to clear it and glanced towards the back door where Jessica and Maria had disappeared.

"Gisele came out in a rage about fifteen minutes after you left and lit into Maria and the manager from Hagerstown. I was a little embarrassed because I was helping a customer. She was screaming and yelling how she was unappreciated and then started telling Maria how to do her job. Somehow the manager …"

"Debbie," I provided.

He nodded emphatically. "Somehow Debbie managed to get Gisele to the back room, but she was yelling and screaming the whole time. About a half hour after that, Mr. Nichols comes out and scoots out the door."

"Chicken shit," I commented and looked towards the back. Would it prove useful for me to go back there and try to listen in? It would have been worth getting caught to hear Gisele being reprimanded or fired - or maybe not.

I think I realized then I probably wouldn't continue working at Wentworths. My new resolve to work at my marriage would interfere with any retail job. I looked up at Tony and he was smiling at me.

"I don't think I can handle all the melodrama any more. What about you?" I said dryly.

He shrugged. "I'm going to stick it out, it looks as though Jessica will be able to run the show whether Gisele stays or not."

I regarded him and found myself wondering if Gisele would give up her position. I didn't think so. In fact, I would think she'd think of all this as just another challenge to her rightful place at the helm. I went back to my locker and found my name tag without even considering stopping in the break room in order to hear what may be going on in the office.

CHAPTER 42

The big pow-wow in the office didn't last much longer than a half hour. Debbie came out first with her purse looking very much relieved to be getting out of the store in one piece. Jessica and Maria came next laughing and making plans to go back to Bertram's so Maria could put in her two cents as to what patterns she thought might fit.

I didn't take offense, it was her job after all.

Gisele didn't appear for some time. She was probably calling everyone she knew at corporate trying to get Jessica canned. Tony cleaned up the detritus Maria and Debbie had left while I took story notes and answered the telephone. There were very few customers.

I was still fiddling with the mystery of how a person could spirit merchandise away from the premises without getting caught. I listed the various possibilities of taking stock before it was checked in, concluding it could only be done if people were in collusion. I wondered if shipping slips could be dummied somehow and figured the only real way I could find out was to ask a manager. From all that I had seen the transaction had to go through a register. Of course, there was the transfer theory. I didn't really want to ask Gisele, but then again, I didn't want to hang around any longer than I had to.

I'd have to sidle up to her, soften her up before I put the questions to her. I knew how to do that, I just wasn't sure I wanted to. I was deep into speculation when Gisele finally appeared. I don't know how long she'd been standing there while I bent over my notebook. I do know I jumped when I looked up and saw her there.

She looked grim faced.

"Hi, Gisele, how's it going?" I slid my notebook shut and stuffed it under the counter. "Just making some notes for a story."

"I saw. I should probably reprimand you for that, but it's not busy."

"Nope," I looked around for Tony to confirm that and he was no where in sight.

"I sent Tony for his break," she replied, smoothing her skirt carefully.

I ducked my head to look at her. "Everything all right, Gisele?"

"It will be I'm sure."

Would now be a good time to give her my notice? "I have some book signings coming up for my latest book, I'm going to be out of town. How should I handle that as far as the schedule goes?"

"You're planning to stay on then?"

I shrugged noncommittally. Are you?

She sighed "You'd better discuss it with Jessica," she said with her lips drawn tight.

"What's wrong, Gisele?"

"Everything and nothing," was her reply.

Hardly sporting of her I thought. A man and woman came through the door and she went off to lend assistance. I had the feeling I was no longer her confidante – providing I ever had been. After I rang up the couple and sent them on their way, she leaned against the bench and sighed again. She wanted me to ask her again what was wrong –

"If someone wanted to steal something from the store, how would they go about it?" I asked instead.

She seemed surprised and then stopped to consider the answer. "Chris said he thought you were writing something. I suppose this is for that."

I nodded. "I've asked Andrew and Jessica, I figured I'd get your take on it, too."

She shrugged and turned to lean over the bench with her arms folded across her chest. "They'd have to know how to reduce the inventory if they didn't want to get caught at it."

"You mean through transfer forms? Something like that?" I asked.

She nodded. "Or damage reports," she said. "Or shipping requests," she added absently. "Is Jessica in on it, too?"

"But aren't shipping requests put through the register?" I asked next and was surprised when I looked up and she wasn't there any more. I looked about and sighed as I heard the warehouse door whoosh shut. Then I frowned. *Is Jessica in on what, too?*

It wasn't long before the light appeared on the telephone indicating one of the lines was in use. It didn't take a rocket scientist to figure that Gisele was using the phone in the back. I nearly picked up the extension when the telephone rang.

"Wentworths," I said as I scanned the parking in the waning daylight. No Peter, no Jack.

"Hi Sam, Jessica here. Is everything going okay there?"

"Do you mean is Gisele still here? Yes, she is."

She laughed. "I didn't mean to leave without saying goodbye – sorry."

"No need to be sorry, she's pretty calm."

"Good, I guess she's considering my ultimatum then."

"And that would be?"

"Shape up or ship out, I don't need her bucking every decision I make."

I wasn't certain, but I thought maybe I heard someone pick up on the extension, then again I have an active imagination. I certainly couldn't tell by the blinking lights.

"What do you think she'll do?"

"I don't care really," Jessica answered. "I wanted to thank you for your help this afternoon, too. I didn't really get a chance. I was disappointed we didn't get to put aside some patterns, but Maria had some good ideas and she and I will work on it tomorrow."

"As it should be."

"Well I thank you anyway, good night."

If I wasn't certain about Gisele listening in, I was pretty sure she had when she came out after Tony's return from break. She was definitely chilly toward me when she sent me on my break.

Oh well.

I debated calling Wayne while I sat in Starbucks and realized I hadn't brought my cell phone with me. I think I zoned out, only realizing how late I was getting back when I saw Tony waving to me from the door. I'd gone well over my allotted half hour and Gisele had sent him to retrieve me. I definitely wouldn't be calling Wayne from the store.

Gisele started turning off lights after the canned announcement came over the speakers stating the store was now closed. I left my post at register one to close and lock the two double doors, standing guard while Tony finished up with his last customer and opened the door for them when they were paid.

"Have a nice night," I said as they passed through.

Gisele came from the back and busied herself with closing out the registers while Tony and I started the clean-up. She didn't look any happier.

"Anything wrong, Gisele?" I asked as I emptied the trashcan near her.

She snorted and shook her head.

"Are we going out after?" I asked next, feeling safe in assuming she'd say no.

"I don't think so," was her answer. "Tony, you can go home when you're done with the sweeping. Sam will stay until I'm finished."

Goody, I thought. And what was wrong with me leaving early?

Tony looked up sheepishly from his sweeping. "I don't mind staying Ms. Fournier. Sam can go home."

Tony was a nice guy. It had been fortunate for us that Gisele had decided to stay in the back most of the night. Gisele looked at him pointedly, but it was wasted, he was back to concentrating on his chore rather than looking at her. I couldn't figure out why she was still pissed off about me being late or even about my conversation with Jessica. The store hadn't been busy.

"No, Tony, you go. Sam will stay," she stated and then bustled off with the cash drawers to her little haven in the back. I guess we didn't have to stand at attention next to her while she counted.

Why did I feel the urge to stick out my tongue? I followed up on that urge -

"You sure you're okay, Sam, I don't mind staying. She's certainly been quite a bitch tonight."

"I'll be fine, Tony," I assured him as he swept. "She just wants to set an example of me, I'm sure. I'll listen to the lecture and take my lumps like an adult."

He stared at the floor. "She was talking to Mr. Nichols on the telephone earlier and she was none too happy. I heard her mention the thefts. You don't think she thinks I had anything to do with them, do you?"

"I don't think anyone would think that, Tony, you're above reproach."

He regarded me blankly for a while and then grinned. “I guess that must be a good thing if you said it, Sam.”

I smiled and nodded. “Yeah it’s a good thing, Tony. Don’t worry about Gisele, she’s just having a bad day. I think all the thefts and murders are getting to her.” And the fact she’s losing control and the fact she’s only an assistant and probably always will be.

He swept the register area and bent low to pick up the dirt with the dust pan while I started to ‘front’ the merchandise adjusting the place settings like Andrew and Louisa had shown me.

I had another stab of sorrow when I thought of Andrew and what Gisele had said about him at our dinner. It seemed as though it had been so long ago now. How she could have suspected Andrew is far beyond me, he was on the same irreproachable level that Tony was. No wonder so many people had quit with her near the helm.

Who knows, maybe someone other than Andrew had accused her of the thefts. I mused on this a while. Ever since our discovery of Andrew’s body that awful morning, she was hot and cold toward me. Gisele couldn’t afford to be pissed at everyone. She had few enough friends as it was especially with Jessica’s ultimatum hanging over her. Well, very soon none of this would be any of my business, would it?

Off in the distance, I heard the back doorbell ring. I think I may have wondered who it was, but I didn't rush back. Gisele was there, she would get the door - had to because it needed a key. I noticed a gaping hole in the crystal vases display and knew there was a case of *Whimsy* vases in the warehouse.

I sighed. Andrew would be proud of me and how I was cleaning and being neat and efficient. Stocking empty shelves and fixing things just the way he liked. I opened the warehouse door and met Tony on his way out onto the sales floor toting his coat and backpack.

"You want to lock the door behind me, Sam?"

I looked into the warehouse and could hear voices coming from Gisele's office. I must have looked puzzled.

"It's Mr. Nichols," Tony said. "He's in a right state over something."

"I'm just going to get a case of vases, you go out and I'll come lock the door when I come back." I leaned toward him. "Just don't tell Gisele or she'll fire me for certain."

Tony laughed. "Night, Sam, I'll see you this weekend."

"Night Tony," I waved and let the door swish behind me. The warehouse was in relative darkness, lit only by the two emergency lights that always burned. Gisele turned lights off whenever she came through; some warped sense that she was saving the company money, I suppose. It was all right, I didn't need them. I knew exactly where the vases were and went for them.

I had just placed my hands on the box when I heard a sharp report followed by a scream. Gisele yelled. "What the hell are you doing?"

The door to the office was wrenched opened and Gisele came running out, alternating pleading and swearing as she ran sideways. Her pleas were those of someone begging for one's life. Her voice wracked with sobs of terror as she stumbled through the break room and turned the corner toward the door that entered onto the sales floor by the bathrooms.

Chris Nichols was running after her. Silhouetted against the light from the break room, I saw a gun in his outstretched hand and, probably if I'd seen his face, there would have been a smile.

"Gisele, make this easier on yourself," Chris said calmly as he fired toward the further door. I heard another scream from Gisele. Me? I molded myself against the boxes in the darkness.

Shit.

I debated going for the warehouse phone, but I didn't know where Chris was or when he'd come looking for me. Maybe he'd think I had left out the front door. I could try for the office phone, just go in and lock the door and make the call. But he had a key. It wouldn't be all that wise to lock myself in a small room with only one way out. I was between Chris and his own office behind me –

I carefully and, hopefully, soundlessly moved a few boxes and slid in between them while I cursed myself for not carrying my cell phone with me like Wayne and Peter always insisted - and Jack had ordered. I didn't even know whether or not it would work back here – probably not. It would have been my eternal good luck to actually have it with me and have it not pick up any service.

I strained to hear footsteps, heavy breathing, any sign that Chris was there.

Double shit. No, this was worse; this called for something more definitive. *Fuck* seemed to fit here. I sat there for what seemed like ages repeating my new mantra in my head and heard nothing but the loud pounding of my heart. I was certain the world could hear it as well. Jack and Wayne and Peter had objected to me working here and I now wished I'd listened to them. I would be sure to tell them all as soon as I saw them again. I held a hand over my mouth to stem any noise that may come out involuntarily and bit back tears.

Chris Nichols' form slid by me in the darkness and I held my mouth tight to keep a startled scream from erupting. I hadn't heard either door and I thought I'd been listening. He unlocked his office door and flipped on the light there. I could just see his profile. He looked angelic with the backlight – almost serene as he laid the gun down on his desk and began opening the drawers. What he did next was nothing short of fascinating in the purely maniacal sense. He systemically and most determinedly emptied each and every drawer in his desk and file cabinet of paper and file; his bookshelves of every book and manual.

I wasn't so fascinated with his efforts that I didn't realize this was as good a time as any to make my escape. Now or never, I said silently.

I guess if I'd realized I still clutched the case of *Whimsy* vases, it would have worked out better for me. My hands were molded to the sides of the box as I shifted position and tried not to cry out from the agony of having crouched in one position for the length of time I had. I thought after I probably should have stayed hidden until he left. The company wouldn't have faulted me for setting off the alarm, but I didn't think that far ahead.

Anyway, the box fell on the floor before me, slipping from my hands without any hope of my retrieving it. I froze in place. I looked straight ahead and scrunched my eyes closed. It was as though I was transported back to my childhood when I did that. I had thought back then (in my distant youth), when we played Hide and Seek, if I closed my eyes and couldn't see anyone, then no one could see me.

Did you ever do that as a child? No? Perhaps that's why I was always the first one found. I couldn't panic. I had to hope that he'd walk right by and look for me elsewhere. I'd just wait for him to search the other end of the warehouse and then I'd run like hell for the front door. How fast does one have to run to outrun a bullet?

CHAPTER 43

I heard the footsteps as he crossed the concrete floor.

"Sammy, are you back here, darling?" Chris Nichols called out softly. "Come on out, Sammy, I know you're here somewhere." His footsteps halted. "Come out, come out wherever you are," his sing-songy voice was not only irritating, it was pretty damned creepy.

I opened one eye and could see his pant legs and the gun he held at his side. I could have reached out and touched them he was so close. I stifled a whimper.

Chris bent at the waist, shining a flashlight toward me and grinned in my direction. He didn't put it full in my face, but rather kept it averted so I wouldn't be blinded. What a nice guy.

"You want to come out of there now, Sammy?"

"No."

"You want to anyway," he retorted as he raised the gun toward me.

No.

I slid from my spot. He actually offered me his hand. I suppressed the urge to swat it away. No need to piss him off needlessly.

"Why did you shoot Gisele?" I asked, as I straightened.

He shrugged and pushed me up against the shelves pressing his body against mine. I never noticed until then how dark his eyes were, even in the weak light they seemed to glisten with evil. I shivered involuntarily.

"What am I going to do with you?" he said.

I knew the question was more rhetorical than not, but I felt compelled to let him know he should let me go, that I was harmless. I opened my mouth to speak and he grabbed my neck, spun me sideways, and slammed my head into the wooden post.

"Jesus, why did you do that?" I screamed pressing my hand against my temple and scrunching my face against the pain.

He grabbed my arm and propelled me toward his office, pushing me inside. As I said, the place was a shambles. Papers and books were scattered across the floor – actually, they *were* the floor and they were slippery. I slid out and down and managed to crack my knee up against his desk.

Chris pulled me up and rather unceremoniously deposited me into a chair. He toed some of the mess about and then bent to retrieve a roll of industrial packing tape.

"Hold out your wrists," he said.

I didn't want to do that either, but I did. He wound the two inch thick tape around and around my wrists and despite my weak attempts at spreading them apart, he secured them close together.

Then he pulled me up again holding me by the neck and pushing me forward. We paused. I knew he did something behind us, but I couldn't tell what before we moved forward again. I thought I smelled smoke and twisted around in his grasp and saw the flames of a fire licking at the mass of paper. I squealed as the bile rose in my stomach.

"What are you going to do with me?" my voice croaked.

"Well, I have to kill you, don't I?" he said conversationally. "I have to, you leave me no choice." He pushed me toward the other office and stood in the doorway.

I thought he had plenty of choices.

"Pull everything off the shelves for me, will you?" he asked as he grabbed the cash that was strewn over the desk and floor from the cash drawers stuffing it in his pockets. I thought I saw blotches of red on the papers and tried not to think where that had come from.

"It was you, wasn't it?" I said as I reached up and emptied the upper shelves sending a rain of books and paperwork cascading down on the floor. "It was you that stole everything."

"Shut up, Sammy," he said, rubbing his face wearily. He pointed to the file cabinet. "Empty that, too."

I finished my task and he grabbed me again as he flicked open a lighter and held the flame to papers until they caught. At least he wasn't going to lock me in here. He could have, he could have shot me then and left me to cremate. I was glad he didn't. I never thought burning would be a good way to die. And yes, I have thought about it.

We exited the office and break room and turned right going toward the back door and the emergency exit by the bathrooms, the door Gisele had just run through trying to escape him. I wondered how far she'd gotten. My tears were falling and there was nothing I could do to stop them, nothing I wanted to do. I thought of Peter and wondered if he would finish my story as the cop had from the scenario I'd told him. I thought of Wayne and wished I'd been able to tell him I'd decided to fight for him. I thought about Jack and hoped he didn't really think I was a stupid girl.

We stood full in the corridor and there he was. Jack Parnell. His left arm reached toward me while the other held his police issue .38.

"You need to let Sam go, Nichols, and we'll talk about your options."

Chris laughed. I took consolation it was a nervous laugh. I felt that was in my favor. "I can't do that, Detective, she knows too much."

"I don't know as much as you think, Chris," I said.

At least I hadn't until he'd shot Gisele and set fire to the offices and slammed my head against the warehouse shelf. I mean I could guess at some things, had, in fact, and even went so far as to discuss them with others - Andrew, Jack, Peter. For the first time, I thought of Tony and was glad he had left when he did. I hope to God he had gotten out. I did a mental head slap and almost smiled. That's how Jack had gotten in.

Chris' breath was warm on my neck. "Gisele saw you taking notes."

"They were notes for a story," I countered.

"They were notes about the Wentworths' thefts," he said back. "You were asking her how things could have been stolen."

"But I didn't know."

"I think it's a moot point now, Sammy."

I mentally shook my head and looked to Jack for some reassurance. I didn't get the message if he was sending any my way.

Great.

Shit.

Fuck.

"Let's talk, Nichols, I know we could work something out for you." Jack moved a bit to his right and Chris tightened his hold on my throat.

"I've killed six people, Detective; I don't think one or two more is going to matter in the long term scheme of things," Chris answered and pulled me closer to him. He was slowly moving backwards toward the emergency door. "Besides, if I don't get you, then the fire will."

Oh yeah, the fire.

It seemed to suddenly get smoky. I swallowed hard and spoke.

"He's set fires in his office and the manager's office, Jack," I said and earned a sneer from Chris. To think I'd thought he was kind of cute. Just goes to show you how bad a judge of character I am.

Jack glanced quickly to his right and then he looked back our way, his jaw was set tight. "Ms. Fournier, do you think you could make it to the telephone to call 9-1-1?"

I couldn't hear an answer, probably because the clanging in my head was taking on epic proportions. Gisele was okay, that was good.

"It's all right, Detective, I know what you're trying to do. I know I killed her."

"But are you certain, Nichols? Can you be absolutely certain?"

We took a couple tentative steps forward and then Chris laughed. "You're trying to bait me, Detective. I shot Gisele in the back and then the head. She's dead."

I strained to hear some sort of noise that would indicate Gisele was crawling towards the customer service desk and the telephone or even toward the front desk. Yes, that one would be better, then she'd be able to open the front door to let in the police and Jack's back-up. He had certainly called in back-up and Gisele wouldn't have to worry about the door, it was already open. Tony had left it for me to close. I wanted to rub my head to make it stop hurting.

Jack stayed silent, still training his gun at Chris' head. Perhaps he should just shoot him and get it over with. Perhaps I should mention that.

"Why did you do this, Chris?" the question came from my lips, but my brain hadn't commanded them to speak. There was a slight upturn in Jack Parnell's lips. He was either encouraging me or I'd pissed him off and he was telling me in his own special way that I should keep my mouth shut for a change. I thought I'd go with the encouragement.

"Why do you care, Sammy?" Chris asked

"I do, I really do," I answered without any conviction. I *really* wanted him to let me go so I could make a mad dash for the door. "Why did you kill Andrew?"

"Because the sniveling little fairy had figured it out. He confronted me – asked me why I had killed Hector. How he knew I had, I can't figure out."

I could have told him that Andrew had just been fishing, that Andrew had thought it all a big game of Clue. I started to shake my head to let him know when I saw a nearly imperceptible shake of Jack's head.

"So you did kill Hector Rodriquez?" Jack said as he took a step forward. Chris waggled the gun he held back and forth.

"Don't try anything, Detective, I haven't gone soft yet."

"Why did you kill Rodriquez?" Jack asked again, not moving back.

"He was a good warehouse manager and kept impeccable records which I, unfortunately, didn't find out until he asked me what he should do about shortages in stock. I had to kill him."

"But he didn't know it was you that was stealing," I said without thinking. "You were his boss."

Chris snorted in my ear. "He would have figured it out."

"And Elaine Newcomb?" I asked.

"She noticed all the empty boxes on the upper shelves, just like you did," Chris answered. "All I did was move the ladder, she was petrified of heights. She told Holly about them - when I'm not certain. Holly called me and said she knew what I'd done."

"She called you at Fridays?" I was watching Jack and he didn't seem to be averse to me asking the questions.

Chris didn't answer, just tightened the hold he had on my neck.

"And Philip Watkins?"

"Who the hell is Philip Watkins?" Chris asked irritably.

"The guy from Barnes and Noble that saw you filling up the van you rented," Jack answered him. "Watkins was blackmailing him, Sammy."

Chris snorted. "He wasn't blackmailing me. He never saw *who* it was that night." He didn't sound convincing.

"That's not what he told his girlfriend, Nichols. She said he knew exactly who you were and verified it when he came to talk with you and Jessica Lupine. He told her you looked guilty. When did you meet him?"

I spun my head around towards Chris. "You ran him off the road?"

"He was a fool to think he could get away with asking me for money."

Jack laughed. "Don't you understand, Sam? Nichols was constantly worried that someone would nail him for stealing even though no one had a clue – save for Watkins. He was so paranoid that he tipped his own hand to a fucking amateur."

What about Gisele? Had she suspected Chris? Something snapped in my head and I realized it wasn't Chris she'd suspected. That's what had left her defenseless against him. She had called him in to confront the person she felt was behind the thefts – or at least *in* on them. She had suspected me. And Jessica.

"Gisele called and told you she knew who the thief was, didn't she?" I said, my voice shaking.

Chris chuckled and nodded. "She was so smug. I couldn't believe it even after all we'd been to each other."

"She thought it was me and Jessica, Chris, not you. She wanted you here to confront me."

He was silent for a while. We stood there at an impasse, him holding tight to my neck and Jack keeping the steady bead on Chris' head.

"Let her go, Nichols," Jack said again.

My mind began to wander. To be honest, I was beginning to wonder about the progress of the fire and must have jumped a mile when Chris' little gun fired by my ear. It scared the hell out of me, not to mention rendered me deaf and probably surprised Jack a little, too. He stared down at the spreading stain on his stomach. I think I screamed, I heard someone and I assumed it was me.

I felt the warm metal against my neck and could smell the acrid scent of fired gunpowder. Oh Jesus, Chris was going to shoot me now. I really didn't think I was ready to die. I tried to move, he had me in a hammerlock - half nelson - some kind of god-damned wrestling move I wouldn't be able to slip from. I closed my eyes as I heard him whisper he was sorry it had to end this way. I felt his lips on my cheek as he kissed me lightly and I stifled a cry.

"I'm sorry that I can't let you go, Sammy. I am truly sorry."

And then I heard the report of a gun. It sounded muted and distant and I marveled at the fact it didn't hurt. I had cut my finger once rather badly while chopping vegetables for a stew and I had certainly felt that right off. It had hurt like hell. I had lopped off a piece of my finger.

I don't know how long I stood there with my eyes clenched shut waiting to drop from the life ending shot, waiting to feel the blood ooze and the warmth leave my body. Waiting for the white light and the angels that my mother had insisted would come.

"Sam?" Jack's voice sounded strained, coming to me in my fog; I opened my eyes.

"Sam? Are you all right?" he asked, still holding forth his weapon as he lay on the floor. I realized then that Chris no longer held me and I looked down and back at him lying on the floor.

"Kick away his gun, Sam?" Jack implored weakly.

I did - sending it skittering across the floor toward the clearance stemware.

I stumbled forward to Jack Parnell, who had by now lowered his weapon.

I pressed my hand hard against the wound and sniffled as I watched Chris Nichols' body twitch, wondering if he was dead yet and hoping he was.

"We have to get out of here, Jack, the fire is spreading," I said through a veil of tears trying to shake my head clear and only succeeding in making it hurt worse than it already did.

He smiled and nodded. "Good idea." He sounded very weak and it did nothing to bolster my spirits. Jack Parnell had never before been shot and now he was. Jack Parnell was supposed to be the strong one here.

Jack Parnell was lying there bleeding because I had come to work for Wentworths. Full circle, I always can blame myself.

"Sammy," he winced in pain as he spoke my name and I searched in the weak light for signs of Gisele. Maybe the two of us could drag him toward the door.

"Sammy?" Jack spoke again a bit more forcibly.

I looked down at him. "What?" I asked irritated.

"We have – to …" the effort to talk was exhausting him. He shifted under my hand and cried out. I think I may have been pressing down too hard. "You have …" he tried again.

I couldn't see Gisele and I wondered where the hell everyone was. Jack placed his hand on my cheek and forced my eyes to meet his. "You have to call 9-1-1, Sammy," he said. "Then get out."

I shook my head. "But Gisele – she called."

Jack's head moved back and forth. "No – you call."

The tears wet my cheeks, soaked my shirt, and fell onto Jack. If Gisele didn't call, then she must be –

I shook my head to clear it of those thoughts and leaned over Jack. "I'll be right back; don't move." As if he could.

He nodded and I surged forward toward the telephone near the front right. I was pretty sure Gisele was to our left, I was damned if I was going to stumble over her body.

My hands shook violently as I dialed 9-1-1 and before I could formulate what I would say, the emergency operator came on the line.

"We need help." I said without preamble.

"Where, ma'am?" she asked calmly.

Why was she so calm? It wasn't right; Gisele was dead, Chris, too, probably, but not unfortunately, and Jack lay dying and there was a fire. Why should she be allowed to be calm?

"It's my job, ma'am. Stay on the line, I'm sending help. What's your name?"

I must have said all that aloud. "Sam, my name is Sam."

"Good, Sam; you're doing well. You're at 122375 on the Pike?"

I didn't know the god-damned address! "I'm at Wentworths. Jack needs help, he's a policeman," I managed. "I have to go help him, he's been shot."

"Leave the telephone off the hook, I'll stay here. You come back on if you need me."

"There's a fire, he started a fire in the back offices."

"You said that, Sam, I've dispatched police, fire, and the EMTs. You doing okay?"

I nodded.

"Jack is bleeding, I have to go help him get out. The smoke, I don't want him to die from the smoke."

"You go ahead, darling, I'll be right here."

I left the receiver on the register – register number four.

I don't remember getting back to Jack, but next I knew I was at his side again and leaning down trying to determine whether or not he was still breathing.

"Jesus!" he cried out. He was breathing all right and I was leaning right on his wound again.

"Sorry; they're sending help." I smelled it now, the first tendrils of smoke were looping around the back door to the warehouse. My head really hurt. "We have to get you outside, Jack, can you move?"

He made an effort, but in the end couldn't move. I first tried to loop my hands under his armpits to pull. Yeah, right like that was going to work you hopeless blob. You don't get a lot of exercise sitting in front of a computer. I searched the immediate area and I remembered the rag rugs and Gisele's and my opinion of them when we were unpacking. I guess I'd test her theory of their usefulness now, wouldn't I? I scrambled to the spot we'd stored them and managed to rap my shin not just once on the corner of the display table, but twice. That certainly felt good.

The smoke was starting to irritate my lungs and I dropped once again to my knees. It was better down there.

"Jack, I'm going to slip this under you; you have to roll to your left." I didn't think he heard me and moved to his side to push him when he grunted, straining to help as much as he could. I don't know to this day how I got the rug under him, but I did. The first tug of the loops resulted in the two I'd grabbed breaking and I swore and took up a bigger hand full. I wasn't going to let Gisele die in vain. If she came up with the idea of using the god-damned rugs for rescue, then I sure as hell was going to prove her right.

I tugged and pulled and was surprised when I'd gained the right front door just as three fire trucks, God knows how many police cars, and an ambulance pulled up to the curb. I don't really know who smashed through the glass door, me or the first responding fireman, but suddenly I was breathing fresh air and I was eternally grateful.

I watched distractedly as they operated, firemen poured through the two doors and rushed through the store to the warehouse. Two paramedics loaded Jack into a gurney and worked over him quickly while police cordoned off the area with their cars and yellow tape, their lights flashing and pulsating. The lights hurt my eyes, but I was comforted by their presence.

Someone came up to me and held me by my shoulders asking questions I didn't think I heard, I don't remember them anyway. In retrospect, I may have answered him, but I don't know for certain. Someone had to have told them who the two bodies were, I assume it was me. I watched Jack lying there and prayed he would be all right. I thought he was watching me, too. I didn't know, but it was comforting to think he was.

It was my fault that he had been shot. If I hadn't gotten the brilliant idea to work at Wentworths, then this wouldn't have happened. The guilt and the tears came again in earnest.

I saw two more gurneys come out with a shrouded body each and knew one was Gisele and the other Chris. They were loaded into some vehicle beyond my field of vision. The smoke had reached me outside now and one of the paramedics came to me and said I should move away. He palpitated my head, said he didn't think stitches were necessary, and asked if it ached. I think I nodded.

"Why don't you sit down there?" he said indicating the curb. I sat down on the blanket he provided.

Peter came presently, stopping long enough at Jack's side to assess his damage before he was loaded into the ambulance. He sank to the curb next to me and gathered me into his protective embrace. I cried more and he let me.

"Jack gave me a message for you, Sammy," he said as he stroked my hair.

"He did?" I raised my eyes to his and he wiped at them with his handkerchief.

Peter smiled. "He said to tell you thank you, he was right, and he's going to live. Then he said to make sure you understood he told you so, you shouldn't have gone to work at this place."

I felt my hackles rise and then just started to laugh. When Jack Parnell was right, there was just no arguing with him, even though *he* actually had encouraged me to stick around.

"How did he know?" I waved my hands encompassing the immediate area. "How did he know to come here tonight?"

"He was waiting in the parking lot for you, I told you that. One or the other of us has been here every night you worked since you found Andrew Barker. You didn't come out and he came looking. He saw Nichols shoot Gisele."

"I didn't see him and I was looking – for either him or you," I sighed and snorted. "I guess that's a good thing then."

"Yeah, I'd say it was," Peter touched my forehead. "Why did the guy hit you?"

"I tried to get away; he got mad," I looked a Peter. "He kissed me, said he was sorry he couldn't let me go. He was nuts, Peter; a raving lunatic."

Peter nodded and surrendered me to the administering of the paramedics.

CHAPTER 44

It was nearly one in the morning when Peter settled me into his car and buckled the seat belt around me. It had been a long night. Some splinters had been removed from my forehead and the wound was cleaned. A butterfly bandage had been applied, no stitches needed just as the paramedic had predicted. I asked for and received some aspirin. I really wanted a drink, I thought that would be a great idea, but Peter had prevailed and I didn't get one, except for coffee.

I told my story at least a dozen times and promised I would show up at the police station the following day to sign my statement. Peter had stayed with me, spending an inordinate amount of time on his cell phone in between interviews.

Checking on Jack, I suppose.

Starbucks had reopened and made a killing on the number of emergency personnel present as much as on the curious onlookers that had gathered. No puns intended (on them making a killing).

Eventually, Peter was allowed to drive me home. I'd retrieve my car from the garage another day.

"Gisele thought it was me, that I was the one stealing and murdering people though I can't figure out why. She saw me writing notes and probably read them. I didn't even know she was there. She called in Chris Nichols and she thought they were going to confront me," I said as I leaned my head against the window. I snorted. "She must have told him she knew who it was without giving him a name. Chris assumed she would confront him – he was pretty paranoid."

Peter listened and nodded and held my hand.

"You going to be all right, Sam?" We sat in front of my house and I was reluctant to get out – I'm not sure why. My head still ached. I touched the bandage on my temple just to assure myself that the injury was still there and still sore.

Yep it was.

I looked at Peter and contemplated my answer and then I slowly nodded. "I thought maybe Wayne and I could go on vacation, maybe to some remote island where there aren't any other women." Women – not people – women, that must have made Freud roll over in his grave. "I've been doing some sole searching and want to work on my marriage."

Peter had that look again, the one where he thought I was incapable of making my own decisions, a lot like the night I'd made the strawberry daiquiris. Maybe I wasn't capable of sane thought when it came to Wayne. I still loved him even though I didn't trust him. I didn't think Peter would understand, things were black and white with him.

"Don't forget the book signing," Peter commented.

"I won't, in fact, I'm holding you to your promise to see Boston." I placed my hand on the door handle and pushed it open. "I think I'll go write this up, see if a new company really wants to take the risk."

Peter smiled. "They will, Sammy; don't you worry about it."

"So what will you do? Threaten to break their legs?"

"If I have to," he answered catching my hand.

I laughed, then sobered. "When Chris had the gun to my head and I was sure I was going to die, I wondered if you'd finish the story."

"I wouldn't have been able to, Sammy, I'm a terrible writer. I'm glad you didn't die."

"Me, too."

"Be careful, Sammy," he said as I slid from the seat. I waved as I watched him pull away from the curb and waited until he disappeared before I trudged up the slope of lawn to the house. I was itching to get writing while it all was still fresh in my mind. I even had a title – *Trial Run* – I hoped I could do Jack Parnell justice. I owed him that much. I smiled wondering where the title had come from. Maybe because it would be the first (and last) of my ventures in detective fiction.

I dragged myself into the house and tossed my keys and bag on the kitchen table as I ran my hand through my hair. I needed a hot bath and then I'd at least take down some notes before I went to bed. I suppose I didn't think much of the snores coming from next door as I booted up the computer. I knew that Wayne was scheduled to come home and just attributed the noise to him.

I thought more about the snoring when I slipped into the bedroom as soundlessly as I could with only the benefit of light from my office and headed for the bathroom. In the weak light, I determined that there was enough noise for more than just Wayne, that there were two forms in the king-sized bed. I flipped on the bathroom light and stared - one was Wayne and the other was definitely female, the covers had slipped off her. I stared at them for a long time - to the point where Wayne awakened and sat up in the bed and swore.

"Shit, Sammy, I'm sorry; I thought you were out of town," I heard him say before I turned on my heels and headed back up the hallway.

They – were - in - my - bed.

I grabbed my keys and purse, scrounging around in it for my cell phone. I flipped it open, turned it on, and walked out the front door. Wayne gained the door as I trotted down the front steps and Peter answered on the second ring.

"Don't go, Sammy, I can explain," Wayne was saying. I knew he hadn't bothered to put on any clothes so he wouldn't be coming outside. I didn't turn around, it took all of my willpower.

"Could you give me a ride, Peter?" I said into the phone. "I'll meet you at the corner of Castaway and Drake." I didn't wait for his answer, closing the phone to disconnect and striking off across the lawn. Wayne continued to call my name, but I blocked him out. I had been a fool to ignore the signs. I knew he'd been unfaithful to me, I just hadn't wanted to know. I certainly hadn't wanted to see.

What can I say, I'm an idiot – and I really hate being alone.

I supposed I cried as Wayne's calls ceased and he didn't try to come after me, even naked. I probably would have done some forgiving if he'd *tried*.

Peter was waiting at the corner and pushed open the door when I neared his car. He didn't ask, I didn't offer an explanation.

"Where to?"

I leaned my head back and fought back sobs as I shrugged.

Peter slipped the car into gear and drove away.

We drove for a long time.

CHAPTER 45

It was a rough month that stretched into two and then three. The book signing trip took up a week and a half and I wrote up the story of Wentworths when I wasn't signing my name and posing for pictures. We toured the crap out of Boston. When we arrived back in D.C., Peter had set up dinner with Tamara Wilton and Hildegard Benson (Tamara and Hildy from Starbucks) and we had a good time. Two more characters for later books.

It kept my mind off Wayne at least.

I didn't move out directly. I would drive by and if his car was there continue on, if not, I'd run in and pick up a few things, do laundry, and then leave again. He would leave me notes with his itinerary, letting me know where he was and how long he'd be gone. Perhaps in doing so, he was saying that I was welcome to stay. I never did.

I had the book done in record time and I dedicated it to Andrew and Jack.

I revisited Wentworths, they were under renovation from the fire. Jessica hadn't closed the store. She had to set up a temporary office in the warehouse to run the place. Jessica is up for promotion to Chris's job, I thought she'd be good at that.

I'm thinking of moving on.

Peter has filed divorce papers for me and won't tell Wayne where I am. If he calls on the few occasions I have my phone on, I don't answer. I have a feeling I'd cave. Andrea and Greg have stopped by, Peter let them know where I was staying. They are leaving Georgia in June and moving to Virginia Beach. Another home to establish –

Maybe when I move - and I'm seriously considering it - I'll buy a house and settle down. I'd like that. A little permanence – the white picket fence and the gardens…

And Jack? He's recovering. He claimed he didn't want to see me ever again, but he, Peter, Jake, and I have had dinner on several occasions. He's taken leave to recover. He talks about Liz a lot and maybe they'll get back together. If he dares -

I think that it's time. Rockville just isn't big enough for Wayne and me. He's extended for another two years; Peter thinks it's a ploy to get me back. Peter won't let me go back and I'm hurt enough that I won't consider it as long as Peter insists.

It was the actual *seeing* you see.

I still don't like to be alone, but I'll survive.

978-0-9840224-1-0